The Faculty Club

The Faculty Club

a novel

Danny Tobey

ATRIA BOOKS

New York • London • Toronto • Sydney

ATRIA BOOKS

A Division of Simon & Schuster, Inc.
1230 Avenue of the Americas
New York, NY 10020

First Atria Books hardcover edition June 2010

ATRIA BOOKS and colophon are trademarks of Simon & Schuster, Inc.

For information about special discounts for bulk purchases,
please contact Simon & Schuster Special Sales at 1-866-506-1949
or business@simonandschuster.com.

The Simon & Schuster Speakers Bureau can bring authors
to your live event. For more information or to book an event contact
the Simon & Schuster Speakers Bureau at 1-866-248-3049
or visit our website at www.simonspeakers.com.

Text designed by Paul Dippolito

Manufactured in the United States of America

10   9   8   7   6   5   4   3   2   1

Library of Congress Cataloging-in-Publication Data available upon request.

ISBN 978-1-4391-5429-8
ISBN 978-1-4391-6310-8 (ebook)

To Jude

Some rise by sin, and some by virtue fall.

—*MEASURE FOR MEASURE,* ACT 2, SCENE 1

1

I remember my mother's reaction when I got accepted to the greatest law school in the world. She dropped the stack of mail in her hand, said, "Baby," and started crying. My dad's reaction was harder to place. He just said, "Oh." Not an indifferent, uninterested *Oh,* and not a surprised *Oh* either. This *Oh* was quiet, a little puzzled, and maybe even a little sad—a recognition that, in less than a second, the possibilities of my life had just radically shifted from those of his own.

We live in a small town in Texas called Lamar. My father is a schoolteacher, loved by his students and popular in the community, yet the years of hard work have worn him down, and by the time I reached high school, he'd settled into the strange conviction that he was meaningless in the universe. This terrified me. Death didn't scare me. Risk didn't scare me. But my father's dissatisfaction—in the face of a good life, a loving family, a meaningful job—that left me lost.

The greatest law school in the world. That doesn't really describe it at all. It's more of a black box with an almost comically small sign, a stone building that turns out presidents, diplomats, CEOs, senators, you name it. The class size is tiny; more people apply per spot than for any other position in the world. There are no tours, no interviews, no brochures. It's not even clear if they actually teach any law. It's a well-known joke that graduates don't know anything, yet somehow they become the most accomplished and powerful people in the world.

I come from a small town in Texas. I don't know anyone famous. I went to a college you've never heard of and live in my parents' basement. But I worked like crazy, graduated first in my class, got a perfect score on the LSAT, and published in a law journal before I was twenty. Was I thrilled to get in? Absolutely. Was I surprised? Maybe I was. Did I deserve it? You bet your ass.

The greatest law school in the world.

That sounded like a pretty good deal to me.

The first time I saw my home for the next three years, it was a crisp morning and there were deep pools of fog between the hills spotted with stone towers and yellow trees, cemeteries and playgrounds. It seemed like you could roll down those hills into a dream and never come out. I was lost in this sudden rush of New Englandness, until the sun came out and burned up all the fog, and then it was a bright September day.

On the way to my first class, I stopped to watch a group of tourists gathered around a statue. Some were Japanese; one couple was speaking Italian. Most were American families on college tours. The high school kids were only a few years younger than I was, but somehow they looked innocent, naive to me.

"As you can see from the plaque, this is a statue of our university's founder," said the tour guide, a bubbly, red-cheeked student who came off like a game show host in training. "We like to say that this statue tells three lies. First, our founder was unfortunately not this handsome. He hired a young philosophy student to pose in his place." People in the crowd turned to smile and chuckle at their loved ones. "The second lie is the date. Here, it says 1647. But our university was actually founded in 1641. No one knows why the wrong date was engraved here . . ."

I looked at my watch. Class in five minutes. I had to run before I could hear the third lie.

My first class was called Justice. It was taught by perhaps the most famous professor at the school, a man named Ernesto Bernini. Professor Bernini wrote the book on the philosophy of law. He was also the former attorney general of the United States.

The classroom itself was a work of art. The lower walls were paneled in dark cherrywood, while the high walls and ceilings were light cream, covered by portraits of past deans and a full wall of stained glass windows, each one coming to life as the sun moved behind it. I sat up near the top; the rows of chairs sloped down in a half-circle to a single lectern at the heart of the room.

I took a seat and watched the room fill with students. There was an electric buzz of excitement, a hundred rapid conversations I couldn't make out. Some students looked like they came from New England prep schools, with ruffled hair and blazers, crisp blouses and smart pants; I saw hipsters with spiky hair and iPods, straight from NYU or Columbia; still others came from Big Ten schools in the Midwest, wearing khakis and button-down plaid shirts, sweats and baseball caps. Everyone seemed better looking than average, with an easy charm that filled the room. And it occurred to me that I knew nothing about these people: the hipster might be from Kansas; the blazered, spectacled prep-schooler might actually be a public-school kid from Oklahoma. This was a place of reinvention. At this school, at this moment, whatever we decided to be was possible.

A young black man in a coat and tie sat down next to me. "Nigel," he said, offering me his hand. I was surprised to hear a British accent. He was crisp and curt, but he had a wry, mischievous smile.

"Jeremy," I said. He grinned, then turned to open his laptop.

I didn't see Professor Bernini walk to the podium. I just heard his quiet throat-clearing, and the room fell silent.

His sprightly eyes moved over the crowd.

"Each year," he said, in a soft, singsong voice, "I come here to greet the new students." He was a small man, but he radiated power—from his eyes, from his hands, the casual way they draped over the lectern. "Each year, I get older, and you remain young, vital, and curious." He had a twinkle in his eyes that reminded me of an elf, something from *A Midsummer Night's Dream*.

"The study of law is a life's pursuit. This is not physics or math, where you are over-the-hill at thirty. Law is reason, but it is also experience and wisdom, and so law is time." He paused to lay a creased, spotted hand across his brow. "Good news for little old men." The class laughed as he gently shook his head.

I realized then how frail he looked, how his spine bent forward and his skin was paper-thin. But his eyes were alive and shining. He consulted his seating chart, tapped his finger on it, then walked to the front row and looked down at a blond student.

"Suppose, Mr. Anderson, you are kidnapped from your room this evening, drugged, and abducted. When you awaken, you find yourself in a mine cart that is hurtling down a track at tremendous speed. Ahead of you, you see five children playing on the rails. You call out, but they can't hear you over the roar of the cart. They are too close for you to stop in time." Bernini shook his head, feeling the weight of the situation. "There is no question they will die."

The blond student met his eyes.

"John Anderson," Nigel whispered into my ear. "Rhodes scholar. Former president of the Harvard debate team."

The professor continued. "Now suppose there is a lever you could pull that will change the direction of your cart, placing you on another track. This track has only *one* child playing on it." His eyes twinkled. "What do you do?"

John Anderson met his gaze confidently.

"I would pull the lever," he said.

"Why?"

"Because five deaths is worse than one death."

"I see. But I wonder, Mr. Anderson, if your logic holds. Suppose you were in a hospital, and you had the chance to kill one patient to provide organs for five others? Would you do it?"

"Of course not."

The professor smiled politely. "The trade-off hasn't changed. One life for five, yes? And yet your answer is now opposite?"

"But a hospital—you're supposed to protect people . . ."

"The child on the track doesn't deserve protection?"

Anderson stared at the professor. His mouth worked to form a response. Finally, he said something so quiet it was lost to everyone but him.

The professor walked a couple of seats down.

"Ms. Goodwin, please help Mr. Anderson out. Would you pull the lever?"

"Daphne Goodwin," Nigel said under his breath. "Former editor in chief of the *Yale Daily News.* Triple crown winner: Rhodes, Marshall, *and* Truman scholarships." And, he failed to mention, one of the most uncomfortably attractive people I'd ever seen. Her hair was midnight black, pulled into a luxurious ponytail. Her lips were painted red against lightly tanned skin. She had blue eyes that sparkled from across the room. Her face was set in a permanently skeptical expression, eyebrows raised, lips somewhere between a frown and a smirk: it was aggressive and erotic.

"I would do nothing," she said, folding her thin hands in front of her.

"Nothing, Ms. Goodwin?"

"If I pull the lever, I am causing the death of a child."

"And if you *don't* pull the lever, five children will die."

"But I didn't *cause* that. I didn't create the situation. But I won't pull the lever and, by my action, kill a child."

"I see. Are you sure?"

She paused, looking for the trap. Then she said, "Yes."

"So, Ms. Goodwin, by your logic, if there were five children on your track, and *no* child on the other track, we couldn't blame you for not pulling the lever, because you didn't *cause* their death?"

She froze. "I didn't say that . . . I mean, that's not what I meant."

"Mr. Davis, can you help us?"

I was still looking at Daphne Goodwin's bright blue eyes when it dawned on me that Ernesto Bernini had called my name. Two hundred faces were now following his gaze and turning to look at me. Silence filled the room. I felt my heart stop like a needle skidding off a record. Four hundred of the most brilliant eyes in the world were now burning holes in me.

"Yes?" I answered weakly.

"What would you do?"

I felt panic in every nerve of my body. My future was sitting all around me, watching.

I paused and chose my words carefully.

"I can't say what I'd do, sir. It's a terrible situation. Either I cause the death of a child by my action, or I allow five children to die by my inaction. Any way I choose, I lose something. If I had to decide, I would. But as long as it's just an academic exercise, I respectfully decline to answer."

Those flickering elfish eyes were boring right through me. I was pretty sure I was about to get sent home to Texas, possibly with IDIOT tattooed on my forehead.

Finally, he spoke.

"Fair enough, Mr. Davis. In here, it *is* just an exercise. But someday, you may have to choose. Should you send soldiers to war? Should you sign a law that will help some and harm others? And I wonder, Mr. Davis. Will you be ready?"

"Amazing," Nigel said to me as we packed up our books. "He actually called on you. You must hang the stars! But who are you? I mean, no offense, but I know everybody, and I've never heard of Jeremy Davis."

"I'm no one. Really. No Rhodes scholarship, no editor in chief of anything. And I botched that question anyway. Refusing to answer! What was I thinking?"

"Hey, I thought it was cool. Buck the system and all that. The point is, he knew your name. On the first day! That man makes *presidents*. All I can say is, you're generating quite a buzz for yourself. She doesn't cast her glance casually."

Nigel nodded across the room. I looked just in time to catch the blue eyes of Daphne Goodwin, before she tossed her hair and turned away.

"Anyway, you remind me of a young Bill Clinton," Nigel said, rising and ruffling my hair on his way out. "And I'm going to ride your coattails the whole damn way."

I spent the afternoon running errands. The campus bookstore was a two-story building nestled between an old-timey tailor and a hamburger place called Easy's. I needed to buy books for the rest of my first semester classes: Contracts (taught by Professor Gruber, a round man with short arms and thick square glasses that made his eyes look a hundred yards away), Property (with Professor Ramirez, a severe woman with a long pinched nose and watery eyes), Constitutional Law (Professor Müeling, accent of undetermined origin), and of course, Torts. It would take me almost a week to figure out what a tort even *was,* but basically, if I punch you in the face, or if you slip on some ice while crossing my yard, that's a tort.

I searched for a book called *Trial Skills* and grabbed it. I planned on trying out for the Thomas Bennett Mock Trial, one of the law school's oldest traditions. Whoever won that was basically guaranteed a Supreme Court clerkship, as long as they didn't find some other way to flame out.

I carried the heavy stack of books, and it seemed like I had the whole universe of human behavior in my hands: what we promise each other and how we harm each other; what we can take and what can't be taken away.

I bought three boxes of highlighters and a package of those colored sticky tabs.

When I checked my mailbox that evening in the student lounge, it was empty, except for a handwritten note:

Come to my office, it said.

Signed, —E.B.

2

Ernesto Bernini's office was filled with books—on the shelves, on his desk, on the floor. It would take a hundred years to read all those books, I thought. There was no computer, but stacks of paper were everywhere. The overhead lights were off, and a lamp cast a small orange circle on his desk. The moon shone in through the window, throwing a blue-white glow over the rest of the room.

"Sit down, Mr. Davis," the professor said kindly, stepping toward me and extending his hand toward a chair. He sat close by on the edge of his desk and fixed me with those rapacious eyes.

"How tall are you?" the professor asked.

"Six-one, sir."

He nodded.

"Can you guess the last time we elected a shorter than average president?" He didn't wait for me to answer. "William McKinley. One hundred and six years ago. Isn't that funny? In a world of ideas, height still matters."

He shook his head.

"I didn't know that, sir," I said, then cursed myself for sounding so stupid.

"That's okay," he said, chuckling. "The potential is there."

I wasn't sure I was being complimented, but I said thank you anyway.

He leaned in closer.

"Good bone structure," he said, his eyes moving over my face. Suddenly, I wished I could somehow move my chair a couple of inches without being rude. There was nothing sexual in the way he was looking at me; rather, I felt like a prize heifer being appraised by a rancher. "Strong jaw. Cheekbones could be a bit more prominent, but oh well. You can't have everything, can you?"

For some reason, I thought of an old friend of mine whose dad was a music teacher. He said his dad could tell what instrument a student would be good at, just by looking at the bones of his face.

Bernini smiled, satisfied, and leaned back.

"I read your article in the *Coleman Law Review*," he said. "Very impressive, publishing in a law review as a college student."

"You read that, sir?"

"You seem surprised."

"I just . . . it's kind of an obscure journal. I'm not sure the people who work there read it."

Professor Bernini laughed and clapped his hands. "Nevertheless, I was impressed. Interesting ideas. I'm thinking of citing you in my next article. That will raise your stock a little, eh?" He hopped off the desk and opened a window, letting a burst of cold air into the room. His breath came out in plumes of white mist, and he pushed the window closed against the wind.

"When did it get so cold out there?" He rubbed his hands together briskly. "Now, you're probably wondering why you're here." He grinned at me. "I think you have potential, Jeremy. I liked your answer in class today. It was honest and thoughtful. I'd like you to be my research assistant this semester, if you're willing."

"Yes, sir. Of course."

"Good. It's settled then. For tomorrow, I'll need a summary of every case that has cited *Marshall v. City of Allegheny.* That's all for now, Mr. Davis."

He turned his attention to papers on his desk, as if I were already gone. I thanked him and backed out quickly. Research assistant? *Holy shit!* I thought. *Holy shit, holy shit, holy shit.* This was it. This was the transformation. I'd always thought of law as a way to help people, the way my grandfather had helped people, but this was something totally different. A window had just opened to power, the good kind of power, greatness even. My grandfather helped a dozen clients a year. I could pass a law and help *millions* of people. I could negotiate peace between two countries and end a *war.* That was the game I was being asked to join now. And—I let my mind wander just a bit—there could be travel, to foreign capitals on important missions, perhaps escorted by beautiful women like Daphne Goodwin who one week ago were in a different universe than I was, but now it was suddenly plausible. More than plausible. I imagined myself in a tuxedo in exotic places with Daphne pressed up next to me—Spanish castles, Italian villas, Greek islands . . .

I had to catch myself. It was a research assignment. I had a long night ahead of me in the library. I wasn't sure I even knew how to do what he'd asked. I hoped the librarians were helpful.

I was halfway down the hall to the elevator, when, from behind, I heard the professor say something strange to himself.

"V and D, perhaps?"

V and D? What was he talking about?

"We'll see," said a second voice.

I looked back, just in time to see the door close.

11

3

"In his *office*?" Nigel was leaning back in his chair in the student lounge the next day, polishing an apple on the lapel of a three-piece-suit. "My friend, you are in the catbird seat!"

"Nigel, did anyone ever tell you you talk like a 1940s movie?"

"Jeremy, I am a renaissance man in an age of specialization."

"I don't even know what that *means*."

Nigel laughed and slapped me on the back. His good nature was infectious. Even strangers on the sofas around us looked over and smiled. Most people were studying. A few were hovering around, watching a chess game by the window.

"Ryan Groon," Nigel said, inclining his head toward one of the chess players. "First in the nation in competitive chess for his age group. He can play blindfolded."

"Where are you *from*, Nigel?"

"England, originally. My father was in the foreign service. My mother is an American actress. Penny James, have you heard of her? No? She was very well known in the seventies. Anyway, I grew up in London and Connecticut, went to Princeton, and now I'm here."

I could picture Nigel on a beach somewhere, splashing around as a kid while people stared at the gorgeous American actress stretched out under an umbrella. Maybe in the background, his father loomed in a white suit and straw hat, speaking into a phone some waiter held for him on a silver tray. I could see both parents in Nigel's face: the strong, forceful features of the diplomat, the graceful good looks of the movie star. It all made sense now.

"Say," Nigel said. "I want to show you something."

He pulled a book from his bag.

"With your permission," Nigel said, "I'd like to ask Daphne out before you get your claws into her. Eh? Of course she'll say no, but I'm not one to look back in eighty years and wonder *what if*? Whad'ya say?"

I admit, the idea of Nigel asking Daphne out annoyed me a little bit. After all, wasn't I the one she was looking at in class? But still, Nigel and Daphne made *sense* together. Daphne and me . . .

"Sure, why not?" I told him.

"Excellent! Good man! I'm going to present her with *this,* as a symbol of my intentions."

He produced a book. It looked like an antique, leather-bound with gold edging on the pages. It was a collection of essays.

"Nigel," I said slowly. "Are you sure *that's* what you want to give her?"

"What's wrong with it?" he asked. He actually looked a little hurt.

"Nothing, nothing. It's really nice. I'm sure she loves political theory. I was just thinking, maybe you could go for something a little more romantic. Flowers, maybe?"

Nigel grinned at me. He waved his finger in my face.

"A Casanova to boot! Yes, that's exactly what I'll do. Flowers. Brilliant!"

I sort of shook my head and changed the subject.

"Nigel, can I ask you a question?"

"Anything."

"Have you ever heard of something called 'V and D'?"

Nigel looked up from polishing his apple. He seemed to pause for a second.

"No."

Then he smiled, an easy, casual smile. "I'm having some friends over for dinner this weekend. Would you like to come?"

"Nigel, did you hear my question? V and D. That seemed to mean something to you. I just thought, with your background . . . you seem to know about everything . . ."

"Nope, never heard of it," Nigel said, rising and taking a bite from his apple. "I think I'm going to watch Groon finish trouncing this young man over here, and then I'll take a walk. Think about my dinner invitation. I promise good wine."

One day, curiosity is going to kill me. Once an idea gets into my head, I can't let it go. What was V and D? Why did Nigel get so weird when I mentioned it? He was such a know-it-all. V and D seemed like the only thing he *didn't* want to brag about knowing.

I searched on the web and didn't find anything useful, mostly sites about venereal disease. The world's largest library was a hundred yards from my room, and I didn't find anything there either.

That night, I met one of my oldest friends, Miles Monroe, in a dark booth at the back of The Idle Rich, a pub near my dorm. Miles was a man of voracious appetites. I found him with a pint of Guinness and a few empty glasses, a basket of onion rings next to a basket of fries, a cigar burning in the ashtray, and his head buried in a thick book of Durkheim essays. His leather satchel sat next to him in the booth, bulging with books. Miles was immense, nearly six-seven with the physique of someone who read philosophy and ate onion rings all day. Miles might not live to be forty, but he was having a great time.

"How's the search for the holy PhD going?"

Miles looked up and saw me. A smile opened in the middle of his shaggy philosopher's beard.

"Great," he said. "Just twelve more years to go."

He rose and gave me a giant bear-hug and slapped me on the back. I smelled a faint hint of marijuana on his tweed jacket.

"It's good to see you, Jeremy."

Back in high school, Miles Monroe always looked out for me. He was three years older, the captain of our debate team when I was just a freshman. They called him "The Beast," because he was a force of nature on the team, throwing his gargantuan body around and jabbing his finger while speaking in his rich, booming voice. We all knew he would go to college, but when he got into college *here,* the news shot quickly around our town. Everyone was surprised, because he was the first person from Lamar to get in. Ever. But no one was surprised that *he* was the one to do it. According to town gossip, passed from mom to mom in grocery stores and carpool lines, he made perfect grades in law school and had an amazing job lined up at a blue-chip New York firm after graduation. And then something happened. At the last minute, he rejected his job offer, grew a beard, and enrolled in the philosophy PhD program. His earning potential shrank from three million a year to thirty thousand. After that, the news about Miles tapered off. He became just another bright kid who peaked early and fell back into normal boring life. But, he'd always had a love for all

15

things gossipy and arcane, so I thought he'd be the perfect brain to pick.

"Ever miss home, Miles?"

"Not a bit," he said. "Why? Do you?"

"I'm not sure yet."

"Hey, you just got here. I've been here, what, seven years now? It's culture shock. You'll get used to it."

He took a drink of Guinness and wiped his beard with a napkin.

"How was your summer?" I asked.

"Excellent. I was a counselor at philosophy camp."

"Philosophy camp? Is that where nerds go when they die?"

"I see you haven't lost your mediocre sense of humor."

"So, you had a good time?"

"Yeah. They wouldn't let me teach Nietzsche, though. They said teaching Nietzsche to high school kids was like handing them a bottle of Jack Daniel's and the keys to a Porsche."

Miles was deep into his dissertation on Nietzsche, whom he liked to call "the bad boy of philosophy." "Nietzsche probably didn't believe half the things he wrote," Miles once told me. "He just liked to stir the pot. Plus, he was crazy. The syphilis went to his brain. One chapter in his autobiography is called 'Why I am so great.'"

"Miles, can I ask you a question?"

"Sure."

"What does *V and D* mean?"

He rubbed a napkin across his beard and started laughing through the french fries in his mouth.

"That's what I love about you, Jeremy. You haven't been here a week and you're already asking about all the interesting stuff."

"I get the feeling it's kind of a touchy subject."

"Let me guess. You asked some law student about it, and they got all weird and quiet?"

"One guy. Yeah. How'd you know?"

"Oh, it's a cliché around here. I guess he thinks he's a contender. Doesn't want to screw it up."

"Okay, contender for *what*?"

"V and D is a club. That's it. Some people like to call it a secret society, but it's really just a club for rich kids. I'm not sure what the initials stand for. Some people say Victory and Destiny. Lame, right? As a former classics major, my personal favorite theory is *Vitium et Decus*: Latin for 'fault and distinction,' loosely translated; or, in modern terms, 'vice and virtue.' But who knows? It's not like they advertise."

"So it's just a club? Why do people get so weird about it?"

"Well, according to rumor and gross speculation, each year they select a group of law students to 'try out,' if you will, for the club. They call it *striking* the club. Ultimately, they induct three students into the society. Think about that. Three and only three out of the most selective law school in the galaxy. Once you're in, you can't say you're in. I guess people who *want* to be in assume they're not supposed to talk about it either. And, if you really do have a shot, you don't want to screw it up, because your life is pretty sweet if you get in."

"Pretty sweet? How?"

Miles leaned back, savoring the suspense and taunting me. He smiled.

"Why do you care so much about this?"

I thought about what he told me, about secrecy and people screwing up their chances. But I trusted Miles.

"Can you keep a secret?"

"Clearly not."

"I'm serious."

"Okay. Yes, I can keep a secret."

"I heard someone mention my name for it. A professor."

"Mention . . . What professor? Who was he talking to?"

"Bernini said it. I don't know who he was talking to. It was weird . . . I thought he was alone when he said it."

"Spooky."

"Are you making fun of me?"

"No, no," Miles said, slapping me on the arm and laughing his booming laugh. "I hope for your sake they are thinking about you. You know what one of the rumors is?"

"What?"

"If you don't make your first million by the time you're thirty, they give it to you."

I nearly choked on my drink. A million dollars by age thirty? My dad wouldn't make a million dollars in his entire life, much less at the beginning of his career. The last few days had definitely planted dreams of power and glory in my head, but somehow I hadn't really thought about wealth too. I'm embarrassed to admit that for a brief moment, an image popped into my mind. I saw myself holding hands with Daphne. Somehow, in this flash of a daydream, it was implied that we were very rich.

"Really?" I managed to get out, doing my best to sound nonchalant and failing miserably.

"So they say." Miles leaned back in the booth and flipped his book closed. "But who knows? It's all speculation." He rubbed his wild, fuzzy beard. "Can I offer some advice?"

"Sure."

"If you want it, forget about it. Whoever these people really are, you can't do a damn thing about it. You don't come to them." He shoved another handful of french fries into his mouth and said in a muffled voice: "They come to you."

When I got home to my room late that night, a little drunk and reeking of bar smoke, I unlocked the door and turned on the small lamp by my desk. A dim light filled the room. I was about to grab my toothbrush when I saw something on my neatly made bed. I paused, then reached behind me to make sure I'd locked the door. I had. I pulled on the knob, and the lock was indeed working. I checked my windows—each one was still locked from the inside. But someone had been in my room. I went for the object on my bed and stumbled over a wastebasket, barely catching myself on my desk so I wouldn't do a complete face-plant. I cursed. Could you imagine the moms in Lamar whispering in the checkout line? *Did you hear about Susie Davis's son? Yeah, he was going to be president. Too bad he tripped on a trash can and died.* I laughed and steadied myself. Maybe next time I'd stop at two Guinnesses.

Lying flat on the middle of my bed was an envelope, plain and white. I picked it up and examined it. Nothing on the outside. No address. No *To* or *From* or *Attn*. I tried to open it quickly, but my hands were shaking. Inside was a card with three lines of text:

YOUR PRESENCE IS KINDLY REQUESTED FOR COCKTAILS
ONE WEEK FROM TOMORROW NIGHT.
2312 MORLAND STREET AT SEVEN O'CLOCK.

I flipped the card over. It was blank.

I traced my fingers over the paper. It felt smooth and substantial.

Finally, I held the paper up to my lamp, and through the grain I saw the watermark, the dim glow of the letters *V&D*.

I should have been excited, but something bothered me as I tried to fall asleep that night. I kept replaying the conversation I'd overheard between Bernini and his unseen visitor:

"V and D, perhaps?"

"We'll see."

We'll see.

Here I was, thinking Bernini was as big as you could get in this world. I thought he was the kingmaker. But now he answered to someone else? Or some group? Who on earth says "We'll see" to Ernesto Bernini? A few hours ago, I was flying high, enjoying the fantasy of a bright and certain future. Now, it was all a question mark again. What was V&D? What hoops would they ask me to jump through? Would I make it?

We'll see, I thought to myself, over and over, until I finally fell asleep.

4

"Get your ass over here," said the voice on the phone.

An hour later, I was on a train to New York, watching the countryside flash by, and then I was riding an elevator to the thirty-eighth floor of a skyscraper near Central Park. I'd never seen Central Park before; when the cab dropped me off, I took fifteen minutes to wander through the woods. They were positively enchanted: the dense canopy of trees; the bridges built with mossy stones; the thin stream moving over pebbles in a riverbed. I even came face-to-face with a bronze sculpture of a wood sprite. All that was missing was the Brothers Grimm, perched high in a tree and watching me over their long noses.

I saw the woods again from above as the elevator shot up.

My brother was standing by the window in his lavish office, in an immaculate silk suit with initialed cuff links.

"Look at you," he said. He grinned. He held out his hand, and when I shook it he grabbed me and gave me a hug. "Look at you," he said again. "All grown up. Fancy school, big shot lawyer-to-be."

"Look at *you,*" I said. I glanced around the room. It was a true corner office—two of the walls were floor-to-ceiling windows. "This is amazing, Mike. I had no idea."

"You haven't seen the half of it," he said. "Later, I'll take you to a bar where I've seen Bono, Al Pacino, Warren Buffett. Everyone."

"You saw Bono?"

"Saw him? I *talked* to him. I went right up to him and said, 'Are you Bono?' And he said, 'Yeah. Who are you?' And I said, 'I'm Mike.'"

"And?"

"And what? That's it. Nice guy, though."

He dropped himself into a cushy leather chair and put his feet up on the desk. It was strange, hearing him talk. He still had a little of his Texas accent, but he'd also picked up a Brooklyn cadence.

"Settled in yet? Like it up there?" he asked me.

"Yeah. The town's great. I'm in the dorms."

"They have dorms in law school?"

I nodded. "They're really nice dorms. More like a fancy board-inghouse. Stickley furniture. Oak cabinet, oak desk. View of the campus. It's all kind of embarrassing, actually."

"Not bad," he said.

I didn't think I was still angry at Mike, but something about seeing him in his fancy office made it bubble up out of nowhere.

"You should've come home when Dad had his heart attack."

"What?"

"You heard me."

My dad's breakdown had climaxed, a few years after it started, with a massive heart attack. All that worry had worn him down; it turned out there were even smaller guys than he imagined himself to be, chewing away at the cords and strings that supplied his heart.

"Jer, that was four years ago."

He waved my comment away and gave a big laugh. But I wasn't ready to let it go.

"Dad needed you."

He sighed and shook his head.

"Jeremy, I get here at five a.m. every day. No fancy degree for me, like you're gonna have. No one handed me anything. I'm competing against the smartest people in the world, every single day. I have to stay ahead of the market. I could be up sixty million one day, and poof, I'm down a hundred mil. That doesn't wait. Not for me, not for Dad, not for anybody."

He was staring out the window as he spoke, and this gave me a chance to really look him over. My brother had always been handsome. He used to have a lean, hungry look, but now his face was rounder and his cheeks were rosier. His hair was slick with gel and combed in a precise part. A full-length wool coat hung from the back of his office door.

"Jeremy, I love Dad. Dad knows that. You and I made different choices, but that's all it is. Choices. I'm still your brother. Remember when you broke your leg?"

"Yeah."

"Who carried you all the way to the house? Ten blocks of heavy lifting?"

"You did. You're also the one who told me to jump."

I had to stop myself from laughing—I was doing a bad job of staying angry. I was four when I broke my leg, he was ten. We were playing Justice League. Mike suggested that if I was a halfway decent Superman, jumping from the bridge over the creek shouldn't pose a serious problem. My scowl broke a little, and the tension was gone. He breathed a sigh of relief and his smile lit back up.

"Come on," he said. "Let's get a drink."

We went to his Bono bar. There was a doorman and a velvet rope, and sure enough we passed right by the long line. He whispered to the doorman, who clapped him on the shoulder and laughed. My brother could always make people laugh. His smile was contagious. The place was swanky, but at the moment the most famous person in the room was Steve the bartender. We settled into a booth. Mike ordered us both boilermakers.

"Whatever happened to that girl you used to date?" Mike asked me.

"What girl?"

"Amy something."

"Well, we never really dated. She was a little out of my league."

"Mom said you guys dated."

"Mom's an optimist. We hung out a lot. It was one of those: you're cute, funny, smart, and awesome, so let's just be friends."

"Ouch."

"That was back in high school anyway."

"Dating anybody now?"

"I just got here! There is one girl, though. Daphne. She's pretty amazing."

"Well, what's the problem? There's no more 'out of my league' bullshit. You're Mr. Ivy League now."

"I *live* in the Ivy League, Mike. Every guy in town is Mr. Ivy League!"

"Still, you want something, you have to grab it. That's what I did. I didn't have a fancy diploma. No one handed me anything."

"So you've said. A couple times now."

"You know how I got where I am?" I did, but that never stopped Mike from telling the story, so I let it go. "I didn't go to Wharton. I didn't have an MBA. I walked right up to my first boss and said, 'I'll work harder than anyone you've got, and I'll do it for free.' I got a second job through a temp agency. Data entry bullshit. It paid twelve bucks an hour. I could do it in my sleep. Actually, I did do it in my sleep. Worked until ten at night, then got home and did data entry till two in the morning. God only knows how many people got the wrong pants size because of me. I lived like a bum. I ate ramen noodles every night—twenty-five cents a pack—until my palms started itching from vitamin deficiency."

"That's messed up."

"You're damn right it's messed up!" he said, laughing and slapping his hands on the table. "And look at me now!"

"That's great, Mike."

"How much debt are you gonna have, after law school?"

I swallowed hard. It was a subject I preferred to handle through total denial.

"A hundred and fifty thousand dollars."

"I could pay that off for you like that." He snapped his fingers. "But I won't. It wouldn't help you a bit."

"I don't want your money, Mike. But you can pay for the drinks."

He laughed and ordered us another round. A little later, Sean Penn and a woman walked into the bar.

"That's Sean Penn," Mike whispered to me.

"I *know*."

"But it's Sean Penn."

"I heard you. It's Sean Penn, not Jesus Christ."

"Should we meet him?"

"What would I say—'Do you like movies?' "

25

Mike grinned at me.

"Well?"

"No, I don't want to meet him."

He shrugged. "I would've done it. I would've walked right up to him."

I watched my brother. He kept looking around the room, from table to table. I leaned in.

"Hey, Mike."

"Yeah?"

"You've done great for yourself. I'm really proud of you."

For a second, he seemed really surprised. Then the cocky expression came back.

"Thanks," he said finally, after a moment had passed. He looked me over, then turned his gaze back to the crowd. "Ten blocks," he said to himself, proudly.

5

Back on campus the next day, I decided to take Nigel up on his dinner invitation. Unlike most students, who lived in the dorms, Nigel had an off-campus apartment in the posh section of town. I knocked on his door and wondered who else was invited.

The door swung open and Nigel appeared, looking like he'd just stepped off the cover of *GQ*. He wore a tan shirt that appeared bronze against his brown skin; on me, the shirt would have looked like mustard on an undercooked hot dog. It hung perfectly on his thin frame, as if he were an alien that could grow a second skin specifically for dinner parties. His slacks were crisp and casual, with brown shoes and a matching belt. But more than anything he just seemed comfortable, totally at ease. I glanced behind him at the other guests, and I thought of the old line: this was the role he was born to play.

He gave me that million-dollar smile and ushered me in.

There were four people in the living room, sitting on the plush couches and chairs. I recognized John Anderson, the Rhodes scholar and Harvard debate champion, immediately. Until now, I had only seen him from across the lecture hall of Bernini's Justice class. Up close, he looked like a high school football star, with broad shoulders and aw-shucks good looks. But high school football stars were supposed to become fat, bald shoe salesmen, while us nerds grew up and became fabulously wealthy. Jocks certainly weren't supposed to stay fit and intimidating and go on to elite law schools. John must have been six foot six, and his hands, resting casually on his legs, were massive. Even sitting, he somehow felt taller than me. I suddenly had the very uncomfortable sensation of being a freshman in high school all over again.

Next to him, holding a glass of wine, was a stern-looking man who fixed me immediately with saggy vulture eyes. As if reading my mind, Nigel whispered, "Dennis Vo. He never sleeps. He's working on some book and he won't tell anyone what it's about." Nigel grinned.

"Do you think it's any good?" I whispered, smiling for the first time that evening.

"Well, he's twenty-seven, and his last book won the Cushman Prize. So, yeah, I guess it probably is." Suddenly, my one publication in a lonely, obscure journal didn't seem so special anymore, despite what Bernini had told me.

I felt someone watching me, and I looked over to the last person in the room. I'd never seen Daphne Goodwin up close before. Her eyes sparkled even brighter, reminding me of that clear blue ocean water you saw in brochures. Her skin was light, the color of soft tan sand, and her lips were painted a rich plum color. She looked away.

"Let's get you a drink," Nigel said, placing his arm around me.

The conversation at dinner was amazing. I'd never heard people move so quickly from one topic to another.

"Of course we should legalize prostitution," Daphne was saying, her cheeks flushing as she made a *what are you thinking?* gesture with her hands.

"That's ridiculous," John replied. "A good society can't allow people to be exploited."

"Okay, fine. Say you have a women who's fifty years old, single, and a millionaire. She likes having sex. And she's really good at it. So she decides to make a business out of it. Is she being exploited?"

"No, of course not. You said she's a millionaire."

"Fine. So you're not against prostitution. You're against poverty. You might as well be arguing against coal mines or sweatshops. You have no problem with prostitution per se."

"Wrong. I don't think we should let your rich lady be a prostitute either."

"Why not?"

"Some things are priceless. Noble. You can't pay for sex without demeaning it."

"Well, doctors heal for a living. That's noble. Does that mean they can't charge for it? Or teachers? Priests? You think people should only make a living doing *slimy* things?"

"No, but . . ." John looked around for help, but everyone was watching Daphne. She leaned in for the kill, her hair a little wild and her blue eyes fierce.

"Let me tell you what I think is *really* going on. You don't like prostitution because deep down, you think women are fragile and need protecting."

"What?" John said. "That's ridiculous. I never said that."

"Is it? First you attacked prostitution because it demeaned poor people. We took care of that argument! Then you said we're demeaning sex. Well, we dealt with that too. So, answer me this. Who do you feel more sorry for: a male prostitute or a female prostitute?"

John looked at her for a moment, then shrugged. Suddenly, Daphne turned and looked directly at me.

"What about it, Jeremy?" she said, fixing me with those startling eyes. "Who do you feel more sorry for: a male prostitute or a female prostitute?"

I didn't know what to say. She had me paralyzed.

"I feel sorry for them both, the same," I lied.

"Really?"

"Yes."

"Then I wonder why you're blushing," she replied, abruptly flipping her gaze back to the rest of the table.

I was gradually aware that I had stopped breathing. I allowed myself to suck in some air before I passed out with my head in my soup.

Nigel came through the swinging doors with a tray of steaks, which were sizzling in red wine and garlic. The room filled with hazy smoke from the kitchen. "On that awkward note . . ." he laughed, setting the tray down. "Let's eat."

Moments later, Dennis the vulture had taken the debate in a new direction.

"The definition of marriage goes back thousands of years. It's the bedrock of western civilization. You don't go messing around with that," he said, jabbing his fork in the direction of the rest of us.

"Why not?" Nigel asked. "Definitions change all the time. 'Citizen' used to mean 'white man with property.' We changed that, didn't we?"

"Marriage means one man, one woman," Dennis shot back, "so spare me the politically correct guilt trip."

"Marriage *used* to mean one man, one woman *of the same race*," Daphne replied. "So even *that* definition has changed."

"It's about equality," Nigel said. "Gay couples should have the same rights as straight couples. Period."

"What's next?" Dennis replied. "Polygamy? Incest? Bestiality? It's a slippery slope. You have to draw the line."

"But," I said quietly, before I even realized I was talking, "by your logic, we would have to ban straight marriage, because it might lead to gay marriage."

Dennis froze. He looked at me for a second, blinking. He looked at Daphne, then back at me. He threw his fork down. "You just don't go messing around with the basics," he mumbled.

"Bravo!" Nigel cried, clapping his hands and grinning my way.

Just for a moment, Daphne smiled at me.

An hour later, the table was covered with empty plates and wine bottles. Dennis and Nigel were arguing passionately about some movie I had never seen. John and Daphne were talking softly to each other at the other end of the table. Earlier, they'd reminisced about their Rhodes scholar days at Oxford: favorite bars, which professors they kept in touch with; but now they spoke quietly, and I couldn't make out the words.

I spent the time pleasantly buzzed, staring at the flickering candles on the table and reflecting on the most interesting observation of the evening: John Anderson didn't seem that smart. Don't get me wrong: at any other law school he would probably dominate the classroom. But here, during the hours of debate over dinner and wine, he was mostly quiet, and when he did speak, he just didn't seem to move as quickly as the others. I wondered how much of his success—his debating championships and Oxford adventures—had more to do with his overwhelming physical presence, his infectious good nature and extraordinary charm, than what he actually said or did. Was John Anderson the ultimate vessel, already being groomed to become a handsome, vacant politician, surrounded by teams of speechwriters, analysts, stylists, pollsters? Now more than ever, I was reminded of high school, of the empty-headed popular kids who ruled the school. It was the same then—it didn't matter what they said or did; it was cool because *they* were the ones who said or did it. As the alcohol worked its way deeper into my brain and the conversations around me swirled into a mild hum, my thoughts drifted back to high school, and for the first time in many years, I thought about Amy Carrington.

Amy was a cheerleader freshman year, but unlike some of our other cheerleaders, she was also exceptionally smart and thoughtful. Her grades were almost as good as mine, and she always treated me with kindness. We were on student council together, and I remember how stunned I felt the first time she walked up to me and asked for a ride home. Soon, it was an afternoon ritual, driving to her house and talking in her room after school, with the door slightly ajar to appease her parents. She had a boyfriend named Russ, the quarterback at another high school, but every afternoon it was me who sat on her bed, talking about our futures and what we wanted to be, or sometimes—though it took all my energy to pretend not to mind—hearing about her sexual experimentations with Russ. There is no single memory more alive to me today than the side of her face, turned away from me, daydreaming out the window of my car, a soft smile on her lips. When I heard the gossip that she and Russ had broken up, I immediately asked her to the spring dance. But, she told me, she had already agreed to go with Bryan Collins, a senior at our school nearly identical to Russ in every way. Bryan went on to take her virginity and then break up with her a week later. I learned about it at lunch, from a bunch of freshmen who snickered as she walked by. I felt no satisfaction then. And I realized now, sitting in this warm room surrounded by bright, fascinating people, that I hated John Anderson. I hated everything about him.

I was awakened from this by a slight pressure on my foot below the table. It was gone as soon as it came. Nigel and Dennis were still arguing.

"*Eyes Wide Shut* was a piece of crap," Dennis said, a look of amazement on his face. "You know, just because Kubrick directed something doesn't make it good."

"Yes, yes, you keep saying that," Nigel replied. "But *why*?"

Again, I felt the pressure on my foot, almost teasing in the way it came and went. It traced itself back and forth along my leg. I looked over at John and Daphne, who were still whispering intensely. Maybe it was the alcohol, but it seemed like either Daphne Goodwin was playing footsy with me, or Nigel had a cat.

"The *acting*, Nigel. Think about how terrible the *acting* was!"

Nigel threw up his hands.

"The acting was *supposed* to be terrible," he cried.

"What! What! Are you all hearing this? *Supposed* to be terrible?"

I was beginning to think I had imagined the sensation, when something soft slid down the side of my leg, then back up, slowly moving past my knee, still creeping up toward my inner thigh.

"Think about it," Nigel explained patiently. "People came to see Tom Cruise and Nicole Kidman play a married couple because they wanted to see what the *real* Tom and Nicole's marriage was like. But instead of something fake—the movie—revealing something real—the marriage—they got *fake* leading them to *faker*—a movie that was less real than most movies! It was a joke, a parody of the audience's desires. Kubrick was mocking us."

Daphne suddenly smiled at me, and the pressure on my thigh disappeared. She turned back to John and resumed her whispering.

"Mocking the audience?" Dennis said, shaking his head. "Yes, Nigel, you've convinced me, that *does* sound like a great movie."

The table was quiet. Nigel sat back in his chair, his eyes half-shut, a sleepy, satisfied look on his face. Dennis poured himself another glass of wine, then thought better of it and pushed it away. Daphne had gone to the bathroom to take out her contacts, and when she came back, she wore thin black frames that matched her dark hair. John sat at the window, staring out at the lights across the valley.

"I'd like to thank you all for coming," Nigel said softly, leaning forward in his chair. "I think we have a special group here, and I'm enjoying getting to know each of you." He paused and met eyes with us, one at a time. "I think we are going to have a wonderful three years together.

"I'd like to propose that we do this again, and soon. Perhaps a meal out next time, no?" He smiled, and seemed to savor what he said next. "In fact, I have a surprise. A friend of my father's has invested in a new restaurant in town. When the review comes out this week, you won't be able to get a table for six months. And, through no small amount of name-dropping and arm-twisting, I've arranged to close down the back room just for us, a private dinner next Friday."

My first thought was *holy shit, this is gonna be awesome.* And then

I felt a jolt. Next Friday. The night of the V&D cocktail party. I felt Nigel's eyes on me.

"Sure," Dennis said. "I guess I can put up with you communists for another night."

"Excellent," Nigel said. "Daphne?"

"Oh, Nigel, I'd love to. It sounds wonderful. But . . . I can't that night."

"Oh, I'm sorry to hear that," Nigel said. "What about you, John?"

"I'd like to, Nigel. I really would. But, I don't guess they could still change it to another night, could they?"

"I'm afraid not," Nigel said, looking at me again, curiously.

"Jeremy? Surely *you'll* join me?"

To my surprise, my voice came out hoarse and barely audible. "I can't," was all I managed to say. Nigel wasn't smiling anymore. There was a strange look in his eyes, and suddenly it dawned on me: Nigel had no intention of hosting a dinner that night. He had a secret invitation to the V&D, same as I did. He just wanted to find out who else would be there.

John was staring down at his hands. Daphne was watching me, her lips barely suggesting a smile.

Four people. Three spots.

The game had begun, and I hadn't even realized it. At least now we knew who the players were.

6

How was I supposed to keep my mind on school? Friday night was coming up! What would it bring? What would they want?

And Bernini! He was heaping more and more assignments on me. I was spending entire nights in the library, running home to shower as the sun came up, then stumbling into class and fighting to keep my eyes open. I came to know every nook and cranny of Edwards Library: the grand façade with columns so high you had to crane your neck to see the capitals; the upper floors with shelves lit by naked bulbs; the shaved-pencil smell of books that hadn't been touched in years.

Soon, Bernini would write his magnum opus: a colossal work, modestly titled *The History of Law*. My job was to summarize thousands of pages of text, obscure works that existed only in the dustiest corners of Edwards: first editions; treatises with margin notes by famous readers; memoirs so frail they were housed in argon and handled by permission of the dean only.

I'd be halfway through one assignment when my phone would buzz and that familiar Italian accent would sing, "Jeremy, do you have a minute?"

The answer was always yes.

Wednesday night I was delivering papers to Bernini's office when he glanced up from his desk.

"Jeremy."

"Yes, professor?"

"Take this."

He placed something in my hand. It was a small key.

"I'm going to begin writing soon. I won't want to be disturbed. Let yourself in when the lights are off to deliver your research. You understand?"

"Yes, sir. Thank you, sir."

I backed out of the office.

My law school training was already kicking in: I immediately starting thinking of worst-case scenarios. He trusted me with a key to his office. What if I lost the key? What if I had to bother him to replace the thing he'd given me so I wouldn't bother him? I decided to go directly to a locksmith in the morning to copy the key and put it somewhere safe.

A day later, the duplicate key was hidden on my bookshelf in the middle pages of *Crime and Punishment.* How could I possibly have known, at that point in time, that this would one day save someone's life?

Arthur Peabody was one of the top stars at the most prestigious law firm in Boston when he cracked. They put him on sabbatical for six months and tried to rehabilitate their golden boy, but it was no use. Whatever had broken in his brain during those 300-billable-hour months couldn't be fixed. It was for that reason, and also maybe because of his storybook face, that students over the years had come to call him Humpty Dumpty.

In the end, he was cradled back into the fold of the law school and given emeritus status as the head tutor of Legal Method. Now

Humpty Dumpty was an old man, with droopy eyelids and hang-dog cheeks. He wore the same soup-stained bow tie every day, and you could usually catch him stomping through the library, muttering to himself. Each year, he taught first-year law students how to do what he did best (and perhaps the only thing left he could do): take a legal question and dive into the endless sea of case law to craft an answer.

You see, in law, it isn't enough to find the perfect case that makes your argument. You then have to find every case that came afterward and that refers *back* to your case. Maybe your case was overturned. Maybe it was expanded or transformed. And it doesn't stop there. Each of *those* cases had cases that came after *them*. What if someone overruled the case that overruled *your* case? It was this endless branching chain of cases that could drive a man insane—or in the case of Humpty Dumpty, hold him together.

In 1873, a man named Frank Shepard was smart enough to create a book that cataloged this chain of citations for every case, making the process infinitely easier. Lawyers have been updating it ever since. Now you could go to his book and see every case that cited your case and whether it helped or hurt. It was such a good idea that his name become immortal: all over the country, thousands of lawyers are Shepardizing their cases every day.

And that's what we were practicing in the gothic main hall of the library, while my mind was on Friday and what might happen. In fact, I was getting pretty grumpy flipping through volume after volume of *Shepard's,* tracking my cases.

"This is ridiculous," I whispered to Nigel, who sat next to me.

"Shh," he said, not looking up.

"I mean, I get it. This isn't rocket science. Do we actually have to go through every single stupid case?"

"Quiet," Nigel said, barely moving his lips.

"Why can't we do this on the computer? It takes seconds on the computer. Why is he making us go through twenty old books wasting our entire day?"

No response from Nigel, but now I knew why.

The stained glass wall behind us made a rainbow across our table, and a pudgy shadow had appeared in the middle of it.

"Suppose, Mr. Davis," said a voice from behind me, "that the electricity fails the night before your motion is due in court . . ." Humpty Dumpty placed his gnarled hand on my shoulder. I looked down and saw wiry white hairs on the knuckles. "Suppose you work not at a large firm, but at a small office with limited computers . . ." His mouth was just behind my ear. "Or suppose, God forbid, that you represent not corporations but actual humans, who cannot afford the thousands of dollars computer research requires . . ."

He was close enough now that he either had to kiss me or bite my nose off. Abruptly he walked away and left us alone with the books.

I walked home in the dark through the freshman quad. The streetlamps were on, lighting each side of the path. I watched the leaves shake and fall in the wind and felt the chill in the air. I pulled my coat tighter. It was late; most of the windows of the dormitories were black.

I saw a woman walking toward me along the same path, carrying overstuffed grocery bags in each hand.

As we passed, I let myself sneak a look at her face. I'll admit right here, I'm a hopeless romantic. Going to college in the small town where you grew up (and staying in your parents' house) isn't exactly a recipe for an active dating life. Maybe I hadn't admitted it to myself yet, but I think the idea of meeting someone incredible was a big part of the appeal of coming here.

I was surprised at how pretty she was. She wasn't striking, like Daphne with her red lips and black hair. She felt, I don't know, *real,* unlike so many of the students I saw who seemed to order their universes by résumés and transcripts.

She had soft brown eyes and brownish blond hair, and full lips that were more warm than sensual. She wore no makeup, and her hair was tied in a simple ponytail. Her coat was too bulky for the fall, and she had on green surgical scrubs underneath. She gave me the briefest glance as we passed.

I know this sounds crazy, but I felt a connection when our eyes met. Like I said, hopeless romantic. I wanted to say something, but as the distance between us grew, everything I thought of sounded more and more absurd. What do you yell from twenty feet away: *Hi? Stop? I love you?*

I shook my head and kept walking.

Then fate intervened. I heard a crash, and the woman cried out. One of her grocery bags had split and oranges were rolling in every direction—down the hill, into bushes, past the statue of our noble founder.

"Shit," she cried, "shit, shit, shit." She started trying to scoop them up, but her other bags were dropping and spilling as she scrambled in too many directions at once. I noticed her eyes were full of tears.

"Hey," I said. "Hey, it's okay. It's just groceries."

She shook her head and put her face in her hands.

"I can get your oranges back," I said, possibly the lamest courtship promise of all time. She began to cry in earnest.

"Are you okay?"

She wouldn't answer me. I didn't know what else to do, so I started picking up oranges.

After a while, she said, "I don't care about the stupid oranges."

"Oh."

Now I felt truly ridiculous.

"That came out wrong. Just, please, you don't have to do that."

"Good. Because some of your oranges are in the creek."

She laughed suddenly.

"Oh, God," she said, wiping her eyes. "You must think I'm crazy."

"No . . . no . . . you just seem like you're having a really bad day."

"More like a really bad year."

"Oh. I'm sorry." I sat down against a retaining wall a few feet away. "Are you a medical student?"

She shook her head and gave a small, unhappy laugh. "No. I'm a doctor, sort of. I graduated from medical school last year. I'm doing my internship now."

"What kind of a doctor are you?"

"No kind, really. I'm training in neurosurgery."

"That's amazing. I mean, isn't that the hardest program to get into? Especially *here*."

She looked at me like I'd slapped her across the face. Her eyes were fundamentally gentle, but there was something else there—a sort of self-reproach, as if the only anger she was capable of feeling was aimed at herself; and it was a righteous, intense anger.

"I shouldn't even *be* here."

Her eyes welled up again. I'm embarrassed to admit it, but she'd become even prettier since she started crying. Her eyes were damp and bright, with gold flecks in the brown irises.

41

"I know how you feel. I think everybody feels that way. It's like, what am I doing here? How did I even get in? But we can't all be mistakes, right?"

Somehow, that was the wrong thing to say. Something in her expression broke when I said that.

"Look, I'm sorry," I said. "I'm saying all the wrong things."

She shook her head.

"No. It's not your fault. It's nice to talk to someone—especially someone new. I don't get out of the hospital much."

"It's really hard, huh?"

"Honestly? It's worse than I ever imagined. I barely sleep. I eat McDonald's three times a day, usually standing up. When I'm not in the hospital, I'm supposed to be reading. I have no friends, no life. I have too many patients, and they're always yelling at me for keeping them waiting . . ." She shook her head. "Sorry. I shouldn't just unload on a total stranger like that."

"It's okay," I said. "I don't get out of the library much. It's nice to talk to an actual person."

She nodded.

"My dad's a businessman," she said. "He works all the time. I barely saw him growing up. Now he's rich and powerful, but he's not happy. He's angry all the time. What's the point of that?"

"I don't know. My dad's a teacher, and he spends all his time wishing he was big and important like your dad."

"Wow, you're really good at cheering people up."

She smiled for the first time. I laughed.

"Yeah, I guess that wasn't what you wanted to hear."

We were quiet for a while. I noticed we were totally alone. The path was deserted, and it was getting colder by the minute.

The silence was almost absolute, except for the occasional rush of the wind through the leaves.

"Listen, I know it's none of my business, but if you want to talk about anything . . ." I was aiming for heroic rather than nosy, and I probably came down somewhere in between. "Like you said, I'm a total stranger. Anything you say is pretty much anonymous."

She looked at me for a minute. It was a curious expression, like she was sizing me up and weighing her options. Was I trustworthy? Could I ease her mind? I guess she decided it was worth a shot, since after a little pause she shrugged, more to herself than to me. She closed her eyes and seemed to focus her thoughts.

"When I said I shouldn't be here . . . I really shouldn't be here. I don't deserve to be here."

She took a deep breath and looked me straight in the eye.

"I'm only here because of my dad."

She sighed and leaned back against the wall. "I've never said that out loud before." She laughed. "I think about it a lot, though."

She smiled at me with those full lips, and her cheeks looked rosy and warm, even out here in the cold.

"I always wanted to be a neurosurgeon. I'm not even sure why. I've been saying it since I was a little kid. I think when I was in elementary school, I said it once and saw how people reacted. I guess they thought it was amazing that I even knew the word. School was easy for me. I got straight A's. College was easy too. Chemistry, biology, I could learn them in no time. Neurosurgery was the best, the hardest, so I knew that's what I was going to do. I never imagined anything else.

"But medical school . . . all of a sudden, everything was different. Nothing came easy anymore. It was like trying to memorize the phone book. I was drowning. I kept my grades up, kept telling everyone I was going to be a neurosurgeon. On the outside, I was fine, but . . ." She paused. "I felt like I was in a fog. One night I called my dad from a pay phone so no one would hear me. I was crying. I said, 'Do you want me to make straight A's?' He was just sarcastic. He said, 'No, I want you to make C's.' I failed every class that semester." She looked down. "A breakdown like that . . . Do you know how many spots there are for neurosurgeons? There's two of us in my intern class. Thirty total in the country. I was finished."

She trailed off, shrugged.

"But . . ."

"My dad worked it out with the school. They wrote it off as a research semester on my transcript. I slept late, worked out, did some easy lab work a couple of hours a day. I took the tests again and got straight A's. They backdated the grades. My F's just kind of . . . disappeared." She looked right at me. "I'm sure there's some nice new building on campus with our name on it."

I let it all sink in.

"You asked him to do this?" My question came out more judgmental than I meant it to.

She shook her head. "No. But I went with it. I didn't say no." She sighed. "So you see, you *feel* like a mistake. But I know I am."

We walked toward her apartment without talking. It was well past midnight, and even in this academic hamlet, it wasn't safe for women to walk alone along the river at night.

I thought about her story. I guess I knew things like that happened, but to *hear* it for sure . . . it's the kind of stuff that makes schools like this an impossible dream for people like me. And yet I couldn't shake the feeling I got from her. Her eyes were kind and playful at the same time; they looked right at you, as if you were the most important person in the world. I couldn't think of anyone I'd rather have leaning over my hospital bed, telling me everything was going to be all right. Or was I just going easy on her because she was pretty?

Finally, I said, "I think you're too hard on yourself. In the end, you took those tests. You made those A's."

"My transcript is a lie."

"I'm not denying that. And I'm not saying it's right. I'm just saying you can't torture yourself like this. It's not good for you. It won't help your patients."

She smiled, but she didn't look convinced.

"Do you have any hobbies?" I asked.

"What?"

She looked at me like I was crazy.

"Hobbies," I repeated. "Things you do for fun. When you're not beating yourself up."

She thought about it for a second.

"I like opera."

"Really? I've never even heard an opera."

"Well, I haven't been in years, since I stopped letting my dad pay for things. Now it's too expensive. But I have my CDs."

She smiled genuinely for the first time that night, then she caught herself.

"So," she said, stopping and looking right at me. "What should I do?"

"I really don't know."

"I could use some friendly advice."

45

"What would happen if you came clean?"

"They'd fire me. I'd never get another job in medicine."

"And if you didn't? Like I said, you made those A's in the end. Can you make peace with yourself?"

"I don't know. Could you?"

"The truth is, it would be pretty easy for me to tell you to do the right thing. It's not my career. It's not my dream at stake. I don't know what I'd really do if I were you."

We reached her stoop.

"This is it," she said.

We were standing below a brownstone with a short staircase up to her door.

"Are you going to be okay?"

"Yeah. It felt good just to say it out loud. That's a start, right? I just need some sleep. A shower, go for a run maybe."

I looked at her pretty face, her warm smile. I didn't like what she had done (or had let happen), but she was so kind, so gentle. I wanted her to stop hurting all the same.

"Some first date," she said.

I hesitated, then took a shot.

"Can I see you again?"

She studied my face. For a second, I thought she was going to say yes.

"What would we do?" she asked, smiling. "See a movie? Grab some pizza? I think tonight kind of exists in its own universe. Total strangers. Moonlight confessions. Isn't that what you said?"

"I guess so."

"We have a secret," she said, holding out her hand.

"We do," I said.

She squeezed my hand, and I felt it through my entire body.

7

Friday the seventeenth. I couldn't stop shaking. My tie was crooked. My jacket looked worn. I cursed my pants, my shoes. It was all wrong, bush league, low-class. Nothing I could do about it now. I wished I'd had the courage to ask Nigel to come with me. I knew he would be there, but just as certainly, I knew that I couldn't say anything to him, that I was supposed to arrive alone.

2312 Morland Street. I didn't even know what that was. Was it the secret clubhouse? Even Miles, my source of all things creepy and Ivy League, didn't know where the physical heart of the V&D was located. There was no famous landmark, no cryptic house for tourists to photograph. At least, not as far as he knew. And Miles ate this stuff up with the delight of a stamp collector. If he didn't know, who else could I ask?

Yesterday, I told Miles about the invitation. I couldn't stand it anymore. I had to tell *someone*. He was a huge help. He stroked his wild beard, patted me on the shoulder, and said: "My advice? If they ask you to have sex with a goat, that's where you draw the line."

"Be serious. I have no idea what I'm doing."

"Jeremy, as a philosopher, I deal in ethics and reason. As a hobbyist, I dabble in mythology and campus lore. I can do both

47

from my couch, and I don't have to turn the TV off. As far as reality goes, you've taken this farther than I ever imagined. So, what I'm saying is, you're on your own."

He smiled and shrugged. I thanked him for the help and huffed toward the door.

"Jeremy?" he called after me.

"What?"

"I *can* tell you one thing."

"Okay," I said. I turned around, a little too eagerly.

"Don't forget to send the goat a thank-you note."

I grabbed the door to slam it behind me. Just before the thud, I heard him yell, "Rich people *love* thank-you notes."

The door closed to the sound of his booming laugh.

2312 Morland Street turned out to be a pale blue two-story Victorian house, with navy trim, octagonal bay windows, and pointy triangular turrets, nestled on a quiet street of similar houses. The lawn was small and well-kept.

As I walked up, I saw two young women lounging on the stoop. They were about my age, but they didn't look local; they were tan with long legs and teased-up hair that reminded me of bored summer girls from my childhood. One of the girls smiled at me as I walked up the steps. The other was inspecting her nails and didn't look up.

"I'm Jeremy," I said.

"O-*kay,*" said the one who smiled at me, in a perfectly adolescent *what's that got to do with me?* tone. She stared me down, and I blinked first.

"Am I in the right place?"

The other girl started laughing without looking up from her nails. It was a haughty, bubble-gum-smacking laugh. "Why are you asking *us* where *you're* supposed to be?"

It was a fair question. I felt my face flush. I mumbled *never-mind* and headed for the door. I heard them whispering behind me; one of them said, "I *know*!" and they both laughed.

I didn't see a doorbell, so I knocked and waited.

Finally, a man answered the door. He looked like a model out of the Brooks Brothers catalog; silver-haired, with a plaid shirt open at the collar and a perfectly tailored blazer. His handsome face was tan and lined.

"Jeremy, please come in. Right on time."

He patted me on the shoulder.

We walked through the foyer into a majestic living room. The house felt larger on the inside than it did on the outside. And the man moved gracefully through it. He was so comfortable in his own skin that I started to feel like an alien in mine. The room was filled with chairs and couches, some gathered around a grand piano. But all the seats were empty now, like a saloon in a frontier town after the mines had caved.

"I'd invite you to sit, but I'm afraid we don't have time," he said.

A woman came through a set of swinging doors and placed an arm around the man. She had a wobbly walk, and as she approached I could smell the cloud of alcohol mixing with her perfume. Her hair was blond with black roots, and it was coiled and springy from a bad perm. She wore a white tank top that exposed a generous stomach. She looked like one of the girls outside dipped in alcohol and baked in the sun for twenty years.

"Hey babe," she drawled to the man, with a Southern twang.

49

The man didn't flinch when she put her arm around him. What was someone like *her* doing with someone like *him*?

"This is Jeremy," the man said to her. Not a trace of awkwardness on his face. "Jeremy, this is my friend Candace. She just flew in this morning."

"Nice to meet you," I said, holding out my hand.

"Ooh, he's cute," she said to the man. She grinned at me. Her makeup was garish, but I could see how she had once been very pretty. "You should meet my daughters," she said. Then she mock-whispered, "The younger one's a *virgin*."

I coughed and choked at the same time.

"Candy, fix yourself a drink. I'm going to take Jeremy upstairs."

He put his arm around me, and we wound up a grand staircase to a landing on the second floor. I soaked in the beauty of the house. Every detail, every touch was perfect: marble archways with smooth-breasted angels leaning out. Antique clocks and lamps whose shapes echoed the bends and slants of the rooms around them. Like the man himself. That woman was the only outlier, like a toddler slapping her finger down on the perfect wrong note in the middle of a sonata. A sly, crazy thought popped into my head. Were they mocking me? Was she some sort of "white trash" parody, meant to remind me of my place? Or was I just totally paranoid and freaked out by the whole situation? Who knows, maybe she was exactly what this guy liked. After all, Bill Clinton was the most powerful man in the world, and you saw the gaggle of misfits he chased. There would always be senators caught with their pants down at highway rest stops, exploring various flavors of self-destruction. So, which was it: parody or lust? Either way it was funny. The only question was: was I laughing at them or were they laughing at me?

.   .   .

We passed through a small door into a study. There was an oak desk in the center of the room and bookshelves on all sides. But instead of books, the shelves were lined with relics from all over the world: African masks, Indian idols, Native American totems, and a hundred other artifacts I couldn't place.

On the wall was a giant map, the kind that showed the whole world spread out into two smashed ellipses, side by side. There were hundreds of small pins stuck into it, marking different cities.

"Have you been to all these places?"

"I have." His blue eyes gleamed. "Over many years, obviously."

I inspected a small, tattered map framed on the wall.

"One of the original maps from the search for Bimini. *That* set me back a bit," he added, chuckling.

He gave me space and let me stroll around the shelves.

"What's this?" I asked, looking at a small bottle. It reminded me of a beaker from high school chemistry, down to the stopper in the top. It contained a yellow liquid.

"Ah." He crossed over and held it up. "Aqua regia. King's water. It's a mixture of hydrochloric and nitric acids. Famous for its ability to dissolve gold."

He took a pen from his desk and jotted something down. He tore the page off and handed it to me.

$$Au + 3\,NO_3^- + 6\,H^+ \rightarrow Au^{3+} + 3\,NO_2 + 3\,H_2O$$
$$Au^{3+} + 4\,Cl^- \rightarrow AuCl_4^-$$

I nodded, as if this meant anything at all to me.

"Are you a chemist?" I asked.

He laughed. "You sound surprised."

"No, I just . . . I guess I thought you were a lawyer . . ."

He didn't say anything.

I stumbled on. "Because of your connection to . . ."

He watched me curiously. I had to stop *talking*.

He finally spoke, breaking the tension.

"Chemistry is a hobby of mine. But I didn't mix this myself. This bottle, like all the objects in this room, has historical significance."

He lifted the bottle off the shelf and held it up to the lamp. It sparkled through the light.

"This was recovered from the Nazis. All the failures of the human mind, the Nazis. The lust for power, the desire to be led. Delusions of superhumanity, put toward the lowest acts of bestial murder. Tell me, Jeremy, have you ever seen a Nobel Prize?"

"No, sir."

"They're quite beautiful." With his right index finger, he traced a circle the size of his palm. "Two hundred grams of 23-carat gold. The front features an engraving of Alfred Nobel and the dates of his birth and death in roman numerals."

He took the scrap of paper from my hand and wrote on it:

NAT—MDCCCXXXIII
OB—MDCCCXCVI

"The back displays the prizewinner's name, above a picture representing their field of endeavor. The medals are handed out each year in Sweden by His Majesty the King."

His eyes drifted off, as if he were picturing a king clasping his shoulder and pressing the medal down into his palm.

"Do you know what the poet Yeats said when he accepted his medal?"

"No," I answered, for the fiftieth time that night.

"He saw his engraving: a young man listening to a beautiful woman stroking a lyre. And he said, 'I was good-looking once like that young man, but my unpractised verse was full of infirmity, my Muse old as it were; and now I am old and rheumatic, and nothing to look at, but my Muse is young.'

"Now," he smiled, "to answer your question. In 1940, the Nazis invaded Denmark. Until that point, the Institute for Theoretical Physics had been a haven for German scientists fleeing the Nazis, including the Nobel Prize winners James Franck and Max von Laue. Suddenly, they had just hours to hide their medals before the Nazis stormed the institute. They had to hide the gold, or the Nazis would use it to fund their horrors. But where to hide it? The Hungarian chemist de Hevesy suggested burying the medals, but Neils Bohr argued that the Nazis would just dig them up. Then de Hevesy came up with a brilliant idea: he would quickly mix together some aqua regia. He dissolved the medals into a beaker—this beaker, actually—and placed it on his shelf among hundreds of identical beakers.

"The Nazis raided the laboratory and walked right by the beaker, God knows how many times, over the years. When the war was over, de Hevesy returned to Denmark and found the beaker untouched. He distilled the gold, and in 1952, the Nobel committee presented Professor Franck with a new medal."

He paused and smiled at me kindly.

"That's amazing," I said. "How did you find the beaker?"

"I purchased it at an auction in Copenhagen. I had to have it. What a magic trick! Good dissolves itself, passes right through

53

evil, and reforms on the other side. Flawless. Come. I don't want you to be late."

Late for what?

We walked through a door behind his desk, into a dimly lit room. All at once I smelled a clean, pungent, hollow smell. The first thing I noticed was the strange chandelier hanging above me, and in a moment of revulsion I realized that its twisting, interlocking shapes were bones, tied and fixed together. It swayed gently as fresher air breezed in from the study. Candles rose from the empty sockets, spilling wax over the bones and illuminating the room with a dull amber glow. The shadows flickered and revealed other shapes in the room: above me, cloaked angels made from skeletons were suspended from the ceiling, giving the impression of flight; bony wings butterflied out from their spines. The walls and ceiling were covered with hideous designs: lines and circles of leg bones, wrists, vertebrae. Then I saw the worst thing of all—a fireplace composed entirely of hundreds of skulls, stacked into a macabre mantel.

"It's a reproduction," he said from behind me. "The Capuchin Crypt, in Rome, under the church of Santa Maria della Concezione."

"What is it?"

"An underground tomb, decorated with the remains of four thousand monks who died between 1500 and 1870. Five rooms, all filled with bones. And when you leave, they hit you with the kicker."

He pointed to the far wall, where a sign was illuminated over a row of skulls. It read:

What you are now,
we once were.

The Faculty Club

What we are now,
you will be.

"Anytime I start taking life for granted, I come sit in here for a while."

"Oh," I mumbled. I wondered how any sane person could sit in here without being chained down.

"Come," he said.

He placed his hand on my back and led me into a long hallway. On both walls, I saw tall glass cases filled with knives, rifles, swords, spears, clubs, maces, crossbows, tomahawks, battle-axes—all mounted to the wall and illuminated with bright lights.

"What's the story here?" I asked.

"No story," he said pleasantly. "I just like weapons."

We came to the end of the hallway. He turned to me, and there was a black cloth in his hands.

"I need to ask your permission to blindfold you."

"Really?" All of a sudden, Miles's goat seemed a few steps closer to being a frightening possibility. "Are you serious?"

He half-shrugged.

"I'm afraid so, if you'd like to go further."

Something told me he wasn't kidding.

Well, I thought, I've come this far.

I nodded.

He moved behind me, and the world went black.

I was suddenly aware of my other senses. I heard the dragging of a heavy door and felt a draft of air.

"One or two steps more," he said quietly.

There was a jolt, and we were moving briskly down in what felt like a prehistoric elevator, the kind with accordion doors. I had no idea how quickly we were going, but the temperature was dropping fast.

When the door opened, cold, wet air hit my face. He led me forward. The ground suddenly felt rough and uneven.

"Stay to your left," he said. "In fact, keep one hand on the wall if you don't mind." He walked directly behind me and kept a hand on my shoulder.

We walked in silence. The air smelled clean and crisp, like limestone and salt. I couldn't tell if we were in a small tunnel or a large chamber, but somehow—I have no idea why—I believed that to my right was an abrupt drop.

My fingers ran over something slimy and warm.

Five hours ago, I was in the library briefing cases like a good law student. Now I was blindfolded underground with a man who collects acid.

As if he sensed my thoughts, the man—call him Mr. Bones—whispered, "Please, just humor me a little longer. You have nothing to fear."

"You don't hear that all the time," I whispered. I was starting to feel a little crazy in the dark.

"I'm sorry?"

" 'You have nothing to fear.' You don't hear that much. The guy at Starbucks doesn't say 'You have nothing to fear.' Someone says that, it's usually a bad sign."

He slapped me on the back like we were old college buddies.

"*There's* that sense of humor I heard about. Relax. I wouldn't bring you here if you didn't deserve it."

Deserve *what,* exactly—the Ivy League version of *Deliverance*?

We finally came to a stop. I realized they did their job well. If I happened to be the unlucky reject who didn't make the cut, I'd have no idea how to get back here—whatever here *was*.

I heard a heavy grinding sound, and then a door opening.

My blindfold was yanked away and my eyes were overwhelmed by a blast of golden light. It was too bright, too fast. I couldn't see a thing. Rough hands shoved me forward. I reached out, trying to keep my balance. That's when I heard the door behind me slam shut and lock.

8

The world came into focus and I found myself in a ballroom, lined on all sides with elegant mirrored walls that made the room seem infinite. Golden chandeliers flooded the room with a warm radiance. I heard music.

The room was filled with men in tuxedos and women in black dresses. I was in a far corner, away from the crowd. I scanned the hall and didn't see Nigel, Daphne, or John anywhere. In fact, I didn't see a single person I recognized. I turned around and there was no door behind me, only a tall panel between two long mirrors. I pressed on it, and of course it didn't budge.

Did I mention I hate parties? Luckily, I had a flash of a memory, something from middle school that gave me hope. I'd taken my friend Vivek to my church's end-of-summer roller skating party. Vivek was the only Indian kid in our town. His house had statues of human elephants and four-armed women who appeared regularly in my dreams. About halfway through the party, the youth pastor asked us to sit at the far end of the rink. He skated up. "Is everyone having a good time?" he asked. We all said yes. "Let me ask you a question," he said. "Does everyone here know for sure that they're going to Heaven?" Again, we all nodded. But the pastor looked puzzled. "Well, my question for you is, how do you *know*? Let's try something else," he said. "Raise your hand if you've accepted Jesus Christ into your heart."

We all put our hands up. Everyone except Vivek. For a second, I watched him look blankly from person to person. Everyone was staring at him. His hand wavered, and then it went up too.

I'm not a particularly brave person. My school was small, and you were either in or you were out. And when you were out, you were really out.

But something about the whole situation rubbed me the wrong way. So, I put my hand down. I looked at Vivek, and after a moment, his hand came back down too.

I figured if God wanted to know what was in my heart, he could just look.

Now I *was* Vivek, in this vast room of strangers of a very different religion. I just hoped some of the karma from that day might swing back around tonight.

I was filled with a sudden sense of liberation. I started thinking of all the things I would do when tonight was over. I thought about that girl I met in the middle of the night and walked home, the one who spilled her oranges everywhere. I figured I might just march right up to her door, ring the doorbell, and ask her out. So what if she'd already turned me down? She was distraught. She thought I was judging her. She was judging herself. I wanted to tell her to lighten up, let it go, come have a slice of pizza and be a normal twenty-five-year-old for once. I mean, does everyone here have to take themselves so damn *seriously*? Is that what we get out of this school—the belief that everything we do is a matter of national importance? If that's the case, I thought, it's going to be hard to ever have fun again.

I looked at myself in the mirror, straightened my tie, checked my teeth, and marched into the crowd.

. . .

Halfway through my second drink, I bumped into a walrus of a man, complete with a comically curled mustache. His tuxedo shirt strained at the buttons, and his woolly hair was parted on the left and traveled away from his cowlick in two heavily gelled waves. I don't know if I walked into him or he walked into me; more likely, the crowd surged us together, until there was no choice but to say something. I would've been okay with "Excuse me," but he raised a plate and showed me a half-devoured piece of cake.

"I shouldn't be eating this," he confided.

"Why not?"

"Just had a quadro six months ago. Know what a quadro is?"

"Not really."

"Quadruple bypass. Fucking doctors cracked my chest wide open. Got a scar from here to here. Nasty. Wife says I look like Frankenstein."

Frankenstein on an all-brownie diet, maybe.

"Know the old saying 'Live fast, die young, leave a good-looking corpse'?"

"Sure. Like James Dean."

"Right-o. My motto is, 'Live fast, see your cardiologist, and leave a fat old corpse!'"

He gave a wheezy, disturbing laugh that involved his hands and shoulders. He mopped the walrus mustache with a handkerchief.

"Beautiful ceremony, no?" he asked, mouth full of cake.

Ceremony? What was he talking about?

"Excuse me?" I said.

"Good grief, man, the *wedding*."

60

What wedding?

I decided to play along, for lack of a better plan.

"Yeah," I said. "It was great." I held out my hand. "Jeremy Davis."

"Ah. Gordon Perry." He crushed my hand in his meaty palm. "Bride's side or groom's side?"

I gave him a chummy smile.

"Guess," I said.

He scrunched his face up and scrutinized me. "Young. Handsome. Employable. Must be bride's side."

"Right-o," I said.

"Ha! Maybe you can inform my wife I'm not a complete fucking idiot."

Let's not get ahead of ourselves.

"And what do *you* do for a living, Jeremy?" he asked, placing another forkful of cake into his crowded mouth.

"I'm a law student," I said.

"Oh, great. *That's* what this country needs. Another lawyer."

Okay, wait a second. Lawyer-bashing? Walrus men? Was I even at the right party?

"Say," he said, pointing his fork at me. "Know what you call ten thousand lawyers at the bottom of the ocean? A good start!"

He poked my chest with the back of his fork-holding hand and gave the wheezy laugh again, louder this time, his head and shoulders bobbing up and down until his face started to flush.

Suddenly, behind the man I spotted Daphne, across the room in a black dress that dipped just slightly between her breasts. I felt a shock of excitement. Her hair was twisted up over her head, showing off the long, creamy curve of her neck. She was surrounded by a crowd of attentive men and unhappy-looking wives. Her eyes caught mine, and I felt a jolt shoot down my stomach.

Without thinking, I took a step in her direction. It was a bit unsteady—how fast had I polished off those drinks?

A thick walrus hand clamped down on my shoulder.

"Wait, wait. A lawyer and a snake get run over in the middle of the road. How do you tell the difference?"

I pinched my eyes closed for a second, took a deep breath, let it out.

"How?"

"The snake's the one with tire marks in front of him!"

The man got even redder this time. Little beads of sweat popped out on his forehead. He dabbed at them with the handkerchief. I started to worry he was going to have another heart attack right here.

I looked back to where Daphne had been, but she was gone. I felt an intense longing for that tan neck, the bright red lips, the blue eyes framed by black hair.

"Myself, I'm in the life insurance game," the walrus was saying. His eyes lit up, like a great idea had just occurred to him. "Say . . ." he said, poking my chest again.

I pointed to my drink.

"Looks like I could use a refill. Very nice meeting you."

I pressed deep into the room, trying to put as much crowd between me and my new friend as possible. Near the bar, I heard a familiar voice. I saw the tall, handsome figure of John Anderson, standing a full head above the crowd. He had his quarterback arms spread, each one around the shoulder of an older, distinguished-looking man.

"Judge Hermann, I found a Raiders fan for you to argue with," he said.

Everyone in their circle laughed, and I felt a surge of envy.

Great, I thought—*he's chatting with a judge, and I'm trading lawyer jokes with Archie Bunker.*

I decided not to pass through John's view. I set out toward the opposite bar instead. I saw a table where a bride and groom were chatting with guests. Behind them was a band on a small dais, bronze horns and a cocktail singer in full swing. *What the hell were we doing at someone's wedding reception?*

A wave of relief spread over me as I spotted Nigel, chatting with a serious-looking older woman in an expensive suit.

"Nigel," I said, a little louder than I meant to. "Hey, Nigel!"

He cast a quick glance at me and said something to the woman. They shook hands, and she handed him a business card from her fancy purse.

He stepped over to me.

"Jeremy," he said brightly, giving me the once-over. "How are you, old chap?" He shook my hand like we hadn't seen each other in years.

"I don't know, Nigel. This party. These people. It's not what I expected."

"I see." He stole a glance around me. A quick one, but long enough for me to catch him.

"These are definitely not the people I expected to be associated with"—I lowered my voice to a pseudo-whisper—"*you-know-what.*"

Was I somewhat drunk? All my words seemed a little harsher than I meant them.

Nigel put his arm around me and led me toward the middle of the room. He said quietly, "I doubt very much that these people have anything to do with the V&D."

He looked at me, waiting.

Danny Tobey

"So what are we doing here?"

I was starting to feel angry, like everyone knew something I didn't.

"They're watching us, Jeremy," he whispered, his lips moving so slightly I could barely make out the words. "On the other side of the mirrors." His gaze held me, keeping me from swinging my head around to the long, graceful mirrors that paneled the walls on all sides of us. "They want to see how we socialize. If we can blend in, find the important people in the room." Nigel came in close. "They're *watching* us, and you need to get your shit together." Suddenly, his voice was full volume and cheery. "I think you *will* love soccer, once you get over your Texan football obsession." He gave a hearty laugh and clasped my shoulder. "My father has a wonderful box. We'll get you over there soon, eh?" He smiled without a care in the world and walked away.

I had a momentary flashback of checking my teeth in the mirror earlier tonight. I cringed. I pictured John Anderson cracking up the judges and politicians, reflected on every wall of the room. I decided to get drunk, under the delusion that I wasn't already.

At the bar, the man next to me smirked, like we were in on the same joke.

"Can you believe this fuckin' party?"

He was one of those short, tense, beefed-up men who exude violence, the kind of guy who would wear a Texas hat into an Oklahoma bar. He was strapped with muscles and his tuxedo strained against them. I decided to give him a *What can you do?* shrug and then look away politely.

"You seen Derrick?"

The hairs on the back of my neck were up now. I should've just said no. I'm not sure why I didn't.

"Who's Derrick?" I asked.

"A big fuckin' asshole, that's who."

The artery on his temple was prominent, pulsing. He leaned into me, and I realized only then how wildly drunk he was.

"He says, you think you can do my job better than me? And I said, yeah, I do. So he tells me to get the fuck out of his office. He doesn't care if fifteen people are waiting for the fucking Care Flight. He's got his own ass to cover, the *fucking jerkoff*. I say enough talk, just *do it*." His voice was rising now, almost to a soft yell. "Just *DO IT*, I tell him. I was ready to tear his fucking *HEAD* off." The artery was really popping now. People around us turned to see what the commotion was. Was he going to take a swing at me? Would his blood vessel explode first?

"Are you *hearing* what I'm saying?"

"Yes," I said softly.

"I'm sorry, am I *disturbing* you?"

"No, you're not. Not at all."

He stared at me then like I'd just told him to go fuck himself.

"Look, can I get you a drink?" I asked, pulling away a little.

"You think I can't afford my own drinks?"

"No . . . I didn't say that. I was just trying to be friendly."

"You some fucking queer?" he said.

At that point, it became clear that I wasn't going to win. More people were looking at us, but they hadn't yet circled us into that timeless point of no return. Bet this was going over great with the boys behind the mirror. Were they munching on popcorn and placing bets?

I backed away and hoped the drunker, more oblivious partiers would fill in between us a bit. He took a couple of lurching steps toward me, then stumbled and caught himself on a surprised man.

I took that moment to turn and walk as fast as I could, as indirectly as I could, toward the other end of the room. I was feeling more sober by the second. The room was still packed, which was good. I prayed that Derrick's friend was so drunk that his rage had already found a new target. Maybe a coatrack or a bar stool.

I came out the other end of the thriving, rowdy crowd, back to the far corner where I'd started. It was still a quiet little enclave, and I stood against the wall and tried to think of ways the night could have gone worse. I felt someone looking at me. The tables around me were empty, except for an old, lonely-looking man sitting by himself. He was staring at me with inquisitive eyes under folds of pearly skin. He had a bad reddish toupee. He didn't look away when I saw him. He held my gaze, and finally I went over and sat down at his table.

"Having fun?" he asked pleasantly.

"Not really."

He smiled.

"Me neither. I don't like parties."

"That makes two of us."

He chuckled, and then we sat quietly for a while.

"Are you a student?" he asked, after a bit.

"I am. I'm a law student."

"Oh," he said, as if he had guessed as much. "So, tell me, why law?"

"That's easy," I said. "My grandfather."

"A lawyer?"

I nodded.

"And you're close?"

"We were."

"Oh." He studied my face. "He passed?"

"Last year."

"I'm sorry. What was he like?"

I smiled.

"Tall. Really tall. He scared the hell out of people, he could seem really serious, but he was a teddy bear. He had this smile that was mostly in his eyes. Kids loved him. The first time I saw his wedding picture, I couldn't believe it. He and my grandmother looked like movie stars. He was that handsome. People were drawn to him. He was shy, but people always came up to him. It's hard to explain.

"When I was a kid, I used to sit in a chair behind his desk and watch him talk to clients. He knew how to talk to people. He could joke with them, get them to open up. When people were upset, he could talk them through it. He was always calm. His eyes told you everything was going to be okay."

"I bet he was excited you were going to law school."

"I remember when he was sick . . ." I was startled to feel my eyes welling a little. I tried to swallow it down. "He said to me, 'I'm sorry I won't be around to help you.'"

"What did you say?"

"I told him . . ." I paused, pinched my nose, and closed my eyes. "I told him he already taught me everything I knew about being a good person." Why was I losing it in front of this guy? Why did I have so many *drinks*? "I told him I remembered a time we went to a football game. This small man in a bow tie took our tickets. And my grandpa said to him, 'I know you. You've worked here a long time, haven't you?' The man said yes. My grandpa said, 'You used to stand over there, but now you stand over here.' You have to understand, this is the guy who tore the *tickets*. Hundreds of people passed him every day and didn't say a word. I saw it in that guy's eyes. It *meant* something. My grandpa was telling that man he *mattered*. That's the kind of person he was."

I didn't know what else to say.

The man considered me for a minute. Then he looked behind me and said, "I think your ride is here, Mr. Davis."

I turned around. Behind me was the man from the house, Mr. Bones, still wearing his jacket and open-collared shirt. He put his arm on my shoulder and said, "Time to go."

I stood, but I turned back to the old man.

"How did you know my name?" I asked him.

"I know everything about you, Mr. Davis."

I felt a chill pass through me, a shiver.

"I know where you live. I know what you do. I just won-der . . ." He said this last part quietly, almost to himself. He looked down at his hands on the table, as if I were already gone.

"Wonder what?" I asked him.

Mr. Bones was tugging on my arm now. He had the blindfold in his other hand. He was unrolling it to put it on me.

"Wonder *what*?" I asked.

Mr. Bones was trying to pull me away. But the old man looked up and met my eyes. The tug on my arm paused.

"I just wonder if you want it badly enough," he said.

The blindfold came over my eyes, and I was left to ponder that question in the dark.

I never saw the person come out of the shadows in the hallway in front of my door, after my walk home from 2312 Morland Street. It must have been four or five in the morning. I really had no idea. I was freezing. My ears were ringing from the cold. I just felt the hands close over my eyes, smelled the alcohol, felt the warm breasts press up against my back. I heard Daphne whisper in a husky voice into my ear that she'd been waiting for me. Her cheek was hot against my neck. Her lips were full and soft, moving in my ear, working her words in soft vibrations on my skin. "I have an offer for you," she said. She turned me around with her hands in my hair, on my waist, until I faced her.

"I'm not going to lose," she said softly, urgently, her sapphire eyes boring into mine. I tried not to look at the deep shadow between her breasts, her dress that clung to a perfect, full body. "I won't leave it to chance," she whispered. "It's too close." She moistened her lips with her tongue. "But . . ." She smiled. "I've done my research. I know how to win." She ran her hand down the side of my cheek, down my neck. She whispered into my ear. "The Thomas Bennett Mock Trial—it's not perfect," she said, her lips humming, "but I've traced the winners. It's an edge. It can break a tie.

"Think," she said, looking down, letting her forehead touch mine, her lips moving inches from my lips. "Nigel and John are the talkers. You and I—we're the brains. Pair the talkers with the brains, you have a competition. Maybe *I* have a good day, maybe *you* have a good day, who knows . . . But . . ." She met my eyes and smiled. "Put the two brains together, and the talkers have nothing to say. We crush them. They're just two puppets with their hands up each other's asses."

I saw it. "We take two spots, they fight over the third," I whispered.

"I knew you were smart," she said, letting her lips graze mine. She pressed me against the door, her body pushing into mine. I felt points of warmth all down my front, her breasts on my chest, her stomach on mine, her thighs hot against my legs. God I wanted her. I wanted her like I've never wanted anyone. I wanted to pull her dress up over her waist right here in the hall, slide into her right here. "I read your article," she said in that husky, teasing voice. She let her thighs slide back down against the bulge in my pants, then up again. "You did?" She let her hand trace lazily down my stomach, over my belt. "A little superficial," she murmured, her nails grazing up the zipper of my pants, "otherwise, it was pretty good." I grabbed her hand and jerked it away. "How many articles have *you* published?" I snapped.

She pulled herself off me, swept her hair from her eyes. "Think about it," she said. "It'll be a good chance to get to know each other."

I watched her walk away down the hall, swinging her ass and taunting me.

When I got to my room, not sober, not fulfilled, horny and furious and thrilled and bewildered, I found another envelope on my bed. This time, I didn't even bother to feel surprised that my doors and windows had been locked. I'd seen bigger tricks tonight. I tore it open and read it quickly.

It said, simply, in typed letters:

NOVEMBER ELEVENTH. SEVEN THIRTY P.M.

And below it, a quick, handwritten addendum:

Get a new suit.

9

I threw myself into the mock trial. Daphne's logic was appealing. Her eyes, her lips, her rosewater scent were overwhelming. I would guarantee our entry into the V&D. I would win her admiration. I would win *her*. Did it matter that I knew, on some level, that these were exactly the ideas she wanted rolling around in my brain?

The case was fascinating: a war hero had suffered a terrible head injury and come home changed. Suddenly, this mild-mannered husband was capable of murdering his coworker in cold blood. It would all come down to *mens rea:* what had *really* caused this violent crime—was it the war hero? Or was it the injury that changed him?

Word had already spread across the class: this year, the judges' panel would include a retired Supreme Court justice, a former United States Attorney, and, as always, the famous professor Ernesto Bernini. Dozens of students were drafting briefs, hoping they would be selected to compete in the final trial, to show off their skills in front of this stratospheric panel. Daphne and I spent weeks in the library, revising our motions and studying trial tactics. Outside, the days got darker and colder.

I passed the ancient man who worked the front door at the library. As usual, it seemed that if I breathed too hard, he'd blow away like sand.

Moments later, I was back at my favorite table, watching Daphne read my section of a new brief, her hair pulled back in a long ponytail, a pen tapping against her mouth. She didn't make a single mark. She read the entire thing and looked up.

"Start over," she said, and went back to work on her own section.

I hadn't slept more than a couple of hours in days. I'd developed a searing headache I couldn't shake. Twice in the last two weeks, when I stood up too quickly I felt the world go blurry. Between the trial prep and the endless research for Bernini's opus, I wasn't even attending class anymore. *What did it matter?* I asked myself. *I've discovered the real channel to success in this place, and it has nothing to do with the straight A's and summer jobs my classmates are pursuing like lemmings.*

Around midnight, I was in one of the darkest corners of the library, looking for a rare volume. But on the shelf, I found an empty space where the book should've been. I felt a surge of panic, then anger: was someone using *my* book? Or worse, had someone hidden it?

I started walking the deserted floor, searching for the book.

That's when I heard the strange sound of crying.

I followed it to a deeper recess, and through a crack in a shelf of books, I was shocked to see Nigel bent over a table, his eyes red, his hands slamming a stack of books off the table onto the floor. The crash was jarring. Without thinking, I walked toward him. He looked up, and a wave of humiliation and anger spread across his face.

"What do you want?" he snapped at me.

"Nigel, what's wrong?" I took a step toward him.

"Don't patronize me," he said.

"Nigel, we're friends, right?"

His eyes burned right through me.

"Friends." He turned the word over like a moldy peach. "I thought you and Daphne were friends now."

"It's not like that."

"You think I don't see what you're doing?"

"I'm not doing anything."

He ignored me and turned back to one of the books he hadn't knocked to the floor.

What the hell, I thought. "Say, you don't have Goldman's *Theory of Criminal Justice,* do you?"

Nigel laughed bitterly. "Like it would help." He smirked. "I've already read it."

"Look, Nigel, it's after midnight. Let's call it a day. We can grab a beer. Get some food. Sal's is still open."

Nigel shook his head without looking up. His movements were quick, jerky. What happened to the suave, graceful gestures of Nigel Manning, son of an ambassador and a movie star?

"How can I call it a day," Nigel said, "when it takes an hour to read a case, and I've got a hundred more cases to go?"

I did a double take.

"Why does it take an hour to read a case?" I asked.

He looked wounded. "How long does it take *you*?"

"I don't know. Ten minutes? Twenty?"

"That's *impossible*. Half the time it's not even apparent what they're talking about. Who taught these judges to *write*? It's all gibberish."

He sounded frantic. All the pressure and strain of three months of law school was pouring out of him like bile.

73

And that's when I realized, at this moment, Nigel *was* Humpty Dumpty: infinitely fragile, a web of invisible cracks running through his handsome face. He was *crushable*. Motions were due in a week. All I had to do was turn around and walk away, and he and John were finished.

Instead, I sat down. I didn't say a word as he wiped his eyes, blew his nose, and composed himself.

Then, I taught him how to read a case. I showed him how to skim through the pages of words and tease out the key elements— the *issue,* the *posture,* the *holding,* the *rationale.* I showed him how meaning could emerge from the chaos, the way constellations emerged from a dispersion of stars.

When we were done, Nigel frowned at me.

"I envy you, you know."

"Are you *kidding* me? I'd give anything to have your life. You've traveled the world. You go to parties with Oprah and Bill Gates. You envy *me*?"

"You're a nobody," he said matter-of-factly. "You never have to wonder if you're here because some professor loved your mom in *Last Affair.*" He smiled lightly. "You're white, so you never have to entertain the thought that you're here to populate the cover of an admissions brochure—you know, the one with the smiling rainbow coalition sitting under a tree?"

"Nigel, that's bullshit. You're one of the smartest people I've ever met. The only reason I can read a case is because I spent the last four years living in my parents' basement, practicing for law school. While you were out having a life."

"Maybe yes, maybe no," Nigel said. "But *you* never have to wonder."

The hell I didn't. I was a category too. The country rube, here at the pleasure of the Northern gods. I tried to think of a way to say this, but Nigel spoke first.

"I want you to know something, Jeremy. I appreciate what you did tonight. But the V and D is my destiny. My dad was in it. And his dad before him. And you can trace it all the way back to the first black man in the V and D, in a time when black men didn't get shit handed to them. So I tell you this out of courtesy for the kindness you showed me: don't be surprised when I do whatever it takes to hurt you."

With that, he picked up his books and left without another word.

10

Daphne and I sat next to each other in the packed courtroom. Her leg was pressed against mine under the table. The chamber overflowed with spectators—hundreds of jealous classmates, chattering professors, curious undergraduates, high school debate teams, townies, press, even a few tourists with cameras—every seat was full, and people stood two rows deep in the back of the room. All here to watch the 203rd chapter of the oldest, most prestigious mock trial in the nation. Actors from the drama school would play the star witnesses: Arnold Reid, the altered vet; Sheila Reid, his loyal wife. Doctors from the university would serve as expert witnesses, providing actual medical testimony and standing on their own credentials. The jurors were upperclassmen, 2Ls and 3Ls eager to decide the fate of the best and brightest first-years.

A warm front had moved in overnight, pushing away the clouds and cold and sending bright rays of sunlight streaming into the courtroom from the wall of windows. Across the aisle from us, Nigel and John sat at their table, laying out stacks of papers. Next to them was their client, the unfortunate Arnold Reid, played by a good-looking young drama student.

The murmuring suddenly stopped, and I looked over and saw the procession of judges enter from a side door. The retired Supreme Court justice was first; he looked more rested and relaxed than I'd ever seen him in pictures, almost embarrassingly so: he had a tan that looked straight out of a bottle. The former U.S. Attorney was next, pudgy and good-natured, with neat prep-school hair, owlish glasses, and a deep dimple in his chin. Professor Bernini entered last. He looked straight ahead, avoiding eye contact with the room. His trademark impishness, that twinkle in his eyes, was completely gone. He was taking his role as judge seriously.

The men marched solemnly and took their seats on the bench high above us.

Dean Thompson addressed the room. He welcomed the crowd and gave each judge a warm, reverent introduction. He introduced the four of us, then closed with a long list of the famous people who'd won this event as first-year students.

Then, the retired Supreme Court justice leaned forward.

"Are both sides ready?"

"Yes, Your Honor," Daphne said, rising.

"Yes, Your Honor," John echoed.

"Okay. The State may proceed."

I felt a shot of voltage from my toes to my fingertips. The State. That was me. And this was real. Holy shit. Holy shit, holy shit, holy shit. Until this moment I'd been watching this like a very pleasant movie. What the fuck was I *doing* here?

I stood up and faced the jury.

I cleared my throat. You could hear a pin drop in the room. I felt every one of the thousand eyes on me.

The jury was composed of random 2Ls and 3Ls—people I'd seen in the halls but didn't really know.

Slowly, I started to speak.

"May it please the Court. Counsel, ladies and gentlemen, good morning. We expect the evidence to show that on September 22 of last year, this defendant had a business dispute with a man named Russell Connor. The defendant drove home. He removed a nine-millimeter handgun from his safe and drove back to his office. He pointed this gun at Russell Connor and shot him in cold blood. He shot him three times. Russell Connor was unarmed. He was sitting at his desk. He died on the spot. Russell Connor left behind a wife and four children."

I let that sink in.

"Ladies and gentlemen, those are the facts of this tragic event. This is a case of cold-blooded murder, pure and simple. I ask you to remember that. This is a case about Jennifer Connor, who will never see her husband again. This is about Stacy, Marcus, Noah, and Blake, who will never see their father again. No matter how complicated this case may become, if you hang on to that idea, then at the end of the day, common sense is going to win. And we will give the wife and children of Russell Connor what they deserve. Justice." I took a breath and nodded. "Thank you."

I walked back to my seat and sat down. Daphne wrote something on a legal pad and slid it over to me. *S*O*L*I*D,* it said.

Moments later, Nigel was standing in front of the jury. He raised his hand, just slightly, like a conductor the moment before a symphony begins, and a silence fell over the room.

"Imagine," he said softly, his clear British accent carrying through the hall, "that you are about to go to jail for the rest of your life."

He wore a three-piece suit, with a gold watch-chain hanging across his vest. He appeared likable, precise, trustworthy. There was no hint of the fragility from the other night. I wondered how many people who looked perfect were secretly a mess on the inside.

"Imagine that every detail pointed to the fact that you were guilty. Every fact. Every witness. No way out."

Nigel sat down on the edge of his table and sighed.

"Now imagine one more thing. *You* didn't do it."

He looked at each juror.

"How angry would you feel? How helpless? Would that be justice?" He paused. Then suddenly, his tone lightened. "Of course not. That's easy. We don't punish people for things they didn't do."

And then he looked directly at me, his face showing a profound distaste. "But that's *exactly* what the prosecution is going to ask you to do. They are going to ask you to send a good man to jail for an act that was not his own."

Nigel stood up and looked at his client. He smiled.

"Witness after witness is going to tell you that Arnold Reid was the kindest, gentlest man they ever met. A soft-spoken husband and father. A small-business owner. A man who dreamed of going back for his MBA. But first he had something to do. He decided to leave his comfortable life and serve his country in a time of war. Two months later, he went to Iraq as a private in the army. He didn't have to go. He didn't need the money or the scholarships. He *chose* to go. That's the kind of person we're talking about.

"And then it happened." Nigel put his hand on the rail of the jury box and leaned in. "One day, Arnold was fixing a tire on the side of the road in Baghdad, when—*BAM!*" Nigel smacked his hands on the rail, startling the jurors. "A rocket landed twenty feet from where he was kneeling.

"Arnold was treated in hospital after hospital. It was a fight for his life. And he pulled through. He was honorably discharged and sent home to his wife and children. But not without scars.

79

"Arnold was left with a strip of metal, a twisted piece of rocket, lodged in his head. That was the price he paid for serving his country.

"And suddenly, nothing was the same. He had constant headaches. He couldn't think clearly. He couldn't concentrate at work. He was suddenly irritable, impulsive. He wasn't *himself*. All because of the piece of metal that pierced his skull as he was serving his country."

There was a righteous anger now in Nigel's voice. His eyes were strong and clear, but they were watering too. He pointed an accusing finger at us.

"And when a man named Russell Connor tried to take advantage of Arnold, tried to exploit his handicap and steal his business, something unpredictable happened. This piece of metal, this foreign object, interrupted the electricity in Arnold's brain and sent it in a direction it never meant to go. And so his body committed an act that this kind, gentle man never would have done in his forty years on earth. *That* was his crime: having a piece of metal shot into his brain while defending his country."

Nigel fixed the jury with a holy stare.

"I ask you to focus your powers of compassion and ask yourself: what if that piece of metal had been shot into *your* head? What if your good thoughts were suddenly hijacked? Would we be right to strip *you* from *your* family *and send you to jail for the rest of your life?*"

Nigel leaned back on his table again, looking exhausted. He smiled sadly, cautiously.

"Well, now you have the power. And I beg you—I beg all of us—to use it with mercy and wisdom."

And he sat down and wiped his brow with a handkerchief.

. . .

The law was clear. If you know right from wrong, if you are awake and you intend your actions, then you are responsible for them. It doesn't matter if you were born angry or mean or impulsive. So why should it matter if you were born kind and gentle and then changed by a bomb?

As with any good mock trial, we were on the verge of blowing our fragile categories wide open. Do we have minds, capable of choice and free will? Or do we have brains, made of cells and electricity, firing like pinball machines with only the *illusion* of free will?

In one fell swoop, Nigel had swept aside hundreds of years of criminal law and asked, how can we punish this man? And he spoke like a Shakespearean actor. His client wasn't even real, and when I saw one of the jurors dab at her eyes, I knew I was in trouble.

11

If Daphne were just gorgeous, or just smart, she would be amazing. But the combination of both seemed unfair, statistically boggling, almost mystical; she took the air out of the courtroom. And yet in front of the jury, she seemed softer than I'd ever seen her—except maybe for that brief, sleepy moment at the end of Nigel's dinner party, her hair down, her contacts out—then and now, she was warm and likable, someone you could curl up with by the fire in pajamas and read a book.

"Mrs. Reid, you told us your husband was a kind and gentle man, is that right?"

"Yes," said the actress playing the defendant's wife.

Daphne was near the witness stand, close to her—just two ladies talking.

"He wasn't violent *at all* before the accident, right? Night and day? That's what you said?"

"Night and day."

"And that's important, right? It's important because you believe it was the accident that made your husband commit this crime?"

For a second, the witness tried to look at Nigel and John, but Daphne stepped casually into her view.

"Right?"

"Yes."

"*Kind and gentle*. Those are the same words the attorney used to describe your husband, aren't they?"

"If you say so."

"Are they your words or the attorney's?"

"Excuse me?"

"What I'm wondering is, *who* decided to call your husband 'kind and gentle'? Was that your phrase? Or did the attorneys tell you to call him that?"

"Objection," John said, standing. "Counsel is asking about privileged attorney-client communications."

"Mrs. Reid isn't the client," Daphne answered calmly. "Her husband is. And she volunteered to testify as a character witness."

"Overruled," the justice replied.

"Thank you, Your Honor." Daphne turned back to Mrs. Reid. "I can repeat the question," she said gently. "Did the attorneys come up with the phrase *kind and gentle,* or did you?"

Mrs. Reid mumbled something.

"Could you repeat that, Mrs. Reid?"

"The attorneys," she answered, glaring at Daphne.

"I see. So you've told us what the attorneys think of Mr. Reid."

"Objection," Nigel and John said at the same time.

"Withdrawn," Daphne said. "Mrs. Reid, would it be fair to say that your husband never raised his voice at you?"

"I didn't say that."

"So he was a kind and gentle man who yelled at you?"

"We had fights like everybody else."

"Big fights or little fights?"

"I don't understand."

83

"Mrs. Reid, please, my question isn't difficult. Did you and your husband have big fights or little fights?"

"Little, I guess."

"So he yelled at you during *little* fights?"

"Well, I mean . . . he only yelled during big fights."

"So you had big fights too?"

"Yes."

"Okay. I'm going to trust that you are answering my question accurately this time. Is that fair?"

"Yes."

Mrs. Reid was starting to get steamed, and Daphne hadn't raised her voice once.

"Mrs. Reid, can a husband be *kind and gentle* if he hits his wife?"

"Objection," Nigel blurted, standing up. "The question is vague, more prejudicial than probative, assumes facts not in evidence . . ." He was talking as fast as he could think.

"Your Honor," Daphne said pleasantly, "the defense is putting a lot of weight on this phrase *kind and gentle.* I think the jury deserves to know exactly what it means."

"Go on," the U.S. Attorney said.

"Mrs. Reid, can a husband be *kind and gentle* if he hits his wife?"

"Of course not."

"And Mr. Reid never hit you?"

"Never. Not once."

"Can a husband be *kind and gentle* if he pushes his wife?"

"No."

"And Mr. Reid never pushed you?"

"*No.*"

"Can a husband be *kind and gentle* if he grabs his wife and shakes her?"

"Nuh—"

Halfway through the word *no,* Mrs. Reid came to a halt.

"Mrs. Reid? It's a simple question. Can a husband be *kind and gentle* if he grabs his wife and shakes her?"

"I don't know . . ."

"Yes or no, Mrs. Reid."

Silence.

"Your Honor, please instruct the witness to answer my question."

"Mrs. Reid?" Bernini looked at her curiously.

"Yes," she whispered.

Daphne cocked her head, confused.

"Mrs. Reid, for the record, are you saying that a husband can be *kind and gentle* if he grabs his wife and shakes her?"

"Yes. No. I don't know."

"Please, answer my question. Yes or no?"

"No," she said softly.

"Good. We can't call a husband *kind and gentle* if he grabs his wife and shakes her. Mrs. Reid, I'm sorry, but I have to ask, has Mr. Reid ever grabbed and shaken you?"

Mrs. Reid shook her head, not yes or no, but as if she were warding the question away. Nigel and John stared straight ahead, betraying nothing.

"Yes," she said finally.

"Thank you for your honesty," Daphne said kindly. "It was on the night of your husband's company dinner, wasn't it?"

"Yes."

"You thought you two were alone in the coatroom, didn't you?"

"Yes," she said, starting to weep softly.

85

"Would it surprise you to know that a man named Arthur Willey, the man working in the coatroom that night, saw you two fighting?"

"I didn't see anyone else."

"Your husband was yelling, wasn't he?"

"Yes."

"He grabbed you by the arms, didn't he?"

"Yes."

"He shook you and shouted at you, didn't he?"

"Yes," she said, and tears started to run down her face.

Daphne leaned in, like a priest or a cellmate.

"What were you fighting about that night?"

"I don't remember."

"Was someone cheating?"

"No."

"Were you in financial trouble?"

"No."

"It must have been something big. Surely you remember?"

Mrs. Reid was shaking her head, wishing the questions away. Then she said, "No."

"Are you saying your husband grabbed you and shook you over something you can't even *remember*?"

"Asked and answered," Nigel called out.

"Sustained."

Daphne spoke softly to Mrs. Reid, ignoring Nigel and the judge. "Just one more question, and then we're done."

Daphne made a sad face, as if it hurt her to even ask it.

"Was this fight before or after Mr. Reid's accident, when the piece of metal went into his head?"

There was a painful pause.

"Before," Mrs. Reid said, so softly you almost couldn't hear it at all.

John faced Mrs. Reid and smiled kindly at her. He looked at the jury, with his understanding eyes and his broad hand on the back of his neck, as if to say: *this woman deserves better than what she just got.*

"Mrs. Reid, how long have you and Arnold been married?"

"Twenty years."

"Did you have boyfriends before Arnold?"

"Yes."

"Did you fight with those boyfriends more or less than you did with Arnold?"

"More, I think. Arnold and I didn't fight that much."

"But you did fight sometimes, right?"

"Sure. We were married for twenty years!"

John smiled sheepishly, as if to say, *you got me, ma'am—that was a dumb question.* He let her answer sink in.

"The night you were just talking about, did you call the police?"

"No," she said, looking confused.

"Who drove you home that night?"

"My husband."

"Did you go to the hospital?"

"No . . ."

"Did you have bruises?"

"No," she replied, with a baffled look that said, *aren't you on our side?*

"Are you surprised by these questions?"

"I guess I am."

"Why?"

"Well, it just wasn't like that. I mean, police? Bruises? He didn't grab me hard. We were just fighting and he kind of, you know, held me here. It didn't hurt. It was just, you know, passionate. We were having a fight."

"Were you afraid?"

"No. I was pissed."

A couple of the jurors laughed.

"Mrs. Reid, we've just heard a lot about one fight. Except for that one night, did Arnold ever lay a hand on you in anger?"

"No. Never."

"Did he ever hit you or push you or do anything physical at all?"

"Never," she said. "He was a gentle man. With our kids too. He was so sweet."

"So in twenty years of marriage, you had one really bad fight. Is that it?"

"Objection, leading."

"Withdrawn. Mrs. Reid, do you think a person should be judged by twenty years of marriage or by one night?"

"Objection, argumentative."

"Sustained."

"Mrs. Reid, before his accident, did Arnold ever do anything, *anything,* that made you think he was capable of truly hurting another person?"

Mrs. Reid sat up straight and looked right at the jury.

"Never in a million years."

12

Mock trials are designed to be dead heats; you play with the facts you're given. Our witnesses say Arnold was a jerk. Their witnesses say he was a saint. Our expert witness, a psychiatry resident from the university hospital, testified that you don't need a scrap of metal to explain this murder. Sometimes, even the quietest, sweetest men just snapped. Sometimes *especially* the quietest, sweetest men.

But when the defense called its expert, my heart stopped. It took me a moment to recognize her, in her professional suit and her neat ponytail. The glasses were new; they were *smart* glasses, with small lenses and thin copper frames. She wore makeup now. But it all came rushing back with the force of a memory triggered by perfume: the crisp night, the split grocery bag, the oranges rolling everywhere. The moonlight confession; that pretty, kind face splashed with tears.

Her name, it turns out, was Sarah Casey.

Her credentials were impeccable. Our mock expert was a budding authority on personality disorders. Their mock expert was a budding neurosurgeon; she was a cruise director on a tour of the brain: cut here and get rage; smash here and lose control. She was patient and clear, modest but confident. She smiled and made jokes. She told us about other brain-injured soldiers who came home suddenly different, as if possessed. She even gave it a name—traumatic brain injury, or TBI—and once something had a name, it was real. By the time she was done, it seemed completely reasonable that Arnold's injury had forced him to act against his heart and soul—whatever those were.

I don't think she recognized me until the judges asked if the State was ready for cross-examination.

"You take this one," I whispered to Daphne.

"What?"

"I know her," I said.

"You prepped this part. You're prepared. Do it."

"I *know* her."

"I don't care."

"Is the State ready?" the judge asked again, irritated.

I rose and said, "Yes, Your Honor." Then Sarah looked at me. I watched the thoughts unfold in her eyes: first puzzlement (*where have I seen him before?*), then recognition, then a recalling of our conversation—and then, of course, ragged, saw-toothed fear.

"Dr. Casey," I said, my voice sounding thin in my ears. "Did you meet the defendant before his accident?"

"No," she said softly.

"Did you interview people who knew him before the accident?"

"No."

"So, you can't say for sure that the defendant's personality changed *at all,* can you?"

"No, I can't."

I should have gone to my next question. But I stuttered and drew a blank. She kept talking.

"But I *can* say, with medical certainty, that Mr. Reid's brain injury is consistent with a personality change."

Damn it, I thought. *Focus.*

"Consistent with. I see. But you can't say for sure?"

"No."

Good. Keep moving.

"Now—is it possible to sustain a brain injury and *not* have a personality change?"

"Of course."

"Could someone fake a personality change after a brain injury?"

"Objection."

"I'll rephrase, Your Honor. If someone claims to have a personality change, is there any way to prove it?"

"Not in this case." *Next . . . Keep moving . . . What next?* "But," she continued, "if someone has a brain injury *and* a personality change, we can ask whether the two are consistent. In this case they are."

Shit.

"I see," I said, trying to sound like I had just scored a major point. But I hadn't. I hadn't at all. I was screwing up, blowing it.

"Why did you appear here today?" I asked her. It was an insane question. For one thing, it was open-ended. I was giving her a chance to make a speech. But that wasn't the half of it. It was crazy, because I wasn't asking for the good of my case. I was asking for *me.*

She met my eyes, as if she understood.

"Honestly," she said, "when I saw the flier, I just thought it would be fun. I spend all my time in the hospital. It seemed like a chance to get away for an hour and do something different."

That's when I saw it in her eyes. Some tiny part of her, deep down, *wanted* to be exposed. Consciously or not, the guilt-ridden part of her brain had come here to flirt with professional suicide. Freud called it the Death Instinct. Poe called it the Imp of the Perverse. Now I knew the answer to the question I'd posed to her that night: she couldn't live with the lie, and she couldn't live without it. So she put herself on trial. And now I knew exactly how to win this case, if I was willing to indulge my own darker instincts.

"I see," I said again, this time without even pretending I had a point.

That's when I realized my mind was completely blank.

I was standing in front of a silent room. I started to hear the rustling of people shifting in their seats. I didn't dare look up at Bernini. A few uncomfortable coughs in the crowd . . .

I stalled.

"Just a moment, please, Your Honors."

I walked back to our table and stood over it, pretending to flip through my notes. Daphne leaned over. "What the *fuck* are you doing?" she hissed in my ear. I nodded thoughtfully for the jury, as if she were giving me priceless information. "Listen to me very carefully," she whispered. "You are *not* going to fuck this up for me. What's the matter," she jeered, "you can't cross-examine a *girl*? You think she can't take it? Don't insult her and don't insult me. You need to *grow a pair of balls*." I pretended to jot something down, but really I just wrote *Fuck* and underlined it.

I stepped back from the table.

"You're appearing here on behalf of the defense, aren't you, Dr. Casey?"

I tried to make *Doctor* sound like a dirty word.

"Yes."

"And they are paying you for your testimony, aren't they?"

"No, sir. I'm being paid for my time. My testimony is my own."

Damn it. It was an old trick, and she dodged it perfectly. Nigel and John had prepped her well. Damn them too.

I looked at Sarah on the stand. I didn't want to hurt her. She'd trusted me. I liked her. Maybe more than like.

I don't want to do this, I thought. *I won't do this.*

I could see it now. It was a dead heat. All those weeks of sleepless nights, endless motions, skipped meals, nightmares, sneaking into the men's room to puke my nerves away. I hadn't talked to my parents in a month. I hadn't gone on a date, seen a movie, had a beer. I was so sure that *this* was the way to the V&D—to success beyond my wildest dreams—that I hadn't studied for my classes or even attended them. God help me if I had to rely on those grades! I had all my eggs in this one basket. This *case*. I couldn't lose. Not to mention Daphne, who hadn't laid a hand on me since that night outside my dorm room. Goddamn her lips! My career, my future, my *life*. The whole damn thing hung in the balance.

I don't want to do this.

On the stand, Sarah looked relaxed now, calm. She caught my eye, and there was a hint of a smile—a shared secret. She'd already decided I wasn't going to hurt her. It was almost smug when you thought about it. So confident in her power over me—that I would throw away my life, my future, everything—to cover up for her lie.

Who did she think she was?

I felt a shock of guilt, or pain—that voice saying *Please, I don't want to hurt her*—but somehow it lost out to other dreams and urges.

I made a decision.

"Dr. Casey, you are appearing as an expert witness, is that correct?"

"Yes."

"And this jury is trusting your opinion because of your credentials, right?"

Suddenly she seemed wary.

"Yes."

She looked at me hard, searching.

"You are a neurosurgery resident in the top program in the country. Isn't that right?"

"Yes," she said softly.

"Getting this position, it shows you had top grades in medical school, correct?"

"Yes."

"And all of this—your grades, your position in a top residency—all of this is the basis for your expertise here today, isn't it?"

"Yes," she whispered, looking at me desperately, trying not to reveal anything, begging me with her eyes.

"And that's not all. Your *honesty*. Isn't that part of your expertise here today? The jury can trust what you say because you are an *honest* person?"

"*Yes,*" she said, her eyes starting to well up, perceptible only to me, standing so close.

I closed my eyes. I took a deep breath.

Daphne was swept up in my new rhythm. She looked curious, excited. I found my own righteous anger and turned back to the witness.

No going back.

"Dr. Casey, isn't it true that your application to this program contained serious misrepresentations about your abilities and accomplishments in medical school?"

John and Nigel erupted.

They had no idea where I was going, but they let out a string of objections.

"Yes or no?" I pressed.

Sarah froze, stunned.

"Yes or no, Dr. Casey? Why are you hesitating?"

She shook her head no.

"Dr. Casey," I said, the word *doctor* now sounding absolutely pornographic, "did you or did you not allow your father to cover up numerous failed classes during your medical school education?"

"I don't have to put up with . . . this isn't *real*."

Her lips were trembling.

"Yes or no, Dr. Casey?"

No answer.

"YES OR NO?"

Her face started to break.

"Did you or did you not get this prestigious residency as a result of lies and cover-ups?"

"Yes," she said softly, her voice cracking.

"Did you allow this cover-up to occur?"

"Yes," she repeated, now sobbing.

"Did you go from interview to interview, passing yourself off as something you are not—to get a job you did not deserve?"

"Yes. Yes. Yes."

The objections were raining down now, washing over me.

I didn't pay attention.

I didn't even listen for her last answer.

The damage was done. The witness was toast.

I sat back down at our table. Daphne gave me a look of such pride it was almost lustful.

I heard Sarah's steps as she left the courtroom. But I couldn't find the courage—not even for a single second—to look up and watch her go.

13

We won. That's what the head juror announced, holding a sheet of paper. The judges critiqued our performances, but I can't remember a word they said. I just kept repeating the phrase—part cheer, part question—over and over in my head: *we won, we won, we won.*

The sun was nearly down, the courtroom filled with purple light. The judges were gone. Most of the crowd had gone home.

"Let's go celebrate," Daphne said.

"Sure. Hang on a second."

I walked toward John and Nigel. "Where are you going?" she called after me.

They were still sitting at their table. John was staring at his notes. Nigel looked ahead blankly, like a kid who has just learned his dog died.

"Come on," I said to them. "We're going out."

They looked at me like I was crazy.

"I'm serious. We're going out. It's over. We've been killing ourselves for a month. Come on. I'm buying."

"I don't feel like it," Nigel said.

"I don't care. I'm buying us a round of drinks. After that, you can leave if you want. You owe me that much."

I wasn't taking no for an answer. Somehow I bullied them into joining us at The Idle Rich. Mostly, I think they were numb. The four of us sat around an oak table with the rapport of funeral directors, until the second round of drinks, when things loosened up a bit.

"Something about this place," I said. "It's corrosive, isn't it? When did we get so serious?"

"You didn't have fun destroying our case?" Nigel asked. His tone was only halfway bitter, a major improvement over the last hour.

"How did you know that about our witness?" John asked, shaking his head. We hadn't met each other's experts before the trial. We hadn't even known their names. He must have been baffled.

"I know her," I said. "We met on campus."

"Lucky her," Nigel said dryly.

I shook off a sinking feeling in my stomach, changed the subject.

"Seriously, though. Did you guys ever just hang out, act stupid? Or were you always future Supreme Court clerks?"

"John used to be crazy," Daphne said.

"Bullshit."

"What are you talking about?" John asked her, making eye contact with us for the first time since the verdict.

"You know, the table story?"

"You are *not* bringing that up."

"If you don't tell it, I will," Daphne said, grinning.

"Fine. Go ahead." John leaned back, closed his eyes, and held a bottle to his forehead.

"It's an Oxford story," Daphne said. "John and his friends decide they want to start a poker game. So after a few drinks, one of his brilliant friends—who was it, Tom?—suggests that one of the big round tables in the dining hall would make a perfect poker table. You have to imagine it: these are giant wooden tables, maybe seven or eight feet wide. It took five of them to lift it. So after dinner one night, when the dining hall was empty, John and his friends snuck back in and carried out the table. That was their whole plan. Just walk out with it. Rhodes scholars, right?"

"Oh no," Nigel said, shaking his head. "You stole a table from Oxford?"

"We did," John said. I saw the hint of a grin.

"They almost made it too. They were halfway across campus, carrying this table in the middle of the quad, when a security guard stopped them."

"No."

"What happened?"

"That's the best part," Daphne said. "As the story goes, everyone's panicking except John. He looks right at the security guard and says with a straight face, 'Do you think I *want* to be carrying this table across campus?' He says it just right. The guard blinks at him for a few seconds. Then he lets them go!"

Everybody was smiling now, even laughing a little. "Confidence," John said happily, "the key to life." He took a drink.

"So you kept the table?"

Daphne laughed.

"They couldn't get it through the door of their apartment."

John turned red and looked down. The rest of us cracked up.

"You put it back?"

"Not exactly . . ."

Daphne shook her head.

"They left it on the squash courts."

I don't know why, but that's when I lost it. I laughed so hard I nearly cried. It was like all the stress of the last two months came rushing out.

I felt the thaw come over our small group. It was almost like we were back at Nigel's dinner party, before everything went to hell with trials and mysterious clubs that can't be mentioned for some pretentious reason.

"This is what matters," I said finally. "Right here. Friendship. At the end of the day, none of the other stuff matters."

Everybody agreed, but nobody looked totally sure.

John and Nigel stumbled toward their homes. Daphne and I hung back. I didn't know what to say next. Somehow "Your place or mine?" seemed wrong.

"I guess I might see you tomorrow night," I said. Tomorrow was the eleventh, the night of the second event, according to the cryptic invitation on my bed.

Daphne smiled. "Maybe. Who knows what they have in store for us?" She rubbed my arm. "You were great today. I knew I was right to choose you."

"You were great too."

I felt a thrill in my stomach.

She made a big production of yawning and stretching. "Wow, I can't keep my eyes open." She leaned in and gave me a brief hug. Then she said good night and walked off, leaving me as confused and deflated as a star witness on the stand, freshly shredded and dismissed.

The next morning I checked my bank account. About a thousand dollars left to get me to the end of the semester and my next loan check. I withdrew eight hundred and bought a new suit.

14

November 11 marked day two of the Indian summer that arrived with the trial. I could almost forget the bitterness of October; the days were now bright and cheerful, warm in the sun, crisp in the shade. I got a haircut and asked for it short. I usually let my hair dry wavy. Today I parted it on the left and combed it straight. I put on my new suit. I looked in the mirror and hardly recognized myself.

Tonight's invitation had even less information than the first. Just a date and time. No address. No instructions.

The only option, I decided, was to return to 2312 Morland Street. I would get there early, in case I was wrong and had to improvise.

On the way, I wondered who I would see tonight. Would I encounter the elegant Mr. Bones again? Would he show me new items in his crazy-man collection?

Would I see the old man with the red toupee, the retired lawyer who asked all about my grandfather? The one who wondered if I wanted it bad enough? He wouldn't have to ask that tonight.

The gingerbread house on Morland Street looked the same. I rang the doorbell. A young woman dressed like a soccer mom pulled aside the curtain and looked at me through the window. Two kids chased a ball behind her.

"Yes?"

"Hi. I'm Jeremy Davis. I'm looking for"—I didn't even know his name—"the gentleman who lives here."

"I'm sorry, *who* are you looking for?"

"The man who lives here? He's about my height? Gray hair?"

"There's no one like that here." She picked up one of the kids who was pulling at her pants. She looked at my suit, sized me up. She closed the curtain and opened the door.

"We moved in two weeks ago. Maybe you're looking for the people who lived here before?"

"You moved in two weeks ago?"

"Yes."

"Are you sure?"

She raised her eyebrows.

"Pretty sure."

I tried to think.

"Did they leave a forwarding address?"

"No. I never met them. I'm sorry I can't be more help."

She started to close the door.

"Are you sure I'm not supposed to be here?"

She looked me over.

"Sorry, sweetie. I don't know what to tell you."

"Thanks anyway."

"All right. Drive safe."

It was an odd thing for her to say, considering I walked here. But when I turned around to leave, I saw a car idling across the street. It was a nice car—I'm no good with names, but I was pretty sure it was a Bentley. The windows were tinted. A driver stood by the rear passenger door. He was straight out of another era—long coat, black chauffeur's cap, leather gloves.

We made eye contact, and he looked away almost instantly, lowering his head and moving to open the door. He stood beside it, holding it open and keeping his eyes down.

I looked around. There was no one else nearby. The street was silent, except for the quiet idling of the car. 2312 was closed again, the soccer mom in another universe behind the drapes.

I walked toward the car. The closer I got, the more the man seemed to lower his gaze.

What the hell, I thought. Why wouldn't I get in the car? It's not like they wanted to kill me. Although, my brain offered helpfully, most movie whackings did begin with the obligatory *Get in the car.* Was I crazy to get in? Was I crazy if I didn't? Frankly, I didn't have anywhere else to go. The interior looked nice. Tan leather seats. It appeared empty—was this all for me? One final question: would the driver karate-chop my neck as I tried to enter the car?

I slipped in. He shut the door behind me.

The windows were more than just tinted, it turned out; they were black. I couldn't see anything. Another amusing feature of this automobile was the absence of door handles on the inside of my doors. The driver sat on the other side of a closed divider. Wherever he was going, I was coming along. All I could do was fix myself a drink at the mobile bar. I sat back and enjoyed the hum of the ride.

By my watch, we stopped an hour and a half later.

The door opened, and I stepped out onto a city block, noisy and bright. A high-rise loomed above me: a gray Art Deco building with flowers and medusas carved into the stone above the first floor of sooty windows. We were in the middle of a long block, and I couldn't read a street sign in either direction. The driver stood back and nodded toward the building's doorway. He lowered his head again, and this seemed like my cue to walk like an important man. *Do you know who I am?* my stride suggested to the indifferent pedestrians passing in both directions. The occasional car enthusiast glanced at my ride.

The doorman waved me in and smiled.

"Mr. Davis?"

"Yes." He said my name like it meant something.

"Twenty-eighth floor, please. They're expecting you."

The elevator actually had an operator. He pulled the door shut and raised the lever. It was a fast ride with no stops. He decelerated to 28 and smiled pleasantly.

"Have a nice evening, sir."

"You too."

Was I supposed to tip? After the new suit, I was pretty sure I had less in my bank account than he did. I'd already decided I couldn't ask my parents for extra money to make it until the spring student loan check. It was bad enough they went into debt to help with my Ivy League tuition. I wasn't going to ask for more.

It occurred to me that I had no idea which room to go to. But at the end of the hall, I saw a door partly opened, with half of a very striking older woman, probably in her sixties, smiling at me.

Her hair was silver-white, cut midway between professional and sensual, swept back behind long ears. She reached up and pulled a few loose strands back with musician's fingers, letting the nails trace along her ear. Her face was aristocratic. She wore a white blouse under a gray suit that clung to her slender, tall figure. As I got close, she said, "Please," and stepped aside to let me in.

. . .

They led me to a plush chair in a sitting room, facing a roomful of women, all in their sixties, seventies, and eighties, all remarkable in their elegance. The woman who met me at the door sat last, in a chair directly across from me. There was a quiet power in the room, like a historical gathering of senators' wives, or the near future's assembly of retired senators. The walls were painted bright red, a shade between scarlet and rose. It was a strange, soothing color, almost pulsatile. The lower halves of the walls were paneled with white wood. I was the only man in the room.

A lady in an apron and bonnet entered, carrying teacups on a silver tray.

"Thank you, Beatrice," the aristocratic woman said. I decided to think of her as Ms. Silver, since actual names seemed to be taboo at these events. Mr. Bones and Ms. Silver. Apparently I was living in a giant game of Clue. She took a cup.

Beatrice held the tray to me.

"Enjoy," Ms. Silver said.

I nodded, and we both sipped.

"So," she said finally, "are you comfortable?"

"Yes, thank you."

"Do you have any questions for us?"

They were messing with me. I was sure of it. I decided to maintain some semblance of control by avoiding the one million obvious questions I wanted to ask.

"What color are the walls?"

She looked slightly surprised.

"Amaranth. Like the poem. 'With these, that never fade, the

105

spirits elect. Bind their resplendent locks.' John Milton." She shrugged.

In retrospect, I felt stupid for asking about paint.

I felt all eyes on me. No one else had spoken yet. There were a lot of women in the room, but a fair number of them were shadowed; I could make out only the lines of their long faces.

I started to fidget.

"Relax." Ms. Silver smiled. "We don't need to rush." Was she channeling Barry White? *Slow down, baby, take it easy.* I thought: if tonight ends with an orgy of eighty-year-olds, I'm out. You've got to draw the line somewhere.

She sipped her tea. I did the same. We sat in silence for a long time and finished our drinks.

I was growing warm, relaxed.

"How do you feel, Jeremy?" she asked pleasantly. Her voice sounded lighter now, breezy.

"Good," I said. I noticed a pleasant buzzing in my fingers and toes. My voice sounded far away.

"Good," she said, watching me with a slight smile. She swept her hair again, those long, graceful fingers riding along the curve of her ear.

The room was rotating slowly. I heard the whoosh of my pulse.

I laughed.

"What's funny, Jeremy?"

It sounded like three people asked me the question at once.

"I don't know," I said.

"That's okay." She smiled broadly. Her teeth were perfectly white. I liked her so much.

She watched me a little longer. One of the ladies nodded. Ms.

Silver leaned back in her chair, draped her slender arms over the armrests, inclined her head.

"Jeremy, we're friends, right?"

"Yes," I said, smiling.

"I have a question for you. You will be honest with me, won't you?" There was a touch of hurt in her voice.

"Of course," I said.

"I'm wondering, have you ever committed a crime?"

I felt a rush of surprise and anger. I opened my mouth to say no.

"Yes," I said.

"Oh dear," she purred. "What did you do?"

"When I was thirteen," I said, "I stole a pair of shoes from the store."

"Oh my. And what else?"

"When I was fifteen, my friends and I cut down a stop sign and took it."

"Hmm. Those aren't so bad. Why don't you tell me more?"

I wanted to close my mouth. I couldn't tell if I did or not. The questions continued. I was sleepy. I drifted in and out of the conversation, but I could hear myself still talking somewhere.

I snapped to when she said, "Jeremy, are you a virgin?" leaning back so her blouse strained against her breasts.

I felt blood rush to my cheeks. I thought *No* in my head, but my lips formed the word *Yes*.

Something about my parents, she asked. I nodded off. When I came awake, we were talking about my secrets. *Is there something I would be upset about if someone else found out?*

Ms. Silver. She was pretty. I kept smiling at her. The other ladies were lost in the shadows. How long had we been here?

"What's your biggest fear?" she asked casually, arching her

eyebrows with polite curiosity, stretching those long thin lips into a mildly interested smile.

I heard myself answer. I was already asleep, which was too bad. I really wanted to hear what I said.

Strange dreams: a Chinese dragon, blue-gold with wobbly eyes. A hand with a door in it. The moon, opening to spill its contents.

I woke up with my face on the floor. It felt rough. I was cold. It hurt to move. My eyes opened slowly. I saw dirt, leaves. My mouth was dry, my throat ached. I coughed dust out of my mouth. I tried to move my arms and legs: fire shot up the tracks of my nerves.

I saw sideways trees, felt wind, nothing else.

My head was clearing. I pulled myself up slowly.

I was wearing only underwear.

I rubbed my eyes, shook off the cobwebs. I could see no buildings, just trees to the horizon, yellow and red leaves. *I'm in the woods.*

After a while, I tried standing up.

Wobbly, but then better.

Pine needles stung my bare feet.

I tried walking heel to toe. Better.

I started off in no particular direction.

My head cleared as I walked. I remembered vague images from the night before: the soccer mom, the limo, a roomful of women. And now I'd been dumped in the middle of the woods, stripped to my underwear.

I'd heard about things like this, back in Texas, actually. In the old days, before lawsuits got rid of the real hazing, fraternities would sometimes strip their pledges down, blindfold them, and drop them alone in the middle of the woods, with only a hunting knife and a quarter. Or so we told each other in high school, since everybody had a friend with an older brother who swore it was true.

Well, I didn't have a knife *or* a quarter. What kind of a budget operation were they running up here?

And then that old, suspicious thought from Mr. Bones's house popped back into my head. This all seemed too boorish for the V&D. Were they mocking me? Another satire of my roots, like the trailer park bimbo hanging on to Mr. Bones? Or was this just another paranoid chip on my shoulder—too little sleep, too much wacky tea?

I was feeling woozy. Judging by the sun, I'd started walking around eight a.m., and now it was past noon. I hadn't eaten since lunch yesterday.

I saw a highway in the distance and stumbled toward it.

An hour later, I approached a lonely, run-down building on the side of the road.

I pushed the door open and stepped into a filthy room, me and my underwear. A few haggard men were sitting at tables alone, drinking. A couple of bikers talked in the back. They all looked up at me.

The bartender wore an undershirt with grease stains on it.

"Son," he said, "you're in the wrong bar."

That's when I passed out on his floor.

15

In the sunlight, the grand hallway of the law school, its main artery, thrummed with life. Giant shafts of colored light—red, green, and gold—poured in from the vast stained glass walls spanning both sides of the hallway. Frescoes of Creation and Wisdom adorned the ceilings, powdery yellows and blues paying tribute to the great ceilings of Rome and Florence. Students bustled in every direction, talking and laughing with the energy of a Monday morning in the middle of the warmest November in recent memory. On most days I passed through the hallway somewhat anonymously, saying hi to the occasional acquaintance on my way to class; but today, the first class day after the mock trial, I was the source of my own energy. A buzz seemed to follow me and precede me, to propel me down the hall; people I'd never met stared at me, grinning, nodding, patting me on the back, offering congratulations and the occasional *It was great, but why didn't you argue X?* I felt like a king coming home from battle.

The journey back from the woods had felt cleansing, like a purification ritual. I had been in the wilderness, but now I was home. The bikers turned out to be great guys. They thought the idea of leaving someone half-naked in the woods was hilarious.

They considered adding it to their next initiation. They even decided not to kill me.

I found Daphne sitting at the front of the classroom, rereading today's cases. Buoyed by the good spirits, I marched right up to her. I felt confident, empowered. She must have felt it too, it must have projected off me, because she looked up and gave me the most dazzling smile I'd ever received, her skin tan and flushed, bright amaranth lips, black eyelashes above the flawless whites of her eyes, the perfect Caribbean irises.

"Hey there," she said, stretching her arms back over her head. "You look like you had a good weekend."

"I did. And you?"

"I slept all day yesterday. I slept like I hadn't slept in months."

"Me too."

"Which reminds me," she said, giving me a sheepish smile. "I'm sorry about the other night. After the trial. I was so tired. I still owe you a celebration."

"It was a big victory," I said.

"It was." She grinned. "Huge." She leaned in. "You were awesome."

"You were pretty amazing yourself. The way you handled Mrs. Reid . . . unbelievable. Two hundred people couldn't take their eyes off you."

"So"—she leaned forward, rubbing her hands together—"what should we do?"

"To celebrate? For starters, we should go out to dinner. Somewhere special. Somewhere expensive. How about tonight?"

"Sure," she said, her face glowing. "Wait. *Tonight?*"

"Yeah."

She was looking at me funny, like how could I possibly be available tonight? A very bad thought occurred to me. I tried to push it away. No way, I thought. It wasn't possible. But, could it be she was looking at me like she'd gotten another invitation from *them* and was wondering—why hadn't I?

No way.

"Maybe later in the week, then," I said.

"Yeah, that could work. Let me check. I'll let you know." She gave me a hopeful smile, but it was thin.

"Daphne, is there something you're not telling me?"

"No. Nothing."

"Daphne, come on. It's me."

The voice of Professor Gruber rang out behind me.

"Mr. Davis, I hate to interrupt the power couple of the year, but I was thinking about starting class. What are *your* thoughts on that?" A few people laughed. I looked around and saw that the room was full and Professor Gruber was at the lectern, his stubby arms crossed. The clock read two minutes past the hour. I mumbled an apology and slipped away to my seat across the room.

Couldn't be, I thought. First event—the cocktail party: I came home and there was an invitation for the next event on my bed. Second event—the tea party: I came home, no invitation. So what? Who said the invitation had to come immediately after the last event? One example doesn't make a pattern! And who said Daphne and I had to get the same invitation for the same event? No one! But that look in her eyes—surprise, disbelief. What else could it mean?

But I won the trial. Relax, I told myself. (Though Daphne's words came back to me: *winning the trial's an edge, not a guarantee . . .*)

I barely heard a word of class. Why start now? I kept turning things over in my mind. Don't overreact. Don't jump to conclusions.

When class was over, Daphne was out the door before I could reach her. A plump, good-natured woman with bright red lipstick and a green sweater was waiting at the doorway. Margaret Gleeter, Professor Bernini's secretary for twenty-six years. As I passed, she held my arm and stopped me.

"Professor Bernini wants to see you in his office."

"Okay." I hesitated. "Margaret, you don't know what about, do you?"

"I'm not sure," she said.

She gave my arm a reassuring squeeze.

When I reached his office, Professor Bernini was on the phone, one hand in his thinning hair. He waved me in.

"Yes, I heard," he said into the phone. "I think it's best you speak now, before the article comes out. Mm-hm. Yes." Professor Bernini scratched his scalp. "You'll need to make five points. First, you are saddened by the situation. Second, your office is committed to honesty and fairness. Third, you are going to place him on paid leave. Don't forget to say *paid*—you're splitting the baby. Fourth, you are going to sponsor an independent and fair investigation into the matter. Say those words: *independent* and *fair*. Fifth, you'll take appropriate action once the results of that investigation are in." Bernini winked at me. "That gets you a month. After that, a human sacrifice may be required. Okay, very good. No, I've seen worse. Call if you need me." He hung up the phone and pointed a remote over my head. He clicked a TV on and muted it. He nodded at the phone. "A former student of mine. Now," he said, smiling, "to the matter at hand. It's finished."

"What's finished?" My voice was weak.

"The draft. My *History of Law*. Nine hundred pages, give or take."

He rested his fingers on top of a pile of paper.

"We did it, Jeremy," he said. "I owe you my gratitude."

He reached behind his desk and produced two glasses. The sprightly man popped open a bottle of champagne and filled the flutes.

"Congratulations and thank you," he said, raising his glass.

"Thank you, sir," I said.

We clinked glasses.

"Do you know what this *is,* Jeremy?" He tapped his fingertips on the immense stack. I was still reeling from my conversation with Daphne; I resisted the insane urge to say: *a book?*

"It's a very important work . . ."

He waved my answer away.

"It's glue. Social glue. There's nothing original in this book. I'm not saying anything John Stuart Mill didn't say. Or Jefferson or Lincoln. I'm just repeating it. We have to *repeat* it, Jeremy. Did you know Germany was the cultural center of Europe before the Nazis came to power? It happens so fast." He leaned toward me. His eyes were wide. "Believe me. I was a child when the fascists took over." I'd heard the stories. His father was a democrat who opposed Mussolini. He died in a political prison—no lawyer, no trial, no press. Bernini was eleven; after his father's death, he fled the country with his mother, first to England, then to America. "It's the same story," Bernini said. "Point anywhere on a map, I'll show it to you. There is always a man who would become a dictator. There is always a crowd that would become a mob. The law is a muzzle on an angry dog. We need it. But it's a cold instrument, fragile and intellectual. Remember that, Jeremy: intelligence isn't virtue. The law needs our goodness to give it life. Ah." He unmuted the television. A prominent congressman was holding a press conference. We listened as he repeated Bernini's words almost verbatim. He looked grave, honest. The wind whipped through his gray hair.

When it was over, Bernini clicked the TV off.

"You should be proud of this book, Jeremy. You are very much a part of it. It was a pleasure to work with you."

I felt a cold sensation.

"Professor Bernini, you said it's just a draft, right?"

"Yes."

His eyes danced around, reading my expression, my body language, betraying nothing.

"Won't you be revising it?"

"Yes," he said after a pause. "Almost certainly."

"Well, if you need more research, I'm happy to do it."

"I appreciate that, Jeremy," he said kindly. "But you've done so much. And a book could always benefit from a fresh perspective in the next round."

He folded his hands and waited.

"I understand." I stood. I felt like layers of myself were melting away. I just wanted to get out of his office before there was nothing left. "Thank you for the opportunity." I started to walk out quickly.

"Jeremy?"

"Yes?" I said, stopping, turning around.

Tell me something good.

115

"My key?" he said patiently, holding out his hand. His kind eyes smiled at me, but the twinkle was muted, out of respect for the freshly dead.

I fished the keys out of my pocket. I had to suffer the indignity of winding his key off my ring, something I fumbled with in the best of circumstances. Finally, I dropped it in his palm, and he closed his hand.

He walked me to the door. He patted me on the back and said, "Best of luck to you, Jeremy. You'll be a fine lawyer."

Coffin shut, nailed, dropped.

I started down the hallway.

Coming in the opposite direction was none other than Humpty Dumpty himself, Arthur Peabody: short, waddling, charging head forward, bow tie askew, long jowls jostling with each step. He looked me over, snorted, glanced past me down the hall.

"Another one of your victories, Ernesto?" he called down the hall to Bernini.

"Good morning, Arthur," Bernini said flatly from behind me.

As Arthur Peabody passed, I smelled the cloud of liquor.

"Was this one too good or not good enough?"

"That's enough, Arthur."

There was a warning in his voice. I had no idea what Humpty meant. I didn't care anymore. I just wanted out of that hallway.

"Why don't you tell him the joke?" Humpty Dumpty said. "Maybe he'll thank you."

"Enough," Bernini snapped. I'd never heard him so angry. "Remember your deal," he said to Peabody.

Two doors slammed behind me, moments apart.

The fucking elevator couldn't come fast enough.

116

. . .

I called my parents for the first time in a month. My dad answered the phone.

"We thought you were dead," he said dryly.

"No, Dad. Just crazy. Too much work." I tried to sound light-hearted. "I won the mock trial."

"Hey, that's great. Way to go. You're not letting the big shots push you around, are you?" This was a common theme for my dad, ever since he decided that he was a speck in the universe, meaningless, powerless.

"No way, Dad. I'm pushing *them* around."

"That's my boy."

"Hey, let me talk to Mom, okay?"

"Sure."

My mom picked up the phone.

"Hi sweetie."

"Hi Mom."

"Honey, what's wrong?"

"Nothing, Ma. How's Dad doing?"

"He's fine. How are you?"

"Is he taking his medicine?"

"Yes, honey. We're taking care of everything. You don't need to worry."

"He hates the beta blocker. Make sure he's really taking it."

"Honey, what's wrong? Is everything okay at school?"

"Yeah. Everything's great. I've got lots of friends. I'm learning a lot." I closed my eyes. "I need to run to class. I just wanted to say hi."

"Honey?"

117

"I really need to run, Mom."

"You call me if you need to talk. Okay, sweetie? Anytime."

"Okay, Mom. I love you."

"I love you too."

I hung up.

Daphne left her house at seven o'clock. I'd been waiting in the park across the street. She was reading something small, then put it back in her purse. I stopped her in the middle of the road.

"Jeremy, what are you doing here?"

"Where are you going?"

"What do you mean, where am I going?"

"Answer my question."

"Jeremy, you're freaking me out."

"I gave you *everything*," I snapped. She took a step back. "I won that fucking trial for you. I *destroyed* that girl. I took her apart. I did that for *you*."

"Jeremy, this isn't going to help anything."

"Help? Help? Bernini just took his fucking key back." I felt my head pounding. "I did everything you said. Tell me what's going on. *Please*."

She paused.

"You know I can't."

She actually looked sorry.

"What's in your purse?"

"Excuse me?"

"Give me your purse."

"Jeremy, don't do this."

I grabbed for her purse. Jesus Christ, what was I doing? She put her hands up, let me take it. She stood back and folded her arms. I went through it roughly: makeup, pens, aspirin, coins. There was a square of off-white card stock, familiar. *We are delighted to request your attendance . . .* Today's date. Seven thirty. Delighted. I handed her purse back.

"Did Nigel get one?"

For a while she just stood there. I felt my fists balling up, clenching. Then she nodded.

"John?"

Another nod.

I pressed my hand over my face.

"Bernini took his key back," I said again. I looked at her. "I'm going to fail my classes. I haven't opened a book all semester. Even if I pass, I won't get a job. Everything I did means nothing now, doesn't it?"

She tried to put her hand on my shoulder.

I had never seen her in direct sunlight before. Always indoors, in the library, the classroom, the ballroom. She was still beautiful, but more real. Her hand was on my shoulder. She looked brittle; how badly she wanted all this!

"What do you think I could do?" she asked me.

I had no answer.

"I'm sorry, Jeremy, I really am."

She slung her purse.

"Please don't follow me."

16

When the weekend arrived, I realized I had no friends. Nigel and John had avoided me all week. I couldn't even think of Daphne without remembering the other night outside her house and cringing. In the first months of school, I hadn't bothered to spend time with anyone else.

I went to the library. I decided to start from the beginning. I opened my Torts book, and it was suddenly clear that it was an impossible task. We were hundreds of pages deep into every class. Exams were in two weeks. Most people were reviewing now. And I was on page one. Humpty Dumpty ruled over the library; tonight, I didn't see him in the flesh, but his ghost was here. The specter of failure.

I felt someone watching me. It was one of the librarians, a painfully shy little man who always looked down and never said a word to anyone. He was more ruffled and ignored than half the books. He saw me looking and went back to stamping returns.

After a while I couldn't take it and went to the Idle for a drink and cheap dinner. A pretty girl sat next to me at the bar. I was lonely. She made me think of the neurosurgeon who spilled her oranges in the yard. "How's it going?" I asked. She mumbled an uninterested "Fine" and looked back to her friends.

"Let me show you," said a voice behind me, as two large hands fell on my shoulders. John Anderson walked around to another of the girls. He was a foot taller than her. He gave a magical smile. "How's it going?" he said amiably. "Good," she said, "how are you?" "Good." He grinned. One of the other girls smiled back. "Hey," she said, "my friend just got her glasses today. Don't they look sexy?" He laughed and agreed. I threw some money down and started to leave.

"See," John said. "It's not what you say. It's who says it."

"Fuck you," I said.

"No, fuck you. I never liked you."

He clapped me on the shoulder. I shrugged him off and walked away.

I saw him go back into the main bar, where he joined Nigel and Daphne. He put his arm around Daphne. He kissed the top of her head.

Something bad was turning in my brain. I walked the campus. All those images: greatness, Daphne, money—all gone. I hated John. I hated Daphne. I hated the V&D. I passed the red-bricked dormitories with cannon marks from the Revolutionary War. I passed the gothic Centennial Church, the renaissance porticoes of Creighton Hall, the statue of our founder, handsome and proud. I hated this place, but it was beautiful. I hated it *because* it was beautiful.

I wasn't tired, and I was sick of feeling sorry for myself, so I went back to the library. I found an empty floor. I opened the Torts book to page one and started reading again. The case was *Scott v. Shepherd*. The defendant had thrown a lit firecracker into a crowded indoor market. A surprised vendor picked it up and lobbed it away from himself to another part of the market. Another vendor picked it up and lobbed it again. Finally, it struck the plaintiff (you have to love old English) "in the face therewith" and exploded. The question was, who *caused* the injury: The initial thrower? One of the intervening lobbers? It occurred to me that since I'd come to this place, I hadn't *caused* a thing. I'd just been swept along.

The shy little librarian passed by, pushing his cart. He must have been on night owl reshelving duty. He took books from empty carrels and placed them on his cart. He grabbed two books off my desk.

"Um, excuse me," I called after him. "I still need those."

He stopped, made a big production of turning around and rolling over to me. He set the books back on my desk and rolled the cart away.

There was a piece of paper sticking out from one of the books. It hadn't been there before.

I pulled it out and looked at it.

It was an article. The word *DRAFT* was typed across the top. Someone had written in pencil below: *Come on, can't you make me sound a little more impressive? —HJM.*

I was surprised to see a picture of the man I met at the first V&D event, the retired lawyer with the bad red toupee. The one who wanted to talk about my grandfather, then blindsided me by knowing all about me.

The picture showed the same face: friendly, a thick rug of hair slightly off-kilter.

I read the text below the picture and froze. I felt my blood run cold. I looked for the librarian, but he was gone.

I was alone on the floor.

Below the picture, the article began:

Henry James Morton, retired law professor and chief White House counsel under presidents Kennedy and Johnson, passed away peacefully in his sleep on November 20, 2006.

November 20, 2006.
That was in two days.

17

Shock was my first reaction. A draft obituary, predicting an exact date of death. And the soon-to-be-dead-man, completely on board. What did it mean? What was the V&D up to?

Very quickly, a new thought shot through my mind like a lightning bolt:

I can hurt them.

I didn't know how. I didn't know when. But in some way, this information was valuable. Someone *wanted* me to see the obituary. I knew better than to ask the librarian. There was an etiquette to these things, a code. I'd picked up that much. Someone shared my anger. Or maybe they just wanted to use me toward some common goal. Either way, fine by me. The big shots push the little guys around. If you let them.

There was only one person to talk to, of course.

I banged on Miles's door. His apartment was a disaster, covered with laundry and papers, dishes piled up in the small kitchen. His beard, normally woolly, was now edging—in its length and curliness—away from philosopher toward holy man. Miles caught me staring.

"I need money for razors."

He must have been disappointed by my reaction; he shrugged and said, "I have a chapter due Monday." Then he pointed a giant finger at me. "I called you, you know. A couple weeks ago."

"I know."

"Didn't hear back."

"I know. I'm sorry, Miles."

"No need. I've got lots of friends." He inclined his head toward the empty apartment in proof. "So, what's new?"

The simplicity, the sheer banality of the question stumped me.

But Miles was studying my face. His eyebrows knitted together, then they relaxed and raised. He spoke to me in a calm voice, like he had all the time in the world.

"Okay. Tell me what's wrong."

I told him everything, except the obituary.

"I'm very sorry, Jeremy. I know how badly you wanted it."

He clapped his large hands.

"Now, on to your more pressing problems. It's time to rebuild. You can't pass these courses now. It's too much material. You'll take a leave of absence and start fresh in the spring."

"And have Incompletes on my transcript? Go through three years of law school, then wonder why no one wants to hire me? No way."

"It's your best option."

"Not necessarily."

He looked at me, confused and maybe a little wary.

"What are you saying?"

"What if I'm not ready to give up?"

"Give up on what? On *them*?"

I nodded.

He shook his head.

"Let it go, Jer. You came a hell of a lot closer than most people ever will. Closer than I ever did."

"Miles, I think that's worse."

He gave me a look that said *Enough.*

"Time to rebuild."

I ignored him.

"What if there's a way?"

"What do you mean, a way?"

"What if I had something . . . a piece of information . . . that might make the V and D reconsider? They can take four people one year. Why not? Then I'm back on track."

Until this moment, Miles had been serious, but he never lost his basic good humor. But now, he spoke very slowly, all the color gone from his voice.

"Tell me exactly what you mean."

I pulled out the obituary. I showed him the picture and explained the story.

His voice sounded strange.

If I didn't know better, I'd think Miles—all six foot seven of him—was nervous.

"Have you told anyone else about this?"

"No. Nobody."

He looked at me hard, then nodded.

"There's someone you need to meet."

Miles and I walked side by side through the university, a cold wind moving in from the north, hands deep in our pockets. The fresh air seemed to lighten his mood.

"*Who* are we going to see?" I asked again.

"Chance Worthington," Miles repeated.

"*Who* is Chance Worthington? Is he a student?"

"Not exactly."

"How can you not exactly be a student?"

"Chance's status with the university is unclear."

Miles laughed and slapped my back.

It turned out Chance had been on campus as long as Miles, without collecting a single degree. This was a rare feat, considering Miles had done undergrad, law school, and now part of his PhD here. Chance was an on-again, off-again reporter for the campus paper and for whoever else would publish his articles: alternative weeklies, alien-invasion tabloids, ranting socialist leaflets. Unlike most college reporters, Miles explained, Chance wasn't satisfied with covering can drives and campus protests over the plight of the penguins. He'd taken numerous leaves of absence to travel around the world, to places with violent conflicts or exceptionally pure weed. He had a pile of letters from the administration that he was afraid to open, but they were still cashing his checks.

Miles was one of those people who collected odd friends. In high school, you could count on him to know every lost soul in the Ol' South Pancake House, our twenty-four-hour hangout after debate matches. He knew the quiet truckers and the self-titled lesbian cowgirls. He knew the Vietnam vets and the old hippies who still occasionally yelled at each other across the room. He knew the black debutantes, who always arrived in gowns from a glittery circuit of events we'd never see. I pretty much kept to my friends at Ol' South, with my coffee and my German pancakes, out of shyness. But Miles could sit down at any booth and talk and laugh for hours.

"You guys are gonna love each other." Miles grinned, warming to the event.

We met at Chance's place, an off-campus "co-op," which was basically a hippie dorm where you cooked your own food and didn't have to shower.

Chance Worthington took a long drag off his joint and passed it to Miles. His eyes were bloodshot. His hair moved in wild curls. He tapped his middle finger nonstop on the table. He bit at a nail, then started tapping again.

Finally, he stopped tapping. He took another quick hit, passed it to Miles, and relaxed back into his chair.

"So, whad'ya have for me?"

"I'm sorry?" I said.

"You guys are gonna love each other," Miles said again, examining the glowing tip of the joint. He laughed and started coughing. "What Chance means, I think, is start at the beginning." Miles offered me the joint. I waved it off.

"Well, I got this invitation—"

"Skip to something interesting," Chance interrupted.

"What?"

"I don't want to hear any tea party crap. Give me something new."

I looked at Miles. He nodded, then wiggled his eyebrows.

"Okay . . ." I said. I thought about my tour of Mr. Bones's house. "How about the Capuchin Crypt?"

"Commissioned by Pope Urban the Eighth's brother in 1631, creepy bones and so forth, blah, blah, blah. What else?"

This guy was getting under my skin.

"I saw a map to a place called Bimini."

"Do you even know where Bimini *is*?"

I had a hint of a memory, something out of elementary school adventure books, but then it was gone.

"No," I said.

Chance made a big show of sighing.

"In the Bahamas, supposedly." He smiled. "But they didn't find what they were looking for."

"What were they looking for?"

"Ah, but *you* were supposed to tell *me* something new. I'm not your teacher."

"Fine. What about King's water?"

"What about it?"

"Well, you know, the Nazis were coming. They dissolved the Nobel Prizes . . ."

"*That's* what you know about King's water?"

"It's not true?"

"Of course it's true. The story's on the Nobel Prize website, for crap's sake. You're not exactly through the looking glass here."

I gave Miles a *who is this guy* look. Miles smiled and turned to Chance.

"The story does relate to passing through."

"But the money's on transmutation."

"All right, c'mon guys," I said, "you know I don't speak Pot."

Chance looked at me. He stopped tapping his finger. He sighed and shook his head.

"You raise an interesting topic. It's just that King's water has a long history. *Much* longer than World War Two."

"Okay. I'm listening."

"Well, aqua regia—King's water, as you call it—was invented around AD 800 by a Persian alchemist named Jabir ibn Hayyan. The same man who discovered hydrochloric acid."

Danny Tobey

Chance lit a cigarette and blew a sour cloud between us.

"What do you know about the alchemists?" he asked me, his face drifting in the smoke.

"Not much. They were sort of New Age scientists, but from the Middle Ages."

"In a sense. They were the first chemists. They invented gunpowder. Metalwork. They made inks and dyes and alcohol. They were also philosophers, physicists, mystics, astrologers, you name it. This wasn't exactly an era of specialization. You can trace alchemy back to ancient Egypt, Rome, China, Greece, India, Arabia. Their motto was *Solve et Coagula:* 'Separate and Join Together.'"

"Okay. So that's King's water, right? Separate and join together? They did it."

"Sadly, no. Hayyan saw King's water as part of a much larger quest; in fact, the *central* quest of alchemy. The transmutation of metals."

"Turning lead into gold."

"Exactly. King's water was like an ancient attempt at reverse engineering. If you could dissolve gold, maybe you could figure out how to *build* gold . . . The alchemists, including Hayyan, were searching for what they called the Philosopher's Stone: a substance that would turn something worthless into something precious."

"So this is all about money?"

"Ha! Never underestimate money. I can crack almost any story by asking: 'Who profits from this?' But, no, in this case I think there *is* something more.

"The alchemists survived a long time. Thousands of years. They survived the fall of Rome and Greece. They survived the Crusades. The Spanish Inquisition. Some people think it's because they were clever about hiding their true intentions."

130

"Which were?"

I leaned in. It was all hocus-pocus bullshit, but the guy could tell a story. Even Miles was quiet now, a half-smile on his face.

"The alchemists' texts are dense. Some of them don't even have words, just symbols. And nothing ever means just one thing. There are whole alchemy books dedicated to *decoding* alchemy books.

"Did they want to turn lead into gold? Sure. Who wouldn't? But what if that was just a cover for something else?"

"Like . . ."

"See Paracelsus. *Alchemical Catechism.* 'When the Philosophers speak of gold and silver, from which they extract their matter, are we to suppose that they refer to the vulgar gold and silver? By no means; vulgar silver and gold are dead, while those of the Philosophers are full of life.' "

"What does that mean?"

"Many people believe 'lead and gold' were metaphors for 'vice and virtue.' What if the Philosopher's Stone wasn't about *material* transmutation? What if it was about something *immaterial,* metaphysical even?"

"A substance that would make evil people good?"

"That's one theory."

"Why would they need to hide that? Who wouldn't want everyone to be good?"

"Soulcraft, at that time, was the domain of powerful institutions. The Church. The King. To lose that kind of authority . . . But . . ." Chance used his cigarette to light another. He ground the butt out on the table. "Maybe you're more right than you know. Maybe virtue and vice were just *another* layer of metaphor, in a quest for something even *more* sought after. What if the Phi-

131

losopher's Stone actually turned weak, vulnerable, sinful flesh into . . ."

The memory clicked. I knew what Bimini was.

". . . into something that never dies," I said. I smiled. "Bimini. Ships in the Bahamas . . ."

"Ponce de León." Miles nodded.

"*'Peter Martyr saith that there is in Bimini a continual spring of running water of such marvellous virtue that the water thereof, being drunk, maketh old men young.'*"

Chance recited it from memory, his eyes stoned, half-closed.

"*'Let us go where we can bathe in those enchanted waters and be young once more,'*" Miles replied. "*'I need it, and you will need it ere long.'*"

"Peter Martyr was secretary of the prothonotary under Pope Innocent the Eighth, archpriest of Ocana under Pope Adrian the Sixth," Chance added. "Friend of Columbus and Ponce de León."

I felt the disconnected pieces swirling, snapping into place.

"What about amaranth?" I asked. "She quoted Milton."

"'Immortal amarant, a flower which once, in paradise, fast by the tree of life, began to bloom; but soon for man's offence, to heaven removed.'"

For man's offense. Adam and Eve—they ate from the forbidden tree: virtue fell to vice, and man was cast from Paradise and became mortal.

"The ancient Greeks ground up amaranth petals to treat infections," Miles said. "Across the world, the ancient Chinese did too."

Immortality . . . to beat death . . .

The obituary!

Were things like this really possible?

I pulled it out and pointed to the picture. To the man who apparently knew the precise date he was going to die and didn't seem terribly concerned about it. What if he didn't plan on dying in two days? What if his "death"—the obituary—was just a cover story, because he had no intention of going anywhere, ever . . .

"What if . . ." I said. "What if the V and D found a way . . ."

"*'What we are now, you will be,'* said the skeleton." Chance smirked.

"What's this 'we' stuff, white man?" Miles replied.

Chance grinned.

"We lost our immortality when we ate from the Tree of Knowledge—and we've been trying to use knowledge to get it back ever since. Kind of ironic, eh?"

He collapsed back into his chair. It had been a masterful performance, weaving together clues from ancient China to modern New England and everywhere in between. And now he was visibly tired. I, in contrast, was filled with new life, a new sense of opportunity—when only a couple of hours ago, it had seemed like every door was closed to me.

"This," I said, pointing to the obituary. "We could use this to get to them."

Chance and Miles exchanged glances.

"I doubt," Chance said slowly, "that the obituary means very much."

"But the stuff you just told me. Bimini . . ."

Chance shook his head.

"There was nothing there. The Spaniards went to Florida next. Guess where they claimed to find the Fountain of Youth? Green Cove Springs on the Saint Johns River. Know how many old people retire to Florida every year? My grandparents included? How many of them live forever?"

"What about amaranth? You said the Greeks used it to cure diseases."

"Check out the *Journal of Toxicology*, March 2003, volume seven," Miles said. "They use amaranth as a dye in manufacturing. Turns out it's poisonous. Great way to live forever, huh?"

"Maybe they found another way—"

"Jeremy, do you know about seer's salt?"

"No."

"Feast of the Blue Boy?"

"No."

"Samsara? Astral charts? Infinite wave functions? The Uhrglass?"

"No, no, no, no."

"Do you know when the V and D formed?"

"No."

"Do you know where they meet?"

"Do *you*?"

"Five years ago I found a clue. A margin note in a book we stole. It said the location was in Creighton versus Worley."

"Those are buildings on campus."

"Yes."

"You checked the buildings?"

"Over months. We even went down into the steam tunnels connecting the buildings. Nothing."

"But the language. Creighton *versus* Worley. It sounds like a court case."

"It does."

"Does the case exist?"

"Yes."

"You pulled it?"

"We did."

"And . . ."

"It was a contract dispute. A stupid old case that no one would ever look up."

"That's suspicious."

"*Everything's* suspicious when you want it to be, Jeremy. That's the point. It never *ends*. I had my math friends go crazy on it. For months. No clues. No hidden codes. It's just a case."

"Fine."

"I spent a semester on it. Nothing."

"I said fine."

"Jeremy," Chance said, not unkindly. "You're showing up late to a game you can't win. I've been pursuing this for seven years. There are people who have tried for as long as the V and D has existed. You're talking to a guy who believes in UFOs, but I can't tell you what these people are really about. Do they have some amazing secret? Maybe. Are they just a bunch of deluded old rich guys desperate to beat the reaper? Could be. Or maybe they're just satisfied ruling the free world. I don't have a clue. Magic or not, bullshit or not, I have discovered one thing. These people take themselves seriously. They have real power. And they don't like being fucked with."

"Why did you waste my time, then?"

"Jeremy," Miles said gently, "we told you all this to take the thrill out of it. It doesn't lead anywhere."

"But the obituary—"

"Someone's messing with you. Don't let them."

"But who?"

"It doesn't *matter*. Maybe it's someone who wants to hurt them. Maybe it's them, seeing if you're smart enough to let it go."

Miles exhaled. He looked at Chance.

"Tell him about Sammy Klein."

"Sammy Klein," Chance repeated.

He shook his head.

"Sammy was a nice guy," Chance said to me. "A really *good* guy. He got interested in the V and D. It happens. The secrecy. The lore. People are drawn to conspiracies, puzzles. Just because I publish bullshit doesn't mean I'm stupid. Something about them rubbed Sammy the wrong way. He wouldn't give it up. He got a lot farther than I ever did. God only knows what he knew. He was going to *show* them."

"I knew him," Miles said. "He was in my dorm, freshman year. Quiet. Always polite to people."

"They found him on the beach," Chance said. "His wallet was gone. Someone stabbed him seven times. The police called it a mugging and closed the case."

"Maybe it *was* just a mugging—"

"Jeremy," Miles said. He actually put his hand on my arm. "Take the Incompletes. Get straight A's next semester. You're going to be okay."

I sat there for a long time. They watched me.

Then I spoke.

"Did you Shepardize *Creighton v. Worley*?"

"What?"

"Jeremy," Miles said cautiously.

"Shepardize. That's where you take a case and see all the later cases that cite it. Did you?"

"No," Chance said slowly.

"*Jeremy*," Miles said again.

"How do you do that?" Chance said.

I told him. We went to the computer and pulled up the case. I showed him how to Shepardize it. Miles was watching us quietly from the corner; he didn't stop us, but I could see he wasn't done. A few citations came up on the screen, but nothing that stood out on first glance. It felt wrong.

I shook my head. "They wouldn't use the computer. Too many eyes. They'd use the books."

"That's ridiculous," Miles said. "If it's in the books it's on the computer."

"Not if someone changed just *our* book," I said.

That shut everyone up for a moment.

Chance stole a guilty glance at Miles, then looked at me. His eyes had a new life in them.

"Where?" he asked.

Miles looked at me, shook his head.

"The law library," I said.

Chance started tapping his fingers again. He started laughing. "Seven months with the math nerds, I didn't ask a fucking lawyer." He shook his head. He reached for the joint, sparked it back to life. He took a long drag. After a while, he closed his eyes.

His breathing slowed. Color came back to his face.

He laughed nervously.

"Forget it," he said. "Forget it."

He took another long drag, then said to himself, "Remember Sammy Klein."

Miles stood up. He was so massive, in that realm between fat and muscle; the room bowed under the authority of his size.

"Then we're done," Miles said. He put his hand on my back and I stood.

"Thank you, Chance. I know it's not easy dragging all this up.

You did a good thing tonight. Jeremy doesn't know it yet, but he's grateful."

"I know." He nodded. "You keep me sane."

Miles laughed and gave him a Russian bear hug, all mass and hard claps on the back.

Miles and I started walking. We were out the door quickly. Chance called after us. "Your article," he said. He was holding the obituary in his hand. I'd left it on the table.

As I stepped back in to get it, he caught my eye and mouthed: "One hour."

18

Miles grilled me until he was satisfied I'd gotten the message.

I thanked him and left to run an errand. Something had been bugging me ever since my failed induction into the V&D.

I retraced my steps on the paths winding across campus. It was quiet now, except for the occasional thumping of a party from an open window above me. Here and there, couples made out in the shadows; small groups sat in the grass, talking quietly or strumming guitars.

I followed the route we'd walked to her house, after the moonlight confession. I passed the site where the oranges had spilled. I passed the retaining wall where we sat on the ground and talked. I remembered her smile, the quiet tears.

The house looked the same. It was a brownstone; a half-flight of steps led up to the front door. I found S. CASEY on the names by the buzzer.

I rang the bell, and an unfamiliar girl answered the door.

"Can I help you?" she said. She looked like an engineering student, short ponytail, no smile. She had a book on bridges under her arm.

"I'm looking for Sarah," I said. Suddenly it felt crazy to be here. My palms were clammy. My shirt was wet under my arms.

"She's still at the hospital," the girl said.

"She's working?"

"No." The girl looked at me, puzzled. "She's *in* the hospital."

"What? What happened?"

The girl cocked her head.

"I haven't seen you before."

"I'm a friend of Sarah's."

She looked at me suspiciously.

"What did you say your name was?"

"Never mind. I'll just see her there."

I started backing away.

"Hey!" she called, but I was already down the steps. I half-ran to Student Health. The hospital entrance was around the side.

It was late, and the floor was deserted. I saw two nurses at the end of the hall, watching TV in the waiting area.

No one was manning the nurses' station. I stole a look down the hall, then went behind the counter to the row of charts on the back wall. I found *Casey, S.* There was a tab marked Admission History. I went to the first page and tried to decipher the handwriting and the abbreviations.

The opening line made the world lurch and reel under me:

Pt is a 26 yo WF c̄ no significant PMH who presented to the ER tonight s/p acetaminophen OD c/w suicide attempt.

I felt my heart drop. I checked the date on the note: four days ago. I had no idea what *s/p* or *c/w* meant, but I got the picture.

My skin was cold and my heart was pounding in my head.

Room 203, the chart said.

I looked at the door. I didn't want to move. But I had this sick feeling that my only way out of this hospital was through room 203. What was my alternative? To just take off, the way you might drop a vase in a store and walk out past the clerks, leaving them to find the pile of glass on the floor? It was tempting.

I knocked, touched my forehead against the cool door, and listened until a weak, sleepy voice said, "Come in."

She was on her back, a stack of pillows under her head. A yellow mirrored balloon hung halfway to the ceiling behind her. It said GET WELL SOON. There was a plastic water pitcher and two empty cups of ice cream on her bed tray. She looked pale.

When our eyes met, it took her a second to recognize me.

"Sarah, I am so sorry," I managed.

"Get out," she said, her voice scratchy and soft.

"I'm sorry."

"GET OUT." Louder this time—it would have been a scream if her throat had been working at full strength, but as she was, it came out like a hoarse moan, and she winced as she said it. I found the door and fumbled my way out, willing myself toward the exit, head down. I left, stealing one last look at the nurses watching *I Love Lucy* down the hall.

Chance was already in the library, with a baseball cap pulled over his messy curls.

"What's with you?" he said. "You look like you've seen a ghost."

"Two in one day." I brushed past him. "Let's do this."

"Geez, what got into you?"

141

Rage is what got into me—something about Sarah, the hospital, the V&D. I was filling with a hot, venomous anger; it had started in my toes on the way over here, and my eyes were about to go under.

"These are not good people. They make people do bad things. Someone should *do* something."

"So now this is public service?" Chance asked, smiling. "It's not about revenge anymore?"

I was starting to hate this guy.

"Why are *you* so interested in them?" I snapped. "Going for a Pulitzer?"

"This is a university. It's supposed to be *open*. I don't like the idea that there are places on campus I can't go."

"Are you kidding me? This whole place is one big club. You think anyone can just walk on campus and start taking classes?"

"So?"

"So you don't hate clubs. You hate clubs you can't get into."

"Are you calling me a hypocrite?"

"Are you calling *me* a hypocrite?"

I had a sudden vision of Miles clapping his hands: *You guys are gonna love each other!*

I took a deep breath.

"Forget it," I said. "It's just . . . I just saw something that rattled me."

"I think you'll find," Chance said, "the more you do this, the more that will happen. Shall we?"

I laughed, a little embarrassed at my outburst.

"Why not? Like I said, someone's gotta do something."

"That's what we humans do best," Chance said, grinning. "Something."

I pulled the Shepard's index, a large dusty tome, from the shelf. We found *Creighton v. Worley*. We pulled the volume and scanned down to the list of citing cases.

They were identical to the ones on the Internet.

But in the margin, someone had added a few more.

My heart started pounding. I saw Chance's face light up.

"I *totally* underestimated you," he said.

I read the first case out loud.

"Michaelson v. Mitchell."

"Holy shit," Chance said.

"What?"

It was exciting, but I didn't feel like we knew anything helpful yet.

Chance said, "Those are buildings on campus."

I stared at him.

"They are?"

"Michaelson. The Michaelson Chemistry Labs. *Mitchell.* One of the freshman dorms."

"Where?"

"We need a map," Chance said. He was buzzing now. I saw a glimpse of the old reporter, the one who must have existed seven years and a thousand joints ago.

We grabbed a campus map from the information booth and marked the buildings: Creighton, Worley, Michaelson, Mitchell.

Four dots.

"Check the rest," he said.

I recognized some of the names. Chance recognized all but one. Each pointed to a building on campus. My heart was racing. We charted nine points on the map.

Chance took the pencil and drew a line connecting them. It

started in one part of campus and snaked lazily—but purpose-fully—toward another.

My fingers were starting to tingle.

But it was incomplete.

We stared at the last case.

"*Zimmer Kettle Corp. v. Industrial Steel, Inc.* Hmm . . ." Chance tapped a pencil on his forehead. "*Kettle* is Kettle Hall. That's easy. But *Industrial Steel . . .*"

He shook his head.

He tapped the pencil relentlessly. It was starting to drive me crazy. I was about to snatch it away when a smile spread across his face.

Then, with the flourish of an artist drawing the final stroke of his masterpiece, Chance put one last dot on the map and circled it.

"*Industrial Steel,*" he said, shaking his head with admiration.

I looked at his dot. It fell right on our path, completing it. It landed smack in the middle of a rectangular building.

"That's a dorm, right?"

"Indeed. Embry House."

"I don't get it."

"Of course not. Only someone who really knew this cam-pus would. That's why they saved it for last. That dot," he said, pointing to his final mark, "sits, give or take, on a famous room in Embry. The only room on campus, in fact, to allow ten peo-ple to live in one space. Party central. The waiting list is out the door. But it always seems to go to legacies. And not just any legacies—like tenth generation, 'my ancestors were on the Mayflower' legacies. You have to hold your liquor to live in that room." Chance gave me a proud look. "That's why they call it the Steel Man."

He beamed, either at his own cleverness or the V&D's.

"You think the V and D meets in a dorm room?" I asked sarcastically.

Chance shook his head, unfazed.

"No," he said, smiling at me. "I think they meet *below* it."

19

Chance and I made a pact. First, tell no one. Second, meet tomorrow night, under cover of darkness, to see where our trail might lead.

The thrill of discovery got me home and into bed, and then reality broke through. I tried to press away thoughts of hospital rooms and half-limp balloons. But her face kept coming back to me. Her strained, scratchy voice:

GET OUT.

I had terrible dreams. I saw a room filled with a thousand baby angels, plump and dreamy, the kind Raphael imagined. They had slow, doll-like movements. There were shafts of light from tall windows. The angels were eating. Their chubby little hands brought spoons up and down, up and down to their mouths. When I entered, all thousand of them looked up at once and started screaming.

I woke the next morning, sweating, raw. I felt alone and lost, sick in my stomach. I reached for the phone in the darkness and dialed.

"Twice in one week? What is this, Christmas?"

"Hey Dad. Is Mom there?"

"She ran out. What's up?"

"Nothing," I said. "I just . . . wanted to ask her a question."

"Why don't you ask me?"

There was a long pause.

"Try me," he said.

Ever since my dad's heart attack, I was afraid to tell him that anything was less than perfect, as if whatever I said might trigger the next big one. But I needed someone. I needed help.

"C'mon, give an old man a chance," he said. "Let me be a dad for once."

I sighed. I wasn't even sure what I'd wanted to say.

"I think I did something really bad."

A pause, then:

"Did you break the law?"

"No."

I heard him breathe out on the other end.

"Did you cheat in school?"

"No."

"You hurt somebody?"

"Yes."

"Because you didn't like them?"

"No."

"Because it helped you."

"Yes."

"Listen to me." I braced myself for a lecture on big shots and little guys: *toughen up, grab what's yours, take no prisoners*. Instead, he said: "If you did something bad, you make it right. You hear me?"

"Yes. Yes, sir."

"Then you decide who you want to be, and you be it."

The line was quiet for a second.

"Okay?"

"Okay. I will."

"Make me proud of you," he said.

The call left me dizzy; startled, like I'd been slapped across the face.

For the first time in years, I'd heard the teacher again—the one everyone in town called on when they didn't know what to do.

Chance wore black from head to toe, as planned. He leaned against a tree away from the light; I could make out only the vague shadow of his form, the white eyes and pale strip of skin under the ski mask. As I got closer, his uniform came into view: cargo pants, hiking boots, backpack, hooded pullover; he looked like a real guerrilla journalist, with none of the idiot flair of my black sweatshirt and dress pants. But with two hundred dollars in my bank account and no career in sight, I wasn't about to spend my ramen money on a new ghost-hunting wardrobe. He handed me a ski mask.

"Thanks."

He rubbed black grease on his face, then pulled his mask back down. I took the tin and did the same. He looked at my feet.

"Dress shoes?"

I shrugged.

"Whatever," he said. He checked his camera, then slipped it into a black pouch on his waist. "Anything visible?" He turned in a circle.

I said no and did the same.

"So. We've got a map, thanks to you," Chance said. "What we need now is an entry point. Thanks to me."

"An entry point to *what*?"

Chance had been cagey about how exactly our map translated into action. I think he enjoyed this little bit of power. It wouldn't be as simple as walking into the Steel Man, that much I knew. Chance was convinced the dorm was a placeholder, not our actual destination.

"Every university has a story about steam tunnels that run underground and connect all the buildings," he told me. "It just so happens that *this* university, being very old, actually has them. Come on."

We walked along the wall in the shadow of a large administrative building. We were in the industrial part of the campus, a world away from student life. It was after midnight and eerily silent.

"The only official mention of them involves a bit of campus lore. When George Wallace came to speak in favor of segregation, the students were ready to murder him. Police had to smuggle him out through the tunnels. It got written up in the paper, fifty years ago."

We came into view of a giant, thrumming building bathed in yellow light, with two vents on the roof, each nearly twenty feet wide. It gave off a clean, electric smell, but the vents released colossal, almost volcanic plumes of white smoke that pulsed and swirled up into the clouded sky. It looked like a factory whose chief product was gloom.

"I had a resident poetry tutor in my house, freshman year, this real old guy. He swore the FBI chased an Austrian spy into the library back in World War Two. They searched for hours. Finally they figured he must've found a way into the steam tunnels. Or so the old guy said. I think he just wanted someone to eat with."

"Is that smoke?" I asked, looking at the white plumes.

"Water vapor. This is the hydroelectric plant. There's the physical plant. And *that*," he said, pointing to a run-down side building with weathered blinds, "is the plant manager's office." He paused and looked at me. "In about five minutes, you'll be guilty of trespassing, breaking and entering, and my favorite, 'conduct unbecoming to a student.' All grounds for expulsion. Last chance."

I smiled. "'Freedom's just another word for nothing left to lose.'"

"Preaching to the choir, my friend," Chance said, and we started toward the back of the building. He took a pair of cutters from his pack and went to work on the hanging lock. Then we were past the chain-link fence and into the gravel and grass of the plant yard. There were numerous metal boxes in the grass, all padlocked as well.

It was so quiet. Every step we took crunched.

I started to question the wisdom of the endeavor. Was it too late? Could I turn around now and run out the gate, throw the ski mask in a ditch, wipe the makeup off, and blend back into the Saturday night flow of the main quad?

Chance pulled on my sleeve.

"Keep moving. We're too exposed out here."

We snuck toward the door.

Chance attacked the lock with a set of picks from a leather pouch. If only my mom could see me now. *What nice friends you've made!*

There was a window a few feet away.

"Screw it. I was never good at this."

Chance pocketed the tools and picked up a rock.

"Chance, *no*," I whispered, but it was too late. He smashed the window. A jingling crash echoed through the empty yard, breaking the silence. I looked around, didn't see anyone. He used the rock to clear away the sharp edges, then looked back at me, poised to climb inside.

"We have to go fast now," he said. "Once we're in the tunnels, it's vast. We'll be fine."

I followed him into the window. We came into an office, then into a cinder-block hallway painted white. Chance was moving fast in no particular direction, glancing in doorways. He started cursing.

"Help me out, *goddamn it.*"

"What are you looking for?"

"Something going *down.* I don't know. A manhole. A stairway."

I found a room with a concrete floor and bare bulb. There was a hatch on the ground; it looked like a misplaced attic door.

"Here," I called.

I tried to pull it open, but it was too heavy.

Chance knelt beside me. We pulled together on the chain, and the hatch lifted. We pulled it to the point of no return, and it fell backward with a crash.

"Jesus Christ, Jeremy," he hissed.

"Come on," I said. I started climbing down the ladder.

I looked up and saw two figures behind Chance. He was stepping down onto the ladder and they pulled him up and back. His eyes went wide.

"What the *fuck*," he cried and fell backward. I looked down. I could just drop. I didn't know how far it was. But Chance had the map. He had the flashlights in his pack. I didn't know where to go.

Just drop!

A hand came down and grabbed my sweatshirt. I clawed at the arm. Another hand got around my neck and yanked up hard. I lost my breath.

I went up and fell over on my back.

I hit the floor hard.

A man was standing over me. He prodded me with his foot.

"Get back against the wall."

I took in the uniform and breathed a sigh of relief. Campus police. Miles wrote me about them his freshman year. He had a roommate who was a local kid from a nearby blue-collar town. One night, this roommate went out for old time's sake with a high school friend. They got drunk and decided to steal license plates. The city police caught them. Miles's roommate was handed over to campus police. No police report. No record of the event. No consequences. The roommate's friend spent the night in jail and had to appear in court the next day. I let myself relax a little.

"Take the masks off," the cop near me said.

I hesitated, then pulled off my ski mask.

The other cop was standing over Chance, sizing him up.

"Start talking," he said.

"Please, officer," Chance sputtered. "It's supposed to be a prank. We're pledging a fraternity. They told us to get into the steam tunnels and steal a plate from the professors' dining hall. Tell 'em, Mike." Chance looked at me. His eyes were perfect imitations of the wide-eyed stare of a scared freshman.

The officer turned to me.

I gave Chance my angriest look.

"You weren't supposed to *tell*. They said not to tell *anyone*, even if we got caught."

"*Please . . .*" Chance sounded downright miserable. "I want to go to law school. This could ruin me forever. Oh God, my *parents*. I knew I shouldn't have pledged."

The second officer looked at me.

"What fraternity?"

"We're not supposed to say," I mumbled.

He leaned over me and poked his finger at my chest.

"You should worry about yourself right now."

I shook my head. I aimed for deeply conflicted.

Chance blurted out, "Sigma Chi."

"*Jesus,* Ryan," I said.

The cop standing over me was the angrier of the two.

"They broke a window," he said, fingering his nightstick.

"Were you guys in a fraternity?" I asked.

The cops looked at me like I was insane.

"I don't mean any disrespect," I said. "It's just, if you *were* in a fraternity, you know how much pressure it is to get in. Maybe you had to do some pretty crazy stuff when you were pledges."

A moment passed.

"Well," the cop near Chance said, looking at my clothes, "you do look pretty stupid."

"Yeah. My first time in commando gear."

"Whad'ya say, John? This could just be some townie kids snooping around, threw a rock through the window?"

The cop near me nodded, thinking.

"Disappear," he said finally. "If I see you again, I might have to take a stick to your head. Got it?" He pulled me up roughly and started laughing. He slapped me on the back. "Get out of here. And stay out of trouble."

They were both laughing now. I felt like I wanted to vomit. Chance and I kept mumbling thank you as we worked our way to the door. We were almost there.

"Say," the calm officer said casually, "what's in there?"

He gave Chance's side pouch a little tap with his baton.

153

Chance winced, involuntarily.

"Just my camera," he said, still moving toward the door.

The cop gave the pouch another tap, harder this time.

"Can I see it?" he said.

The other cop was circling calmly around, between us and the door.

"Sure," Chance said. He opened the pouch and tilted it toward the officer.

"Why don't you take it out," the cop said.

Chance exhaled. He took the camera out.

The cop took it and turned it around in his hands.

"Pretty nice camera," he said.

"Big, too," the other cop said from behind us. "Not one of those little pocket ones you see the kids with."

"True," the first cop said, cocking his head. "Not one of those camera phones either. That's what I notice these days."

"Can I see it?" the cop between us and the door asked.

"Sure," Chance said quietly. He passed it over.

"Wow, this is a real camera. It's got lenses and everything."

The cop in front of us said pleasantly, "You a photographer, son?"

"It's just a hobby."

"That's good. My son's hobby is being an asshole. Still, though . . ."

"Why bring such a nice camera on a prank, I wonder . . ." the other cop finished.

Chance mumbled something about taking a picture in the dining hall.

"Huh," the cop said.

"Say, Officer Peters," the man behind us said. "If I'm not mistaken, this is one of those James Bond cameras, good in the dark and so forth."

"Huh," the officer said again.

Ever so slightly, I saw Chance rise up on the balls of his feet. I felt voltage building in my arms and legs.

The officer reached back into Chance's bag. His hand came out holding a piece of paper.

My heart sank as I realized it was our map.

Chance started to say something, but the cop raised his hand. He unfolded the paper. His eyes scanned the page. The corner of his mouth flickered.

I felt a body close behind me.

The cop looked up. His face was still a mask of pleasantness, but all the warmth had drained from the eyes, the smile.

"What were you boys looking for down there, exactly?" he asked, raising his eyebrows.

There was a moment of perfect stillness.

Chance ran.

There was a crack as the cop behind us rammed Chance into the wall. The camera fell and slid along the floor. The other cop went for me. I saw a baton rise up in the air above Chance. Without thinking I jumped toward it and knocked them apart. Chance leapt up and ran blindly into the other officer. "Go," he yelled.

I ran out the door and down the hall. The hole of the window came closer and I jumped, hit the ground outside, and tumbled over the rocky grass. I saw Chance pass me and keep running. Back on my feet I ran through the gate and didn't stop, didn't even think, took off in the opposite direction from Chance and ran until the gloom factory was out of sight behind me. I kept running across the far edge of the campus, on service roads and then through the woods of the west side, looping around to the edge of the river. When I couldn't run anymore I walked, cutting a winding path through the woods until I was sure no one was following me. I rubbed the black off my eyes with my sweatshirt and threw it into the river. Now I was in a gray long-sleeved T-shirt and black pants. I still looked like an idiot, but now it was the kind of idiot who just stumbled drunk out of a club. I cut toward the middle of the campus. I passed an upper-class dorm and heard a party upstairs. I went to the party and blended into the anonymous shoulder-to-shoulder crowd in the small room, purple and red lights, loud bass, everyone jumping to the music, the smell of orange juice and liquor saturating the air. I stole a green coat from the pile in the bedroom by the door. Now I was an alcohol-soaked, green-coated student blending into the throngs of Saturday night revelers on the main campus. I wound my way to the quiet side street of my dorm. No one followed me. I waited in the hallway around the first corner for ten minutes. No one came in the door after me. I got to my room, locked the door behind me, switched off the lights. I checked the lock on every window. I doubled-checked the lock on my door. Remembering the invitations placed on my bed, I moved my chair to the door and wedged it at an angle under the knob, the feet digging into the floor.

I sat on the floor below the window and peeked out the blinds. No one on the street below. No one in the yard beyond.

I looked at the poster of Albert Einstein on my wall. *What are you smirking at?* I asked him.

I was safe.

In the plant, my face had black paint smeared all over it. And no one had followed me home.

They didn't know who I was.

This was my warning. This was my rock bottom, my chance at salvation. Done. Finished. Take the Incompletes. Work hard, get straight A's in the spring.

A normal career. A normal life. No fame. No glory. No secrets. No power.

That was fine.

I could be a person again.

20

The next morning, I felt lighter than I had in months, confident and full of purpose. I called Chance to make sure he was okay, but he wasn't in. I called the hospital and learned that Sarah had been discharged. I walked to her brownstone and rang the bell. Sarah's roommate answered the door, still glum, with thick glasses and a pink barrette in her hair.

"Can I help you?"

"I'm here to see Sarah."

A slight pause.

"She's not here."

"I know she's here. She got discharged yesterday."

She leaned toward me and puffed out her chest, ready for battle.

"I know who you are."

"Look, um . . . what's your name?"

She eyed me suspiciously, as if revealing her name would grant me some secret power over her. Finally, she said, "Carrie. But she doesn't want to see you."

"I understand. I wouldn't want to see me either. And you're a good friend for trying to keep me out. But I'm here for a reason. I want to make things right."

"Oh. I didn't realize you were Jesus," she said.

A voice called down from the stairs beyond their living room. "Carrie, who is it?"

"It's the guy," she replied. "The *lawyer*."

"Law student," I said.

"He won't go away," Carrie explained.

There was a long pause, and then Sarah said, "It's okay. Let him in."

Carrie narrowed her eyes at me.

"Whatever," she said, stepping aside.

I walked into a neatly appointed living room, the complete opposite of Miles's philosopher's cave. They had self-assembled modern furniture, the kind that comes in a box and lives in a world halfway between student and adult. There was one bedroom off the living room; the staircase led up to a second. Sarah waited at the top of the stairs, her door cracked. I could see half her face, one bright hazel eye, one rosy cheek.

I took a breath and started up the stairs.

When I got to the top, I saw her in a blast of sunlight from the window. She glowed, without makeup or jewelry, her cheeks flushed, eyes iridescent. She was somehow ordinary *and* enchanted at the same time: the tomboy you know your whole life before you see her at the prom and realize she'd been beautiful the whole time.

"Sarah," I started to say, but she walked away from the door, leaving it open.

She sat down on her bed and hugged her legs. She nodded at a chair by her desk.

"Thanks," I said.

All the speeches I'd practiced on the way over seemed inadequate now, flimsy and childish. Instead, I just looked at her.

159

She was watching me, quietly. Her room was cheerful, with light yellow walls and framed Delacroix prints of Parisian life: Ferris wheels, hilltop churches, kids with scarves in the snow, warm orange windows. But then I saw the cardboard box filled with books on the floor, next to other boxes, with sweaters, socks, folders: she was packing? On top of the books was a model brain, with every hill and valley labeled, though they all looked the same to me.

When our eyes met, there was a tense energy between us, but also, I noted, curiosity. Whatever else, she wanted me to say *something*. I noticed my hands were shaking.

I pointed at the model brain.

"May I?"

She sighed into her folded hands. "Why not?"

I turned it over in my hands. It was made of rubber and felt pleasantly spongy.

"Is part of my brain really called the Sylvian fissure?"

She nodded.

"Sounds like a place where you'd meet a witch. Or a talking wolf."

Stop talking, I willed myself. She looked at me for a long time. Then she nodded at the brain.

"There's also an anterior commissure."

"Where soldiers buy toothpaste."

"And a cingulate gyrus."

"A dance craze. The Cingulate Gyrus."

"Everybody's doin' it," she said. For a split second, the corners of her lips flickered into a smile. Then, as if she suddenly remembered why we were here, a wave passed over her face, her eyes hardened, and we were back to square one. She didn't say anything for a moment, and when she did, her voice was strangely bland.

"I quit my program."

There was no rebuke in her voice, but it felt like a hard slap anyway.

"I'm sorry, Sarah."

She shrugged.

"It was that or an investigation. I didn't want my dad to get in trouble."

"I don't know what to say. I'm so sorry."

She closed her eyes and rubbed her temples.

"After the trial, all I could think about was how much I hated you."

I started to tell her I understood, but I saw her face and shut my mouth.

"Not just minor hate, understand. I wanted to . . . I spent a whole week wanting to kill you. I blamed you for everything wrong in my life. By the time I got home yesterday, I was *tired* of hating you. That's when I realized something . . . I felt relieved."

"What?"

She smiled.

"That secret. It was killing me. A little bit, every day. Like my whole life was based on a fraud, and everything that came after made that fraud heavier, more impossible to escape."

She looked at me.

"What I'm trying to say is, I forgive you."

The strange thing was, I didn't feel better. I felt worse.

"I'm not sure I forgive myself."

I saw that look again, the one that made me imagine her in a hospital, caring for patients. "You were just doing your job," she said.

I shook my head.

"Was I? Was that the way to do it? The only way to do it?"

"I was lying."

"I know."

I closed my eyes. "This could take a while to figure out."

"Well," she said, smiling, "your life's not over yet."

I nodded. If it weren't for my recent burst of good sense, she might have been wrong about that. But now I saw a different path. I took a deep breath and hoped I wouldn't screw up what I was about to say.

"I brought you something."

She looked surprised, even skeptical.

"I can't change what I did. I know that. It's just a token. To say I'm sorry."

"Okay," she said slowly. She waited.

"Well, it's not here."

"What?"

"We have to go get it."

"You're kidding, right?"

"No."

"Where is it?"

"I can't tell you. But we have to take a train."

"Are you crazy?"

We waited for someone to flinch. No one did.

"You're crazy," she said.

"Know what I thought, the night we met?"

She shook her head.

"I thought you'd forgotten how to have fun."

"Oh. I thought you were going to say I had nice eyes."

"You seemed so sad. I wanted to fix that."

"Why?" she asked.

I think I must've blushed. She just said Oh and looked away.

"Listen. This morning I had two hundred dollars in my bank account. Now I have twelve. I'll probably have to give blood under a couple of names to make it to the end of the semester. At least come see what I blew it on."

"So," she said softly, "my choices in life are: one, go off with the guy who ruined my career, or two, stay home and think about the fact that I have no job, no friends, no money, and no plan? Does that sound right?"

I said it did.

"Big day," she said.

I waited.

"Well," she said finally. "I'm curious." She stood up and looked around the sad, half-packed room. "And curiosity beats *this*."

We rode the train for an hour and a half. Mostly she looked out the window at the towns and fields passing by. I saw the orange blue light reflect on her face.

She spoke only once. She turned to me and said, "If you're some psychopath who's planning on killing me, don't bother. You already did." Then she turned back to the window.

When we left the train we took the subway, then went the final blocks on foot through the bright, crowded city. Everything felt fresh, alive. She didn't ask where we were going. But when we came to the broad plaza with the central fountain and the glass temple beyond, her face went to recognition, then surprise.

"Do you know where we are?" I asked.

She nodded.

"Have you been here before?"

She shook her head.

She looked around, taking the whole piazza in: the men in black tie, the women in regal dresses. There was a look of wonder in her eyes. It *was* wonderful. Before us was a glass wall, enclosing two giant paintings of angels, each a hundred feet tall, one red, one yellow, both swirling and arching up toward heaven. We walked past the fountain to the Metropolitan Opera's grand entrance.

"It's beautiful," she said.

"Come on."

"We're going in?"

I nodded.

"*In* in?"

I nodded. Her face lit up.

"You look like a kid," I said.

We walked through the immense atrium. Everything was upholstered in red and gold. We waited as an ancient man in a tuxedo tore our tickets. Then we took our seats under the glass chandeliers that looked like splintered stars, bursting with faint white light.

Sarah kept looking around, soaking it all in.

"How did you know," she asked, "how I felt about opera?"

"You told me. The night we met."

The opera was Mozart's *Magic Flute*. It was a fairy tale, with dancing animals, a Sun King, and a pair of flirtatious parrots named Papageno and Papagena.

It all would have been ridiculous if it weren't for the music. I'd never heard anything like it: celestial, pure, gliding like a hummingbird. When the curtain came down, the audience leapt to its feet, roaring with applause. I watched Sarah. She faced the stage, smiling and clapping, tears streaming down her cheeks.

Afterward, we walked the city. We came to a bright street filled with Indian restaurants. Each one was decorated with Christmas lights, inside and out; entire walls and ceilings were covered. Every restaurant seemed to be trying to outdo the ones around it until the whole street was flickering red, yellow, purple, and green in a beautiful, benign arms race. We sat on a bench and watched the people pass in and out of the restaurants.

"Can I ask you a question," Sarah said.

"Sure."

"When did you decide to be a lawyer?"

"When I was thirteen."

"How did you know?"

"I was working at my grandfather's office for the summer. There was this one case. This little girl was being abused by her mom. The dad came to us. He was scared. He didn't know what to do. My grandfather made it right. We went to the judge and got the little girl away from the mom. She wasn't allowed anywhere near her ever again. And I thought, wow, the law did that. It saved that girl."

"That's nice," she said.

"My grandpa was a one-man practice. He had a little office with a shingle in front that said William Davis, Attorney and Counselor."

"He actually had a shingle?"

I nodded. "It was a small town."

We were quiet for a little bit.

"When I was a teenager," she said to me, "my mom used to say, when you feel lost, remember the last time you really liked yourself. I was thinking about that today."

"Did you come up with an answer?"

"I did. The year before I went to medical school, I worked as a librarian at a neighborhood library. I loved that. I loved the little kids, the books."

She smiled at the memory.

"What about you?"

I thought about it.

"Four years ago," I said. "I got accepted to Princeton for college, if you can believe that. I was all set to go. And then my dad had a heart attack. A really big one. He was out of work for weeks. My mom needed help. So I decided to skip Princeton and stay at home for school. Help them out."

"Do you ever regret it?"

"Best decision I ever made."

"Did you ever wonder if maybe part of you was scared to leave home?"

I should've been mad. If anyone else had said it, I probably would have been. But there was something so gentle about her that it seemed like an honest question, without any judgment attached.

"I don't know. Maybe that was part of it."

It was getting cold. Sarah shivered and pulled her coat tighter.

"Do you get the feeling," she said, "that in some alternate universe we'd be engaged by now?"

I was so surprised I started laughing.

"What's so funny?"

"Nothing. That just seems . . . I don't know . . . I mean, could we have gotten it more messed up? Not *we*. Me. Everything I've done in the last few months . . . I wish I could go back and do it over."

"I should have said yes when you asked me out. I wanted to."

It felt like a portal had opened up, from my present world to a world of husbands and wives, houses and children. I remembered the windows in her Delacroix painting, warm and orange.

I wanted to kiss her, but I decided not to. We just sat there, and after a while she put her hand on mine.

21

I got back to the dorms and saw a homeless man out front, right by the steps leading up to my entryway. He wore a long gray coat and steadied himself on the railing as he leaned into the bushes, throwing up. I was never sure how to act around homeless people. The town was full of them. What could be more magnetic than five thousand undergraduates with a student's conscience and a parent's bank account?

As I approached the stairs, the man swung around and held up his arms defensively. I saw it wasn't a homeless man at all but Humpty Dumpty, the crown prince of the library, looking like a train had hit him—his bow tie was undone and hanging in two limp strands; his thin white hair was scattered, the part long gone. He reeked of gin. He sheltered a bottle in a brown bag under his arm.

When his eyes fixed on me, they went wide.

"I've been *looking* for you," he said hoarsely. He wiped an arm across his mouth.

This was not good. That much I knew already.

I glanced around. The yard was quiet. I grabbed his shoulder and pulled him into the shadows behind the bushes.

"What are you talking about?"

"You know what," he said.

"No I don't."

"You *know.*"

"I don't have time for this."

He just grinned dumbly and starting laughing.

Enough games.

"Listen to me," I said. "I'm done."

He shook his head like a toddler about to say *Don't wanna.*

"I'm *done,*" I repeated. "I don't know anything. I have no interest in them. I pose no threat. You tell them that."

He laughed wheezily, and a plume of sour breath hit me.

"They know it was you."

A cold shiver went down my neck.

"I have no idea what you're talking about."

"Last night." His eyes were wide, crazy. "Trying to get into the tunnels. You had a *map.* They know it was *you.*"

I shook my head.

Keep it together. Get a poker face, goddammit. But I felt it—the walls crumbling. The skin under his right eye was twitching madly.

"You're not safe," he said. "You need to see the dead man."

I felt fear drip down my back.

What was he talking about, see the dead man? But there it was, the logic unfolding: *The V&D party. The red-haired professor. The obituary. Who gave me the obituary? The library clerk. And who ruled over the library?*

It was Humpty all along, trying to guide me. I thought of his angry exchange with Bernini in the hall; how he seemed like he was half-in, half-out of Bernini's secret world; maybe half-insane from what he knew. And now he would take me to the man with the red toupee. Maybe *he* could help me out of this. If I trusted this nut.

What choice did I have?

They knew it was me. They *knew*.

That portal, that vision of family, the bliss of a normal life, suddenly collapsed like a dead star. I felt a hand on my shoulder, pulling me out of my thoughts.

"I'm trying to help you," the old man said.

I followed him to the library. He was stumbling and muttering, taking swigs from his bottle, making less and less sense as we went. I tried to stop him from drinking, but he knocked my hand away. After a while, I had to help him walk. I held him by his thin arm, and the skin moved loosely under my hand, like a cocoon about to give birth to a skeleton.

We reached the front entrance of the library, with its grand columns, but he took us around back to a door I'd never seen before. He selected a key from a crowded ring, and we entered a loading bay and went down a spiral staircase two floors below ground level.

He looked at me.

"Turn around," he said.

I heard him perform a complicated set of maneuvers: things being pulled and replaced, something large dragging across the floor. When I turned around, I found a door where a wall had been. He used another key, and we went through the door.

So these were the steam tunnels! They weren't at all what I'd expected: no dirt floor, no cobwebs, no blue phantoms passing in and out of the air vents. Just a long white hallway, covered in a complex angiography of pipes, wires, gauges, and dials.

"Don't touch," he muttered. He clinked his bottle on a pipe. "Hot."

Humpty barreled forward with that head-down walk, swaying a bit, no noise but the occasional mumbled curse. We went several minutes in silence until he blurted out *Fuck!* and barreled on again.

We turned into a narrow side hall and stopped.

There were several metal panels on the wall. Humpty scrutinized them and finally tapped his finger on one.

Written on the panel, in neat print, were the small letters DM.

He grinned. His smile looked like a garage-sale xylophone.

He told me to pull off the panel. It led into a tunnel, much smaller than the one we were in. I'd have to crawl, he explained. He handed me a small penlight. The tunnel was dark, and the penlight cast a faint sphere of light that reached about a foot ahead of me. Just follow the signs and I would get there, he told me. Stay quiet. Don't divert.

"Understand?" he snapped.

"I do."

I started to climb in, but he stopped me. Something in his face broke a little, came into focus. For the first time, he actually looked like more than a bitter, addled old loon.

"What if I told you I was better than the things I've done?" he asked me. "Would you believe that?"

I thought, *that's impossible.* But he looked so desperate, I just nodded.

"I saw you in the library. The night you helped your friend. I was watching." He was trying very hard to communicate something. "I am not a bad man."

His eyes were almost lucid.

171

"What have you done?" I asked him.

Humpty shook his head. Apparently he wasn't ready to go that far.

"Just let me help you," he said.

He urged me into the tunnel.

Humpty Dumpty watched me start the crawl. Then he replaced the panel behind me, killing the last of the light.

I crawled on my hands and knees. Every so often I would come to a branch point, and one route would have another sign like before: DM. I felt like I was moving deeper into the belly of a beast; it grew warmer and moister. Eventually I came to a split in the tunnels. To my left, I saw the familiar notation DM, this time by a seam in the brickwork. To my right, I was struck by something I hadn't noticed anywhere else: the faintest hint of light and the softest thrum of noise, almost a pulse, coming from around the corner at the end of the tunnel. I wasn't supposed to deviate, of course, but then again, that was the advice of a drunk lunatic. I looked back at the small letters on the brick. I could always explore here, then come back and follow my original path. I'd just have to be careful, keep track. I had my keys in my pocket. I took them out and tried scratching a brick. It left a faint mark. Fine. I made up my mind and turned away from DM toward the light.

When I came to the corner, it was another fork. I left a small mark with my key pointing me back to where I started, and I took the turn toward the light.

It was stronger at the end of the tunnel, a flickering salmon glow. The sound was slightly louder now. It was a beat, a thumping. I went toward it.

Another turn, another fork. I paused and listened. I looked back toward the other tunnels. Silence. No one. I scratched the wall. I turned and the light was brighter, a pinkish tone, the color of clouds in the last seconds of a sunset. The pulse took on an organic feel now, not exact, slightly wild, even erotic, like a beat that should come *now* but—wait—wait—boom—wait—boom—boom . . .

A strange smoke was drifting down the tunnel around me. I smelled a mix of aromas from my childhood: cinnamon, pepper, gunpowder, peach, and some others I couldn't place—musky smells like having your nose in a warm pocket of someone's body.

I stopped for a moment and let the smoke pass over me. I breathed it in, tried to isolate the different memories it evoked.

There was a square of light ahead of me now, a glowing box of pink-orange light through slits of a vent. I felt lighter now, as if that smoke were working its magic on the networks in my mind, slowing me down, lifting me up, placing me in a smooth, rocking pool, letting my vision shine and spread like a fan of cards. If I went all the way to the light, I would be at the end of a length of tunnel. Nowhere else to go. If someone came from behind, I would be cornered. But I hadn't come this far for nothing. I crawled forward to the light. I pushed my face against the vent, let my eyes line up with a slit.

I was high above, looking down on a scene of odd beauty. The salmon light flickered, lit the room then *poof,* darkness—then a flare and sunrise again. I let my eyes roam across the scene. There was a man with a long beard moving a metal canister around, plumes of salmon smoke pouring from its holes as he traced patterns in the air. I saw people I recognized: Bernini in a high chair, his chest exposed, white hairs curling out around a yellow silk

173

gown that was luxurious and oriental. Nigel standing rigidly in front of onlookers, naked, the musculature of his thin body defined and illuminated by the strange light. The smoke was burning my nostrils. Everything was an electric version of itself, the colors unnatural, neon, strident and explosive like the energies between people you feel but never see. The pulsing came from drums around them, men pounding and letting their bodies collapse and rise over the tuned skins. The beating grew faster. The man in the center threw his head back. There were dancers, moving naked and loose, letting their breasts swing, and behind them a device that mirrored their movements that pulsed and churned as they moved faster and looser, their heads whipping around, hair flying and sticking in clumps to their sweaty, flushed skin. The man in the center was calling out now. His beard was electric, neon green, his stare lost behind round eyeless yellow light. He held up his hands and his palms glowed red with wet electric blood. He opened his mouth and tossed his head completely back and let out a terrible noise in a merciless voice that sounded animal, made a sound like *a ca ca* and everyone was moving.

I tore myself away. The smoke was burning my eyes. I heard a noise down the tunnel. Fuck, I thought, *fuck I should've paid attention.* Someone was coming. I turned away from the salmon square, slid back as fast as I could on my elbows and stomach toward the end of the tunnel, back to the branch point. Whoever was coming was coming fast, getting closer, louder. The echoing of the tunnels, those drums still pounding, faster and faster, building toward some unnatural orgasm. I reached the branch point. I looked down both tunnels. Where was the person coming from? Which branch was mine? I waved the penlight around the bricks. My key mark seemed lost in the scratches and nicks on the hundred bricks around me.

There it was! I heard the crawler, coming from the other tunnel. I took off on my elbows down my original path, following the key marks, turning again, the sound of the crawler advancing, but I tore forward, fueled by pure fear, following the branches until the sounds grew softer, more distant. I worked my way back until at last I found the very first key mark and across from it the letters DM written on the brick. I started back toward my original goal, the one Humpty set out for me, the end point that might save me from whatever hell those people had in store for me.

I went from path to path, following the marks for DM. It went on for God only knows how long, until I came for the first time to a hatch above me in the ceiling of the tunnel.

DEAD MAN, it said.

I pressed the hatch up and it gave easily and slid away to the side.

I climbed up through the hatch into a narrow crawl space. It was dark, but light poured in on three sides. I moved toward the bright light and came out from under an object into a room. My eyes adjusted. I looked back and saw that the object I had crawled out from under was a bed. I looked around.

I was standing in my room.

22

What fear! Fear like I had never felt before. I remembered myself checking locked doors, locked windows, putting chairs under the doorknob—worthless! What a fool I was, thinking I could ever be safe with them against me.

I had to get out of my room. I needed somewhere to hide while I thought this through.

I cut a wild path through campus, walking with my head down and hands deep in my pockets, a wool hat pulled low over my eyes.

I knocked on Miles's door and prayed he would answer.

Finally, I heard rustling. He opened the door, looking like I'd roused him out of a very deep sleep. Miles in pajamas—all six foot seven and three hundred pounds of him—was an unnatural sight. And considering my night up to that moment, that was saying a lot.

"You've got to be kidding me," Miles said, rubbing his face.

"I'm sorry, Miles."

"What *time* is it?"

I started to say something.

"It's a rhetorical question. I have a clock. What I mean is, what the fuck?"

"Miles," I said, "we need to get inside."

That surprised him.

"Miles, I'm in trouble . . ."

He studied me. I watched it dawn on him.

"You didn't," he said softly.

"Miles, I—"

"You *didn't*," he said.

I couldn't say anything. I just nodded.

"Damn it," he shouted, and his voice thundered down the hall.

"Miles, we have to get inside . . ."

"IT DOESN'T MATTER," he shouted at me. I saw a look in his eyes, one that I hadn't seen in years. It was the look he used to get in debate matches. The one that said *I'm going to destroy you.* Forget his size. Forget his mass. That *look* was why they called him The Beast.

"I warned you," he growled. "I told you not to mess with them. Didn't I? You didn't listen. *Goddamn* it. What did you *do*?"

I started to explain, but he talked over me.

"You came *here*?"

I paused. I hadn't thought about that.

"You fucked up and then you come *here*?"

"Miles, no one followed me."

"How do you know? You don't know *anything*."

He smacked the door with his massive fist.

"I could send you away right now. You haven't told me anything. I could shut the door right now."

"Miles, I don't know what to do."

He squeezed his eyes shut, rubbed his face.

"Fuck," he said. *"Fuck."* He slammed the wall and I felt it shudder.

He walked inside, but he left the door open. I followed him and locked us in.

He sat on the futon. The old thing groaned under him. He rubbed his face with both hands. He took several giant breaths. Some of the angry flush went out of his cheeks. When he spoke, he was calmer.

"It was Chance, right? You and Chance met up again."

I hesitated, then said yes.

He nodded a couple of times to himself. The heaving of his massive shoulders slowed.

"It was a mistake, putting you two together. I thought I could control it. It's my mistake." He rubbed his neck. "It's okay," he said finally. "You're frightened. It's okay."

"No. I shouldn't have come."

He shook his head.

"I know you *and* I know Chance. I'm the connection. They would've put it together anyway."

"Miles," I said. "I'm really scared."

He looked at me, and the beast was gone from his eyes. They were calm again, philosopher's eyes—warm, wrinkled at the corners.

"Scared," he said, nodding. "That's a good start."

We called Chance. No answer.

"We need to go over there," I said. "He might be in trouble."

"Slow down. We need a plan first or you're going to get us all killed."

"We should call the cops," I said. "Tell them everything. It's the only way."

Miles smiled at me, and it was an annoying, patronizing smile.

"Jeremy, these aren't the kind of people you just report to the police. Or the FBI, MI6, Sydney Bristow, or Batman, for that matter."

"Then *what*?"

Miles picked up a Rubik's Cube from the table, smacked it down hard, then started pacing and fiddling with it. It was a nervous habit that went back to childhood. His dad had given him his first cube on his tenth birthday. Whenever he had a problem to solve, Miles would pick up the cube and start fidgeting with it.

It seemed so simple. Just nine squares on a side. In high school, Miles used to tell me there were forty-three quintillion possible configurations of the cube: forty-three followed by *eighteen* zeros. The Earth would fall into the sun before our fastest computers could find the best solution for every position.

It begged the question: how could something so simple get so screwed up?

He sighed.

"You're in a bad position. You know enough to be in trouble, but not enough to protect yourself."

"What does that *mean*?"

"Think about it. A secret can get you killed, but it can also save your life."

"You sound like a fortune cookie."

Miles glared at me. "*You* came to *me*."

"I know. I'm sorry. But you did sound like a cookie, a little."

"Yeah, well try this one on for size: there's only one way to kill a shadow."

He looked at me without a trace of humor.

"How's that?"

"Turn on the light."

Miles outlined a plan. I would find Humpty Dumpty and get him to tell me everything he could about the V&D, as quickly as possible. We would document everything in writing, make copies, and address them to all sorts of people—reporters, investigators, conspiracy theorists, anyone we could think of. Then, we'd seal those envelopes in larger envelopes and send them to Miles's most trusted friends at big law firms. Firms that knew about offshore accounts and information that had to be invisible yet accessible. Miles would reach out to them quietly, informally. They would never even know what the information was about. They would just know that if something happened to us, they were to open the envelope and drop the package inside in the mail. That was the leverage: we would live in a precarious balance, like Schrödinger's cat; the information would exist and not exist, and everyone could go on living. I had no idea if the plan would work, if it even made *sense*. But I couldn't think of anything better. And I was so tired, so scared, that I grabbed on to it like the revealed word of God.

"Now," Miles said, slipping into a sweater. "Who else have you been with since the night at the plant?"

I felt my heart stop.

Sarah.

23

I went to see Humpty Dumpty. I had no idea where he lived, but the last time I saw him, he could barely walk. My gut told me I'd find him passed out in his office chair at the library. If he made it that far.

I called Sarah and begged her to meet up with Miles. She sounded tired and confused, but I managed to convince her. She had no idea what was going on, and when she did, she would probably hate me, but at least she'd be safe. That was good enough for now. There was a sick feeling in my throat that kept pulsing: *you did this.* But I swallowed it down. Right now, I was the investigator. Humpty had reached out to me. I was the one he would talk to. I had a job to do.

The library was open twenty-four hours, but it was after midnight on a Sunday, and it was deserted when I got there. I kept my hat low and tried not to look over my shoulder too much.

I headed for the administrators' wing: forsaken on a busy night and now positively gravelike.

There was a soft light under the door of Humpty's office. A good sign. The nameplate announced ARTHUR PEABODY, HEAD TUTOR OF LEGAL METHOD.

I knocked softly.

No response.

I knocked again.

Nothing.

I tried the door.

It was unlocked. I slipped into the room. I saw the dome of Humpty's head over the back of the chair. A few liver spots. Some wisps of white hair.

"Mr. Peabody?"

Nothing.

"Mr. Peabody?"

Passed out, I thought. I wondered if I could rouse him.

Then I heard it.

A soft, gurgling noise. I thought of a child blowing bubbles in milk with a straw.

Oh, no.

What was it? Was he choking on his own vomit, like a drummer in a rock band? Or something else . . .

No.

I pushed the thought out of my head and walked closer.

The office was perfectly silent, except for that faint gurgling noise. I was suddenly slapped across the face by the sound of a clock chime.

I jumped, let out a nervous little laugh, and kept walking.

Still no movement from Humpty.

"Mr. Peabody?"

I got close enough to touch his chair.

I reached my hand out. My fingers were trembling.

The chair wheeled around slowly as I pulled on the leather arm.

Arthur Peabody was holding his neck. Rivers of blood spilled through his fingers.

"Oh my God."

I grabbed for the phone on his desk. He caught my arm and squeezed it.

"No," he hissed.

"I'm calling 911."

He tried to shake his head. With every turn, the river between his fingers surged.

"Please," he whispered.

I could barely hear him. His fingers clawed into my arm. He was trying to pull me in. He whispered into my ear.

"Now or later . . . they'll . . . get me . . ." he wheezed.

"I can protect you."

When I saw his face, I knew what he thought of that.

". . . let it . . . happen . . ."

"Please. I can't."

His mouth worked in my ear.

"I missed . . . my . . . chance."

"Chance for what?"

His mouth felt wet. Pink froth appeared at the corners.

". . . not . . . dying . . ."

His whole body started to shake. His lips were turning blue. His eyes were fading. They were distant, blind. I was losing him.

"Please, Arthur, I need your help."

He made wild, incoherent noises. His eyes rolled back in his head.

"*Please*. Tell me something. *Anything*."

His life was spilling out all over me. The desk was rapidly turning dark red in an expanding pool. *I needed his help. Now.*

"*Arthur say, something.*"

Just hissing; twitching muscles.

183

I had a vivid memory. In the hallway. The day Bernini fired me. Peabody said something about a joke. Bernini was furious.

—*Why don't you tell him the joke?*

—*Enough. Remember your deal.*

That *meant* something to him. Something *important.*

"Arthur, listen to me. What was the joke? The one Bernini didn't want me to hear?" I shook him hard. *"The joke, Arthur."*

For a split second, his eyes seemed to focus. The memory pulled him back.

"The joke . . ." he whispered.

"Yes. YES. The joke. Tell me."

He started moaning. His eyes rolled back up—all I could see was white, the tiny delicate veins.

"What's the joke?" I shouted, cupping his face and pushing my nose into his.

He was moving his lips, just the last echoes of a memory. Mindless. Gone.

I pushed my ear right against his foaming mouth.

". . . if . . . you . . . want to . . . know . . . about the V and D . . ."

"YES? *YES?*"

". . . look . . . at . . . it . . . with . . . four . . . eyes . . ."

And then his stare went blank, and the gurgling stopped.

Arthur Peabody was dead.

I couldn't stop shaking. A man had just died right in front me. Someone who'd risked his life to help me. Whatever they were up to, Humpty had found the courage—at the very end of his life, in his own crazy way—to turn on them.

Except that now he was facedown in a pool of blood on his desk, and I didn't know *anything*—except a stupid childish riddle with no answer. What now?

I rendezvoused with Miles at a seedy motel on the outskirts of town, the one families never used on Parents Weekend. Miles had paid in cash and used a fake ID from the bowels of his wallet, a vestige from his college days. Lenny Wurzengord, it said. Miles had been so proud of it back then. He even wrote me a letter explaining his genius: no one would ever suspect it was a fake ID, because no one on earth would *choose* to be called Lenny Wurzengord.

I knocked on the door to room 18 and prayed Sarah would be in there. Seeing Humpty Dumpty had pulled back the last curtain between myself and death, which frankly had never seemed that scary to a young guy who lived in his parents' basement. But now it wasn't a concept anymore. It was red and sticky and all over my hands. One more night sleeping in the Dead Man's room and *I* would've been the one gurgling and grabbing my throat.

Sarah was there, sitting at a small table, next to a stack of papers—Miles's first attempt at writing everything down for our protection. For a second she looked relieved to see me, like I was there to tell her it was all a joke. Then her eyes went wide. She stared at my arms, which were spattered with Humpty Dumpty's blood. She ran to me and turned my hands over and over, looking for a wound to fix. She asked me what was going on. I tried to explain, but everything came out jumbled. I kept apologizing. More than once she said, "But I don't know anything about this."

185

"I know, but we spent the last twelve hours together. We went out of town together. See how it *looks*? To *them*?" She shook her head again. "I'm sorry," I said, again and again.

"Listen to me," Miles said. His voice was sharp and it popped the bubble Sarah and I were in. "We don't have time for this."

I looked around the room.

"Where's Chance?" I asked.

Miles shook his head. "I don't know. His roommates haven't seen him."

That hung in the air for a moment.

A phrase popped into my head: *no way out.*

"Miles, they killed Peabody. I didn't get what we needed."

"Okay, *focus*," Miles said. "*Think.* What do we *know*? What do we *assume*?"

The words were magical—this was just a trial, a case we could break apart and analyze. For a moment, the image of Professor Peabody coughing up blood was gone.

I tried to lay it out, like a courtroom time line.

"We know there's a club. We know Bernini is in it. We assume Nigel, Daphne, and John have just been initiated. We know Humpty Dumpty"—*Who?* Sarah blurted—"was involved somehow, but he turned on them, and they killed him."

"Good," Miles said. "We know they're obsessed with immortality. We know they studied failed quests for it: Bimini, the alchemists, etcetera . . . What else?"

"We know Peabody wanted me to see that obituary. We know it had a picture of a man who supposedly knew the exact day he was going to die. We know I met that man at a V and D event. Let's suppose, then, that his death was merely a cover. He was old,

186

and it had to *appear* like he died. But he wouldn't, really . . . He would keep on living, hidden somewhere . . ."

"So," Miles said, "we assume that they found a way, where so many others failed . . ."

"But *how*," I said. "Every quest they studied was a dead end . . ."

Miles nodded. "If we knew *what* they're doing, maybe we'd have some idea how to stop it . . ."

He was pacing around the room, rubbing his hands through his hair.

"What are the loose threads? We know what you saw in the tunnels—some kind of ritual—but we don't understand it. Nigel was there . . . and Bernini . . . and now we have this riddle . . . what was it?"

"If you want to know about the V and D, look at it with four eyes."

"Right. Right. What does that *mean*?"

"I have no idea."

"Four eyes. Four eyes."

"Glasses," Sarah offered. It was the first thing she'd said in a while. We both looked at her. "You know, *four-eyes*. That's what kids call someone with glasses."

"I don't know," Miles said.

Sarah shrugged. Then her eyes lit up.

"Maybe it's an optical illusion. You need some kind of special glasses to see it."

"Um, okay . . ." Miles said. "But see *what*? We don't have anything to look at with 'special glasses.'" He pronounced "special glasses" with a healthy dose of sarcasm.

"How should I know?" Sarah shot back. "Maybe Jeremy

187

knows. Did you see any kind of object or writing in that room? Something that might have an image in it, if you looked at it the right way? Through a prism or a special lens or something?"

"I'm not sure," I said. "It was dark."

I thought about it.

"Maybe *four eyes* means two people . . . Maybe it takes two sets of eyes to see it right . . ."

"See *what* right?" Miles said, throwing up his hands. "There is no *it*!"

"Maybe it's the letters themselves," Sarah said. "*V* and *D*. What if you look at them with two sets of eyes, one from the front and one from the back?"

Miles shook his head, annoyed.

"What's *V and D* backward?" Sarah asked.

She took the yellow pad from the table and wrote *V&D* on it. She tore off the page and held it up to the light.

Ɑ⅋V

Miles squinted at it.

"That's it!" he cried.

We both looked at him. He shrugged. "Just kidding."

Sarah flipped him the bird.

"I think we might be on the wrong track," I said. " We're approaching this like scientists . . . visual tricks and all that. These are lawyers. They're logicians. Linguists. I think we're looking for a verbal puzzle."

"Okay," Miles said, rubbing his hands together. "Now we're getting somewhere."

I smiled at Sarah. She rolled her eyes.

"Maybe," I said slowly, "it's a pun. Not four *eyes,* four *i*'s. The letter *I*."

"Ah," Miles said, pulling the pad toward him. "That gives us six letters to play with."

"Six?"

"*V, d,* and four *i*'s," Miles replied, writing them out on the pad.

Viiiid

"It's all so clear now," Sarah said.

"What can we spell with that?"

Miles started playing.

Vidi, he wrote.

"Latin," he said, "for 'I see.'"

"Not bad. But see what? Only two *i*'s left over."

"Yeah," Miles said, tapping the pen on his mouth. "Not good."

He began writing below:

Iv. Ivid. Divi.

"Come on. Look for words," he said.

"What about *id*?"

"In Latin: *this, him, her,* or *it*."

"That's helpful," I admitted.

"Maybe it's *id* in English," Sarah said. "The Freudian subconscious."

"Okay," I said. "But *id* what?"

Miles started writing.

Id vii. Id ivi.

He shook his head. "We don't have enough letters to spell anything useful."

"Maybe they're not letters," Sarah said.

We both looked at her. I slapped my forehead. "*V, I*, and *D* . . ."

She nodded. "Roman numerals."

Miles grinned and started writing.

VIII ID. DIVIII. VDIIII.

"Maybe it's an address . . ." he said.

"Or a date . . ."

I grabbed the paper from Miles and started listing more numbers.

Sarah leaned over, next to me. I felt her arm touching mine.

We looked at the list.

"There's so many possibilities . . ."

We tried to make dates, addresses, Dewey decimal notations for books, latitudes and longitudes—anything that might point us to an answer. It was too much! We made dozens of numbers just by swapping letters around and inserting spaces. There was nothing to guide us. Nothing to tell us what we were looking for or how to know it when we saw it.

I was starting to feel a sinking sensation—that we weren't a bit closer than when we started.

Sarah was still hammering away when I noticed Miles had been silent for a long time. Then he started chuckling. He said, "Oh, that's good."

"What's good?" I asked him.

He shook his head and smiled.

Now Sarah was looking at him too. He was staring off, with a satisfied look on his face.

"What's good, Miles?"

"Say what you want about the V and D," he said to us, "but they haven't lost their sense of humor."

I felt a tingling in my arms and legs.

He was taunting us, enjoying the victory. I felt the thrill of a mystery about to be revealed.

"*What's* good?"

"You saw drums. You saw a ritual. We just didn't know *what* ritual . . ."

He grabbed the pad from us.

"Not four *i*'s. Four *eyes*," he said.

"Huh?"

"You still don't see it? Just like they told us. Look at the V and D with four eyes. Four big *round* eyes."

Sarah and I just stared at him. He wrote something triumphantly on the pad and pushed it toward us.

V ☉ ☉ D ☉ ☉, it said.

Miles tapped on his pad and smiled broadly.

"We need a witch."

191

24

We came to a store called the Flying Mushroom, a place I'd passed many times but never actually entered. It was a brick building painted with broad wavy zebra stripes. During business hours, the neon sign flashed purple and pink; white shoe polish on the windows promised "vintage albums, psychic readings, and more . . ." In my lonelier moments, I had sometimes considered finding out what the *more* was.

We came at it from the back, reaching the Mushroom through the dark service alley that ran behind the stores. If anyone was following us, we would've seen them coming up the narrow path after us. At least, that's what I kept telling myself.

We followed Miles until he disappeared behind a Dumpster. Moments later, he came out with a key.

"How did you know where the key was?" I asked him.

He shrugged, unlocked the door, and ushered us in.

There were rows of wooden shelves, with dusty vinyl records in no discernible order: Beethoven's Emperor Concerto, Neutral Milk Hotel's *Aeroplane Over the Sea,* a Steve Martin stand-up album, Miles Davis's *Bitches Brew*. I thought it would be a great store to visit if you had no idea what you were looking for.

Miles motioned for us to be quiet. He left the lights off and kept us away from the front windows. We went through a beaded curtain into a back room. Miles reached up and unhooked a thick black drape. It unrolled behind the beaded curtain and fell to the floor with a soft thud. We were in total darkness until he flipped a switch, and then I heard a soft bubbling sound and saw black lights illuminate the room from under the high cabinets. Planters with overflowing vines hung from the ceiling. An iguana stared at us blankly from a terrarium. There were lava lamps, of course; one yellow, one red. There were little fountains everywhere: spheres with smoky lighted holes, piles of wet pebbles, tiki volcanoes with water flowing like lava.

We sat at a small card table and waited. Miles looked nervous. The excitement of the puzzle had worn off a bit; the cold air had let a little chill of reality back in. Miles kept scratching his beard. I had no doubt he was dreaming of his Rubik's Cube, twisting his imaginary squares under the table. I stole a glance at Sarah. She didn't look happy, but at least she didn't have that *how many times can you ruin my life in one week* look that I kept expecting to see. Actually, when we were working the puzzle, I saw something totally different on her face, something that bothered me. She looked like she was *enjoying* herself. I admit a certain thrill in solving the riddle, but in *her* it scared me—because I was coming to the conclusion that I might care more for her than I did for myself. She hadn't asked for this. And I had a sneaking suspicion that the moment this became a game to us—that would be the moment someone got hurt.

Miles's phone rang. He snatched it up, looked at the caller ID, and breathed a giant sigh of relief. "It's Chance," he said. They spoke softly, then he closed the phone.

"He's fine," Miles said. "He's heading out of town to crash

with some unnamed social rejects." Miles shrugged. "He wishes us luck."

"Great. That's very generous of him."

A door opened somewhere in the building, and all three of us turned to the black curtain at the same time. Heavy footsteps came toward us. I saw Miles slide his chair back. I looked down at my hand, which was clenching itself so hard the knuckles were white. I let it relax and watched the blood return.

Then the curtain was pushed aside and a large figure came into the room. She was giant, almost as big as Miles. But where Miles looked messy and distracted, she looked like the magnificent queen of a warrior people. Her hair was a wild tangle of thick black curls, with a long elegant strand of silver in the front. Her skin was a warm caramel brown, and her eyes were green, glowing with absolute confidence, almost on fire. She wore a full-length coat dusted with snow, and a Dr. Seuss scarf, striped with a dozen shades of blue, tossed around her neck like an aviator's. She filled the room. You couldn't take your eyes off her.

"Everyone," Miles said, grinning, "meet Isabella."

"This is your store?" I asked, after we had all shaken hands.

"My father," she said, "was a graduate student at the university. One of the first black international students. My mother"—here she gave Miles a smile—"was a local celebrity: a townie philosopher, agitator, free spirit. The first person to sell Janis Joplin records. The first person to read palms and do tarot. I was the little girl running around behind the counter in a moon dress. You wouldn't believe the famous people who came in here as students—as a joke of course—wanting to know if the stars

194

predicted greatness for them." She sat and draped her arm on my chair.

"My mother and father were an improbable couple. An African man and an Irish woman, at a time when that was still scandalous. A university scholar and a red-haired hippie. The only problem was, the longer my dad was here, the more he resented his past. His new religion was economics, political theory. No matter how much they loved each other, she was obsessed with the one part of him he couldn't wait to leave behind. She became something of an embarrassment to him. He turned into a celebrated professor, and she disappeared to San Francisco." Isabella took in the room, seeing it through our eyes, like an alien zoo. "My mother never left me a forwarding address. But she left me this store."

"How do you and Miles know each other?" I asked.

No one said anything, and I think they both blushed a little.

Miles leaned toward her. "No one followed you?"

"Of course not. Now would you please tell me what's going on? Calls in the middle of the night, Miles? Make sure no one follows me? What is this?"

"Okay," he said. He looked at Sarah and me sternly. "Ground rules. No one say a word to her about what we're doing. We're just asking general, hypothetical, academic questions. The less she knows, the happier I am.

"Now," he said, turning to Isabella, "what can you tell us about voodoo?"

She slapped her forehead.

"Miles, what did I say when you asked me to marry you?"

I felt the room stop, as if all the fountains froze at once.

Miles turned bright red.

My mouth dropped open. So did Sarah's.

195

"Well?" Isabella demanded.

"You said, when I grow up," Miles mumbled.

"Sweetie, does *this* seem grown up to you?"

He shook his head sheepishly.

I'd never seen Miles chastened before. He lowered his head, like a puppy waiting for its punishment.

Isabella sighed, running her hands into her hair. It was midnight black, a nest of unruly, graceful ringlets. Her green eyes sparkled. She closed them, and it was like a light went off in the room. She hummed to herself. Finally, she laughed and shook her head.

"Okay, okay, my sweetheart. What do you want to know?"

Miles let out a giant sigh of relief. He gave us a goofy grin.

"Everything. Izzy, tell us everything."

25

"First of all, forget every ridiculous thing you've ever heard about voodoo. Forget zombies. Forget voodoo dolls. Our story begins four thousand years B.H.—Before Hollywood—in the ancient civilizations of Egypt, Assyria, Ethiopia. Their accounts of the stars, the planets, the human soul—these gave birth over millennia to the religions of the African tribes: the Fons, the Igbos, the Kongos, and dozens more. The slave trade brought these ideas to the New World: to Brazil, Cuba, Haiti, Galveston, New Orleans. Religions mixed and transformed, as slaves from different tribes were integrated . . . if you'll excuse the term . . ." Isabella leaned in and gave us a smile that was as large and majestic as she was.

"Of course, it all starts with the word itself. In the language of the Fons, *Vo* means 'introspection.' *Du* means 'into the unknown.' Voodoo is therefore the investigation of mystery. Not just of gods and heavenly bodies, but of our own souls." Isabella drew a line with her finger across the table. "The voodoo temple is the *oum'phor,* held up by a central post—the solar support—and balanced by the moon, a small boat hung from the ceiling, which represents the voodoo goddess Erzulie. The top of the sun-post is the center of the sky. The bottom is the center of hell. The post itself is the wood of justice, with a whip strung from it to symbolize penitence and redemption. The post is the physical center of the temple—it is, as they say, the cosmic axis of voodoo magic. The oum'phor has many chambers: a holy of holies, and symbolic 'tombs' for the uninitiated—death before rebirth. On the altar are *pots-de-tete,* small jars that contain a bit of the soul of each person in the room.

"Everything flows from the power of the gods—the *loas*. You legal types may be interested to know that *loa* comes from the French word *lois,* or 'law.'" That smile again, magnetic. She leaned in. "Ask me where the gods live."

"Where do the gods live?"

"In the astral city Ifé, in a star that bakes at thirty thousand degrees Celsius. You've heard of the ceremonies. Drums. Incantations. An animal sacrifice, or sometimes a plant. The *loa* comes down to earth to mount a voodoo practitioner, who becomes the god's horse. This is an act of possession, so that the gods may perform an earthly task: heal the sick, accept a sacrifice. The mounting begins with a violent struggle but ends moments later with a whimper: in a flash it's over."

Isabella went to a cabinet. She pulled a small object out of a box, unwrapped the felt cover, and placed it on the table.

"Perhaps the most powerful item in voodoo is the *baka*." She traced a circle around it on the table with her finger. "The baka is a talisman, but with a very special and dangerous composition. It is the fusion of two souls: the *ka,* the terrestrial soul that stays with the body after death, and the *ba*—the celestial soul that ascends to heaven. It is this combination that makes the baka's power so volatile: it is whatever the holder wants it to be. A healing charm. A weapon."

Isabella paused. She put the charm away. She walked to a

cupboard, took out four glasses, and filled them with an almond liquor.

"For a time, voodoo did quite well in the New World. But you have to imagine the slave tent on a quiet night. The glow of the flames. The hint of drums. Rumors of rituals, miraculous seizures. The slave owners came down brutally, even for them: hangings, beatings, even flayings, punishments for the slightest whiff of voodoo.

"And so the religion evolved again. It cloaked itself in secrecy. Catholic saints were used to signify voodoo gods. Rituals were cloaked in other rituals. Erzulie becomes the Virgin Mary. Legba the Lion becomes Christ. Is it so surprising? Religions are always borrowing, mixing. Some believe that Moses himself was inducted into voodoo, under the tutelage of a black scholar named Pethro. Some even say Moses married a black woman briefly, until his family intervened. Who knows? But that is how voodoo, cloaked in a new skin, survived four hundred years of slavery in the New World. And how it exists to this very day."

Isabella sat back in her chair and spread her hands.

"That, my friends, is all I know about voodoo."

Miles, Sarah, and I each seemed to have the same reaction. Interesting—but what did it have to do with us? What did it tell us about the V&D? How was it going to save us? I weighed my words.

"Isabella, tell us about voodoo and death."

"Well," she said, thinking it over. "It's common to honor the souls of your ancestors. And to prepare one's soul for death. Penitence and redemption, like I said."

"Okay, but what about . . . preventing death?"

"You mean healing the sick?"

"Not exactly . . . I mean, like, *cheating* death."

Isabella wrinkled her brow.

"I don't understand."

"I met a man who was planning to live beyond his own obituary. To live forever. You didn't say how someone would use voodoo to do that."

She shook her head.

"They wouldn't."

"How do you know?"

"It's just not a part of it."

"Come on, there must be *something*."

There was a strain in my voice. This was our last thread. Our only remaining clue. And it was unraveling before my eyes.

"What about zombies?" I tried. "That's a way to bring people back from the dead, right?"

"I told you, forget about zombies."

"Do they *exist*?"

"That's Hollywood stuff. It's not part of the culture."

"But do they *exist*?"

Isabella pulled back. My voice sounded wild, plaintive. She sighed.

"I don't know. There are stories, rumors. Once, some Harvard scientists claimed to find chemicals in Haiti that would knock a person out and bring them back, sleepy and submissive. But you know the legend as well as I do. A zombie is mindless, empty. If I wanted to live forever, it wouldn't be like that."

A fair point. Running around with my tongue hanging out might be fun for a Saturday night—but eternity?

"Please, Isabella, *think*. There has to be something."

Isabella closed her eyes for a moment. She filled the room with her warmth, her calm. In the fluorescent light her strand of gray hair seemed to glow. She appeared to be searching for an answer to my question. Then she opened her eyes and held her hands out to me. She rubbed the tops of my hands with her thumbs, like she was reading my fortune. Her expression was kind, but she shook her head.

"At some point, every culture has to choose between the circle and the line. The circle seeks contentment: the seasons, the tides, sunrise and sunset, birth to death and maybe even death to birth, who knows?

"The line . . . the line seeks progress: acquisition, mastery, re-finement of the world around you.

"Neither is intrinsically good or evil. That's the thing most people don't realize. It's the *balance* that matters . . .

"But to live forever, as one person, through all time? To cheat the cycle? That's the line, Jeremy . . . that's the line out of control. What you're describing isn't voodoo. There's no magic, no belief to make that happen. I'm sorry, but I think you're looking in the wrong place."

I felt frantic. This was our last clue.

"But what if someone found a way to *use* voodoo—someone from outside the culture—in a way it was never intended?"

Isabella thought about it.

"Well, if that's the case," she said, with that magnificent, wry smile, "then my black half is *very* disappointed in my white half."

We left, with our final clue in shambles.

I was devastated for about an hour, and then I cracked the whole damn thing wide open.

26

"Why don't you tell him the joke?" Humpty Dumpty said. "Maybe he'll thank you."

"Enough," Bernini snapped. "Remember your deal."

I kept turning those words over and over in my head. We were missing something. Something that was right there, hanging in front of us.

I couldn't shake the feeling that we had everything we needed to save ourselves.

Miles was spread out on the comforter of the shabby bed in our shabby motel room. He was mindlessly twisting his Rubik's Cube—scramble, solve, scramble, solve. Miles wasn't quite what they called a speed cuber, but he did go to a few conventions in high school, where math nerds, sci-fi fanatics, comic book collectors, and other of our fellow virgins would commune to break international cube-solving records. The fastest people today could solve a scrambled cube in fifteen seconds or less. Amazing how the world changes—it took Erno Rubik, the Hungarian mathematician, an entire month to solve his own cube for the first time.

"Why don't you tell him the joke? Maybe he'll thank you."

Why would I thank him?

Miles was the only action in the room. We were holed up, stuck in a holding pattern. Scramble, solve, scramble, solve. His fingers were large but nimble.

Sarah was watching him too.

"How do you *do* that?" she finally asked.

Miles looked up, surprised, as if we'd woken him from a particularly deep dream.

"This?" He held up the cube.

"Yeah. How do you do it so fast?"

"It's not that hard, really. The secret is the middle square. It never changes. Once you see the middle square, you know what color that side has to be. Everything else turns around that. From there, it's just pattern recognition, clockwork."

That's when it clicked. The whole thing.

Why don't you tell him the joke?

What was our middle square?

It had to be the dead professor who wasn't dead. Everything turned around him.

It occurred to me: what if we had the wrong middle square? What if our clues didn't fit together because everything flowed from the middle square—and we had the middle square totally backward? We saw red and thought it was blue . . .

The whole puzzle fell into place, like water molecules snapping into ice.

"Oh my God," I said, and they looked at me. I told them everything. I couldn't see my own expression, but I saw it reflected in their faces.

I saw fear.

Immortality was one thing.

But *this*?

For our sake, I hoped I was right. And so help me, I hoped I was wrong.

There was only one way to find out.

I hadn't been to Nigel's apartment since the night of his dinner party, and that felt like another lifetime. I walked up the steps to his brownstone. It was almost four in the morning, and the cold was so intense, so harsh, that my nose and throat burned every time I took a breath. The streets were perfectly still. I hadn't seen a soul on my way over. And believe me, I was looking—for any shadowy figure that might be in the vicinity.

I was surprised to see a light already on in Nigel's window. The doorbell echoed through his apartment. Lights flipped on from room to room, closer and closer, and then footsteps came my way. Nigel opened the door. He was fully dressed and didn't seem at all surprised to see me. That, I think, was the moment I knew just how stupid I was. Why didn't I just chain myself to the bell tower in the center of campus, with a sign that said HEY SECRET EVIL CLUB: COME AND GET ME! But this was the only way. We had to know. I told myself that and heard another voice, that class clown in the back row of my brain, calling out obnoxious comments. It was Arthur Peabody's voice, and it said: *Now or later . . . they'll get me.*

There you go. Now or later. Let it happen.

Wise words from the late, great Humpty Dumpty.

"Jeremy," Nigel said pleasantly. "Come in."

We passed the dining room to the last door in the hallway, the only one I hadn't been in before. On one end of the room was Nigel's bed, a canopy with four elegant spiral posts; at the other was an oak desk, next to a limestone fireplace with a roaring fire. Behind the desk were rows of books. I sat in the leather chair he in-dicated and started scanning the bookshelves. I found what I was looking for easily enough—it was part of a set—the antique he'd shown me on the first day of school, a leather-bound collection of political essays. The one he'd wanted to give Daphne in his crazy quest for her affection. The one I'd talked him out of giving her, back when I was giving love advice to Nigel even though *I* wanted Daphne. Back when altruism and friendship seemed like virtues to me. Well, the book was there, anyway. At least he listened. I also saw, perhaps too late, that the phone on his desk was off the hook. It was an old-fashioned phone with a rotary dial and a ver-tical shaft like a lamppost that cradled the receiver. But not now. Now the receiver was sitting facedown on his desk, and the first thing he did when he sat down was lift it up to his mouth.

"I need to go now," he said into the phone, looking at me. "Yes," he said. "Yes. Quite." He smiled. "I will."

He hung the phone up.

"Who was that?" I asked, trying to sound casual.

"No one," he said, smiling back at me.

The clock had started. Fine. Fuck the clock. Fuck whatever was waiting for me on the other end of that call. Right now, it was just me and Nigel. I couldn't rush this. It was a dance. A magic trick, even. And I wasn't going to get caught with a rabbit halfway out of my sleeve. Not tonight.

I was going to take my time, because that was the only way.

Nigel stared at me, waiting for me to say something. I stared back. His desk was covered with books, and he appeared to be writing a paper or even a book in longhand. There were stacks of handwritten pages, with cross-outs, marginal notes, insertions, all in the same urgent script. Not a computer in the room.

Stress is an amazing thing—an hour ago it was bringing out the worst in me, and now it was bringing out the best. When I spoke, my voice didn't crack. It sounded deeper and stronger than it had in weeks.

"Is it everything you hoped it would be?" I asked him.

Nigel didn't flinch.

"Is *what* everything I hoped it would be?" he asked with a straight face. "Law school, you mean?"

I reclined in my chair without taking my eyes off his. I aimed for just south of angry and repeated, very clearly: "Is it everything you hoped it would be?"

He gave me a dead-eyed stare, raising his eyebrows.

"Yes," he said. "Everything and more."

"I'm happy for you."

"What do you want, Jeremy?"

"Nothing, Nigel. I don't want a thing."

Take it slow.

"So why are you here?"

"I think you know."

Easy, I thought. Less anger, a little more hurt.

"We used to be friends . . ."

Nigel sighed. His guard went down just a hair. But not the coldness that was just behind his eyes. The people on the other end of that call were still coming, and he knew exactly what they'd do to me when they got here. And he didn't care.

"I know," he said. "We were."

"I *helped* you. That's the part that kills me. I helped you."

He rubbed the dome of his head.

"What do you want me to say?"

Okay, swipe one:

"That night in the library, you were a mess. Didn't even know how to read a case. I *helped* you. What a fool I was!"

Let it sit.

Reel him in.

"Did you come here to insult me?" Nigel said, pushing away from his desk. "Tell me I'm stupid? That I don't deserve whatever it is you think I have?"

Good. Keep his eye off the ball.

Then the wagon jumped the tracks.

"I got you something," he said.

"What are you talking about?"

"I ordered it a while ago. It just came. I was going to give it to you at school. But since you're here . . ."

He gave a little sarcastic shrug.

I needed to get him back on track. Time was running out. They were coming. And he was stalling me. But I couldn't show fear. I couldn't let him see what I was up to.

"I don't know what to say."

"Don't say anything. Just take it."

He paused. He waited me out.

"Where is it?" I asked finally.

"Over there," he said. "Under the bed. In a box. Go get it."

A chill went up my spine. We weren't in the dorms after all, we weren't even on campus—but my mind was spinning like an out-of-control clock, and I couldn't help but wonder: Was there a hatch under his bed? Another link to that maze that seemed to connect everything in this town? I imagined myself walking to the bed. Getting down on my hands and knees in the plush carpet. Peeking under the edge of the bed, seeing only black. Reaching my hand under, feeling around in the soft darkness. The strange fist with the knife gliding out, chopping my hand like a master chef working down a carrot. Another hand grabbing into my hair, yanking me under the bed, swallowing me down into the hole.

I was starting to sweat. I doubted Nigel could see it yet, but maybe he could smell it. Maybe he could smell the fear.

Now or later, I thought.

I stood up.

I went to his bed. He was watching from behind me. I could feel it. He didn't say a word. I had a sudden image in my head. Not my life flashing before my eyes. Just a single memory. My mom, holding that envelope in hand, that letter of acceptance. *Baby,* she said. She dropped the mail all over the floor.

I knelt down. It was dark under the bed. The only light in the room was the fireplace, crackling over by Nigel. I lifted the comforter and tried to see under the bed. Where was the box? I couldn't tell—it was pitch black in there. I reached in and felt for it. My fingers touched woolly carpet.

No hand with a knife slashed out at me.

My fingers felt the edges of a cardboard box. I sighed. The ground below me suddenly hardened and felt more solid, more comforting. I pulled the box out and carried it back to Nigel's desk.

"Open it," Nigel said.

I hated this. He was running out my clock. But the whole gambit depended on flow. He couldn't see what was coming. I had to follow the rhythm.

Inside the box was my article. Nigel had paid some company to bind it in a nice leather cover. It was thin, but it looked grandiose, important. I felt a flash of pride. On the cover, my name and the title were embossed in gold letters.

It was a stroke of luck.

I looked at the article for a second, ran my fingers down the smooth leather.

"This reminds me," I said—*easy now*—"of the day we met each other."

I smiled at him, and he smiled back with that joyless, thin smile. I shook my head and even laughed, tentatively. "You were going to give Daphne that beautiful book and ask her out."

"She said no, of course," Nigel said, grinning.

"Well, at least she got a nice book out of it."

"Yeah, lucky her," Nigel laughed.

My stomach dropped three stories.

The center square . . . the center square . . .

Why don't you tell him the joke? Maybe he'll thank you.

Nigel wouldn't be thanking anyone, because Nigel—the Nigel I once knew—didn't even exist anymore.

I took off so fast I'm not sure he knew what happened until I was out the door. I heard him yell after me, then pick up the phone and shout into it.

I skipped down the steps of his brownstone three at a time and almost fell head over heels down them.

Everything fit.

Our center square *had* been wrong. The professor planning his own "death," the one I met face to face—we had assumed his obituary was a cover, a hoax to hide the fact that he was already immortal. I guess I'd pictured a bunch of three-hundred-year-old men living in a cave somewhere, pulling the strings and ruling the world. But that wasn't the center square at all. His "death" was a hoax all right, but not in the way we thought.

Because there were two ways to be immortal, really. You could make your body live forever. Or, you could jump ship when your body was about to give out . . .

Three new spots every year.

Three new students, the best and brightest, initiated into the V&D.

What was the central ceremony of voodoo? What had Isabella told us?

Not immortality but possession. The *loa* mounts the *horse*.

What if someone found a way to use voodoo—someone from outside the culture—in a way it was never intended? I thought of Mr. Bones, in his office with artifacts from around the world. A pushpin in every inch of the map! How many continents had they searched for their path to eternal life?

My God—what had Bernini said to me in his office? It had seemed so strange at the time. *How tall are you? Good bone structure. Can you guess the last time we elected a shorter than average president?* It was inspired. If you lived forever in your own body, you had to hide. But *this* . . . stealing a new body every generation . . . How many centuries to amass wealth? How many turns to be president? You could build dynasties. *Empires.*

The *loa* mounts the *horse*: his mind, your body.

A line of the most brilliant people in the world, waiting to cheat death, over and over . . . And every year, a line of fresh students, clawing past each other to be initiated. What fools! Victims of the world's most exclusive faculty club. And I'd been queuing up right along with them, placing my head on the chopping block with a big hopeful smile . . . But I didn't make the cut, did I? And that's when Humpty had said, *Tell him the joke. Maybe he'll thank you.* Yes—thank you for not taking my body, my life. (But maybe, just for a second, did I feel a crazy pang: what was so wrong with my body anyway?)

I had to get back to Miles and Sarah.

But then I saw him. Across the street, walking toward me with his head forward. The road was perfectly empty, silent except for that figure cutting a quick path in my direction. I tried to scream, but my throat locked up. I was blowing air. I felt it streaming from my lungs, but no sound came out—just a weak hiss.

I took off running, away from the man.

At the far end of the street, I saw another figure step out of the shadows and come toward me, at the same fast clip. I cut down a side street that ran between two rows of brownstones, beautiful old homes. I hit a patch of black ice and slid wildly, knocking into some trash cans that broke my fall but slammed my arm and shoulder, stinging like hell. Pure adrenaline was driving me now. Somehow I jumped up and kept running. I risked a look behind me and saw the two men converge and move toward me, side by side. Not running so much as loping toward me with long strides. I was thirty feet from the end of the block. Once I got there it was a major intersection with at least three ways to run. If I could just make it far enough ahead of them, I could lose them. I willed myself to run faster. Twenty feet. Fifteen. And then my heart stopped as another two figures appeared at the end of the street. They blocked the exit. Silently, they started moving toward me.

I did the only thing I could. Without thinking, running on pure instinct, I broke left into an alley and tore down it faster than I've ever gone in my life.

It was claustrophobic; lightless except for a thin strip of starry night above me.

Then I saw what was waiting for me at the end of the alley, and I realized they hadn't been chasing me. They'd been *herding* me.

Three figures stood at the far end of the alley, blocking the path, not moving, waiting.

Between us was an open manhole. A small wisp of water vapor curled from the black circle. They were closing in behind me. I tried to stop but I was running at a speed that sent me slipping and sputtering on patches of ice. And then some sort of primitive math took over—*four behind me plus three ahead equals fuck it, take the hole.* So I stopped trying to brake and let my hands shield my head and I jumped through the hole, feeling it slam my shoulder on the way down, feeling the empty air, a pale blue disc pulling away until all my senses were pulled to the wet slamming under my feet. I hit the ground and felt the shock run through me.

I picked myself up. There was a burning in my leg, but I could walk. At first, all I heard was the trickling of water. I shook from adrenaline and cold. I was standing in a small gentle stream. I watched water an inch deep move in a current over my shoes. Every twenty feet or so, grating slits above me let in faint street light.

In that dim glow, I saw the figure, ten yards away, cloaked and hooded, staring at me.

He was tall. There was a slow heaving in his shoulders, a calm low breathing.

He took a step toward me, then paused.

I couldn't see his face. He said nothing, made no noise.

He took another step forward.

I willed my legs to move. They wouldn't.

I want to see his face, a crazy voice inside me offered.

Another step. Deliberate. Methodical.

Move, I hissed to myself.

Nothing. Glue legs. Useless, wet, and dead.

The steps came faster then, the stride long and precise. Each step smacking into the thin stream under our feet.

Move. Move!

Now he was charging me.

Without stopping he reached a hand into his cloak, and it came out a moment later with a metallic ping. When his hand returned to his side, there was a long blade pointing down from it.

I moved.

My legs popped out of their paralysis. I took a few steps backward and then turned and ran like hell.

Every step splashed. The water, the stone, the slits of light, it felt like a tomb, and I wondered if I was a ghost who hadn't gotten the memo yet. My side was screaming—one of those "stitches" you get in high school gym from switching between walking and running. A voice, low and seductive, whispered in my head: *You could just stop. It won't hurt. Now or later. Come on, it's easy.*

I didn't stop. I pushed through the stitch and it went away. But the hooded man was closer. I don't know if my legs were giving out or if he was warming up, but I heard his splashing steps faster and nearer. His blade must've scratched the wall—I heard a *ching*! Was he raising it? Was that the sound of the blade up over his head? As I ran, what kept coming into my head was an image of Sarah, standing in that shaft of light at the top of her stairs, her eyes brilliant and hazel brown, almost gold, just after she'd been crying. I wanted to see her again. That's all I knew. I had to get out of this tunnel. In a straight chase, he would catch me.

The brain is an amazing thing. It wants to live. You know that garbage about how we use only ten percent? Well, I think that other ninety is roped off for moments like this. I heard everything, saw everything. I ran past a gutter and saw the water running into it, and just above, too minor to be noticed by a ten percent brain, I saw the small painting of two eyes on the bricks over the drain. That drain led somewhere. And *somewhere* was better than *here,* because I was about to die.

I stopped on a dime and threw myself backward, my hurt leg screaming, aiming low for his ankles. It was a direct hit and he went forward over me, his cloak whipping across my face. It smelled musty. I dove toward the drain, kept my head down, and grabbed the inside and pulled myself through.

I fell into a crawl space, deep in water. There was a ladder, and I took it up. I pulled off a panel and threw it hard down into the shaft, onto the head of the figure who was pulling himself through the gutter below. Light poured out through the opening behind the panel, and I dove into it.

My hand came down on a wall to steady myself, and I felt a searing pain. It was a hot water pipe. I was back in the steam tunnels. I took off down the hall.

Would it have been too much to ask that the panel—not heavy but not light either—might have stunned the person when I slammed it down the shaft onto his head? Knocked him out cold? But it hadn't. As if in slow motion, I saw his long pointed hood come through the panel into the tunnel. Then his spindly arms unfolded like spider legs and bootstrapped his long body through. The knees unfolded into the hall and he was at full height.

In the light, I could finally see him. A pointed hood and scarlet robes. His face hidden behind a crude mask carved out of wood. Pointed bark teeth, like some hungry demon. Rough triangular cheeks. The wood painted stark white, with streaks of orange and

purple around the eyes and mouth, like an eighty-year-old whore out for one last john.

The Puppet Man, I thought.

Then *ping*, and the blade was back at his side, pointing down.

He started the relentless walk toward my execution.

I wanted daylight. I cut right and left, found ladders and took them up, and when I couldn't find a single damn open door I finally saw a panel like the one Humpty had shown me. I pried it off and dove into a smaller tunnel that seemed to slope up. I took it until it leveled out and just kept going, and my heart sank, just absolutely broke, when I saw the dead end ahead.

I spun around to backtrack, and he was there. I saw his bright mask at the far end of the tunnel.

There was nowhere to go.

I turned on my back, eyes on him, and started sliding myself backward. If he came close, at least I could kick at his face, maybe smack that wooden mask into whatever soft or skeletal nose was hiding behind it. But I knew that was crazy when I saw the reach of his long thin arm extending that blade toward me. My leg was no match—it would only make a nice little shrimp on the skewer.

I had to stay out of range. I kept sliding backward, gaining speed. The wall was coming closer behind me but what could I do? That knife was hideous—long and covered with markings. He was gaining on me. It slashed closer and closer. I didn't think. I just slid faster and faster and let the wall come. The blade was so close—it slashed my shirt. I went faster, faster, faster—knew the wall was seconds away and maybe God at least I'd knock myself unconscious before the end and the pain and then I felt the wall slam into me, an instant of explosion and tearing and then I felt cold air sweep around me and I was falling, falling through the air and then there was a great explosion below me, a mushroom cloud of wood and dust and a terrible cracking, stripping noise.

I saw a starburst of yellow flashes as my head hit something and then my vision dimmed and cleared. I looked on either side of me and saw that a long wooden table had broken my fall and exploded under me. I was in a dining hall of some kind, long rows of oak tables in a vast room. I looked above me and saw a wall of hundreds of portraits—dozens and dozens of oil paintings of old white men. And in the center, high above me, was one empty frame, the shreds of a portrait flowering out from the edges. Leaning from the empty portrait was the Puppet Man, clutching the frame and peering out, the blade still in his hand, the face still masked, blank and demonic. He seemed to be sizing up the jump. He turned his dark eyes right at me, and I felt the hollowness sweep through me. Then he disappeared back into the frame.

I stood up, slow and shaky, and limped out of the dining hall as fast as I could, out the exit and into a quiet campus that was just starting to wake up. There was a dim strip of blue on the horizon, under a purple sky. I had no doubt that in half an hour, a crowd of students would marvel at the soon-to-be-legendary Smashed Table Prank and wonder which fraternity had the balls to pull it off.

And I had no doubt that above them, the frame would not be empty—in half an hour, there would once again be a perfect wall of unbroken portraits.

27

When I limped into the motel room, Sarah was sitting on the bed. She had just showered; her hair was wet, and her body was wrapped in a towel. Her eyes were red. When she saw me, she said, "Oh thank God," and ran to hug me. I squeezed her hard and buried my nose in her hair. I breathed in deep. She stepped back and looked me over.

"I thought something happened to you."

"I'm okay."

"Are you hurt?"

"I don't know. My leg, maybe. I think it's all right." I looked around the room. "Where's Miles?"

"We wrote everything down while you were gone. Just in case you didn't . . ." A guilty look crossed her face. "It was Miles's idea . . ." She let the subject die, but I still felt a shiver. "He went to make copies. Come over here. Let me see."

She led me to the bed. Without a word, she sat me down and unbuckled my belt. She slid my pants down and pulled them off. She moved with the precision of a doctor, and it wasn't awkward or embarrassing. She sat down on the bed next to me.

"Lean back," she said.

She examined my leg, pressing her fingers along different

lines and spots that seemed to have meaning to her. Each time, she asked if it hurt, and when I said yes or no, she'd nod. It was somewhere between professional and delicate—each mechanical touch ended with a slight linger; once or twice, almost a caress. I closed my eyes and focused on her fingers moving up and down my leg, bending it, tracing on the inside of my thigh.

She paused, leaving the tips of her fingers just over my hip.

"It's bruised," she said quietly. "Nothing's broken or sprained."

"Oh. Good."

"Good," she whispered.

My lack of pants suddenly seemed more awkward. They were sitting on the other side of the bed, behind her. I reached for them, but I think she thought I was reaching for her. She took my hand and put it on the towel over her breast. She put her other hand in my hair and pulled me in and kissed me. Her lips were soft, still damp from the shower. They opened and I felt the soft hint of her tongue. She pulled back and looked at me.

"I was worried about you," she said.

I tried to say something, something that had been bothering me, but I couldn't get it out. Her eyes moved over my face, reading it. I put my hand on her chin and held her gaze right at me.

"Sarah, when I was in the tunnels, I realized something."

"What?"

I told her that tonight, for the first time in my life, I understood what it meant to be afraid of death. I'd lost people I loved before, but all that did was let me understand loss. Death had still been a concept, nothing more. It was impossible to *feel* that it had anything to do with me. Once, a year ago, I was looking in the mirror and saw my first gray hair. I pulled it out and examined it. It wasn't fear exactly, what I'd felt then. It was like someone had plucked a string deep in my abdomen, an unsteady vibration in my body. But this, tonight—this was a million times stronger. Now, I understood what my dad had tried to tell me about being fifty: I'd had an acute blast of the dull, chronic terror of real age.

And as a result, for the first time I understood the situation we were in. What we represented to the white-haired members of the V&D, waiting in line for their chance to live on. We represented death.

"Sarah, they're never going to stop hunting us."

She gave me a stern look.

"Yes they will. We're going to stop them."

"We are?"

"We are."

She took my face in her hands.

"Do you know why? Because I know what I want. And they're in my way."

There was real power, a force in her words. She stood and took the bottom of my shirt in her hands. She pulled it over my head and dropped it on the floor. Then she reached to the corner of her towel tucked above her breast and tugged, letting it fall in one fluid movement. She stood a foot away. I looked at her full curves. I felt the heat coming off her skin. She pressed my face into her stomach.

I looked up at her.

"I've never done this before," I said.

She arched an eyebrow. I started to explain, but she put a finger over my mouth.

"I know, I know. You lived with your parents in college." She grinned. "You're a smart guy. You'll figure it out."

．　　．　　．

Later, she smiled at me with her head propped on her hand.

"Do you think it's possible?" she asked me.

"What?"

"Possession. Stealing someone's body."

"I don't know. Do you?"

She shrugged.

"I had this patient once. A nice old man. He had a stroke. Every morning, I'd walk into his room and have a totally normal conversation with him. Then I'd point at his right hand and say, 'Whose hand is that?' And he'd say, in a completely casual voice, 'I don't know.'

" 'Well,' I'd ask him, 'it's connected to this wrist, isn't it?'

" 'Yes.'

" 'And that wrist is connected to this arm, right?'

" 'Right.'

" 'And this arm is connected to your shoulder, isn't it?'

" 'Uh-huh.'

" 'So whose arm is it?'

" 'I don't know,' he'd say. 'Is it yours?' "

"You're kidding," I said.

"I've seen patients with multiple personalities. People who smell colors and taste sounds. What I'm trying to say is, we don't know anything about the brain. Not really. All our technology, all our research, we're just scratching the surface. It's still basically a black box. So, yes, I think it's possible. But I've been thinking, lying here."

"About what?"

"Jeremy, if we're right, then they're killing people. Strip away all the bullshit and chanting and superstition, that's all they're doing. It's human sacrifice. We can't let that go. If we do . . ." Her smile was completely gone now. "Then we deserve whatever they've got planned for us."

28

By the time Miles got back, Sarah and I were dressed and sitting at the small table in the kitchenette by the window.

He barreled in with a smile on his face.

"Done!" he said, "done done done done done. Twelve copies, stamped, addressed, ready to go . . . assuming you got what you needed . . ."

He looked at me.

"I did."

"Our theory checked out?"

I told him the story.

"Holy crap," Miles said, rubbing his woolly beard. "Curiouser and curiouser. Call me crazy, but I love this place. The rest of the world, it's all Starbucks and Subway. We are into some seriously macabre shit."

"Miles."

"Yeah?"

"You're crazy."

He clapped his hands.

"I owe it all to you, Jeremy! I was just a lonely grad student until you brought magic into my life! 'Oh go do, that voodoo, that you do, so well . . .'" he sang, channeling Tony Bennett.

"Miles. What now?"

"Now? Now we go mail these bad boys. I want them mailed from out-of-town mailboxes. The more the better. Brownsville, Mason, Orange . . . Once the horses are out of the barn . . . we're golden . . ."

Miles paused. He looked at Sarah. He looked at me. Then back and forth between us.

"Wait a second . . ."

He wrinkled his brow.

"Something's different here . . ."

I hadn't noticed it, but there'd been a looseness between Sarah and me at the table. I was suddenly very aware of my body language. I let my arm slide a millimeter away from hers. My legs had been crossed in her direction. I crossed them the other way. But it was too late.

"Oh," Miles said, feigning indignation. "Oh, I *see*."

"Miles . . ."

"Well I'm just very happy for you both."

"Miles, stop it!"

He grinned ear to ear and gave us a double thumbs-up. I saw Sarah turn bright red.

"Mazel tov!" Miles burst out, which was odd since he was Episcopalian, and he did a little dance.

"Are you four years old, Miles?"

"If I were four years old," Miles said, "I would've done this."

He made his index fingers kiss passionately with a giant smooching sound. He wiggled his eyebrows up and down.

"Don't we have a job to do?" Sarah blurted out, not quite making eye contact with Miles or anyone.

"Yes, of course!" Miles said. "Let's take three cabs. We can cover more territory that way. And an hour from now, we'll be home free!"

Miles divided the packages between us.

And I headed to the train station for a last trip to New York.

On board, I tried to focus on the small towns and lakes passing by, but I couldn't keep my mind off Humpty Dumpty. It was like quicksand in my brain: the harder I tried to fight the image of Humpty collapsed on his desk in a red pool, the deeper I sank into it. He turned on his club, and they killed him. What would they do to me?

I thought of my grandfather, the only other person I'd really known who died. After his funeral, the family entertained visitors in his small house until the last one left, and then we sat in the living room. My mom and dad were on the sofa. My little cousins played at my aunt's feet, oblivious of the whole thing. My brother wasn't there, of course. My grandfather's easy chair, the one he always sat in with an old plaid bedsheet over it, was conspicuously empty. Nobody had the heart to sit in it. What was strange about that moment was that I didn't feel the slightest bit sad. I missed my grandfather terribly, and I'd grieved up to that moment and for weeks after it; even to this day, I still sometimes received unexpected pangs that were gone as fast as they came. But in that moment, sitting in his room looking at my family, I felt inexplicably, outrageously happy—a happiness that I can describe only as a buzzing through my whole body. *Happy* might be the wrong word. It was giddiness. Elation. I've never heard anyone else describe something like it. Frankly, I'm too embarrassed to ask.

I wondered now, on the train: what would my grandfather think of me today?

I left the train and called my brother from a pay phone.

"We need to meet."

"Why? What's up?"

"Nothing. I just need to see you."

"Fine. Come to my office."

"No. Someplace random. Where no one knows you."

"What are you talking about?"

"Just do it. I'll explain everything."

A pause on the line.

"Intersection of Clinton and Delancey. There's a little place called Mico's. They serve burritos that taste like sand. Is that crappy enough for you?"

"This better be good," Mike said to me. He looked tired.

"Late night?"

"I'm in the Model-of-the-Month club."

I took a breath. The restaurant had shades over its small windows, and we were in the back in a dark booth. The service was so surly no one had even acknowledged our existence. I had to admit, it was perfect. We finally got two coffees.

I leaned in.

"Okay. You have lots of bank accounts, safe deposit boxes, right?"

"What's this about?"

"Please. Just answer my question."

"Of course I do."

"You're rich. Crazy Wall Street rich. I know that. And you're kind of paranoid, right? Always have been. So you've probably got offshore accounts, things like that?"

"I'm not paranoid."

"Mike, I don't have time for this. Do you or don't you?"

He shrugged and loosened his collar.

"Let's just say I'm diversified for all contingencies. Including the total collapse of the U.S. banking system."

"Good . . . Good."

I pushed an envelope across the table to him.

"I want you to keep this somewhere discreet for me. Don't open it. Get it off your hands right away."

"What is it?"

"I can't say. But if something ever happens to me, get it and open it. There's another envelope inside. It's already addressed. If something bad happens, mail it. That's it."

"Jeremy, are you on drugs?"

"Please. Just do this for me. It's important."

He leaned back in his chair and sighed.

"I'm not an idiot, Jer. Whatever you think of me, I didn't get where I am by being stupid. This is insurance, fine, I get it. But you want my help, you gotta tell me what I'm getting into. What is it, gambling debts? Is this mob shit? Young fucking cocky lawyers, think they're so smart, get into poker, I've seen it before. That's what you get for going to school so close to Atlantic City. Listen, if you're in trouble, I'll pay off your debts. But it won't be free. You'll pay me back with interest. You have to learn *consequences*. But at least I won't break your legs, right?"

"Your money can't fix this."

The words came out harsher than I meant. I sounded bitter. I saw his face twitch. His composure came back quickly, but the words hung in the air between us.

"Mike, I need your help. Please."

He blinked a few times and ran a hand through his hair. It was thick but the hairline was definitely receding. I noticed he had the hint of a double chin. *This is my brother,* I kept thinking to myself. Jesus, he looked like a middle-aged man.

He smiled, but it was weaker, less cocky. Strangely enough, I found myself missing the cockiness.

"Remember when we used to play at the creek?" he asked me.

"Yeah."

"There was that dog. Belonged to Mr. Reynolds. Remember that?"

"Mean animal," I said.

"He was. Remember the time he was lost, and we found him down in the creek?"

"After a big storm, right? He was pinned down, under a tree."

"You tried to help him."

"I did."

"And what did he do?"

"He bit the shit out of my hand."

Mike nodded at the memory.

"I'm gonna help you," he said. "And I'm gonna play it any way you want. You want me to hold this letter in a mystery bank and never read what's inside? Fine. I'll do that for you. You're a smart guy, Jeremy. Smarter than I am. No, don't say anything, I know it's true. I busted my way through. I'm a bull in a china shop, I know. If you think this will fix whatever's out to get you, I believe you. But you have to promise me one thing."

"What?"

"If this package gets them to leave you alone, then you're finished with them, right?"

I didn't say anything.

"That's it. You understand? Get them off your back and go live your life. Is that what you plan to do? Can you promise me that?"

I looked down at my hands.

"I know you," Mike said. "You have rules. Principles. Always have. Well, I have a different philosophy. Look out for number one. Because no one else is going to. You don't understand that, because you've been lucky. You've never had a real problem. Mom and Dad always babied you. I'm sorry to put it like that, but it's true. If I'm gonna help you, you've got to promise me you're not gonna keep messing with these people. You have leave it alone. Live and let live. Okay?"

I took a deep breath.

I thought of Sarah.

We can't let that go. If we do . . .

"I'm trying to help you," he said. "I'm trying to save you from yourself."

"I know, Mike."

"Promise me. Jer, promise me."

I felt my whole life branching, tearing in half. I shook my head.

"I can't."

He closed his eyes. I watched his face. His good looks, a little worn but still there. I could remember the smell of the grass, playing down in that creek with him, even twenty years later.

"Then I can't help you," Mike said. He slid the envelope back across the table.

"Are you serious?"

He nodded.

"Mike, I need you."

"No. If you won't help yourself, I can't help you."

We stared at each other for a long time. No one flinched.

"I'm sorry," he said, finally.

I nodded.

"I know."

I put the envelope back in my bag and stood up.

"I'll see you," I told him. I started walking away.

He grabbed my arm. He looked like he wanted to say something, but then he let my arm go and turned back to his coffee.

I dropped my packages in the mail, half in random mailboxes I passed, half in the Penn Street station. I felt totally, radically free. For the first time in my life, I knew exactly what I had to do, even if I didn't have the slightest idea how I was going to do it.

29

Miles handed me the phone.

"Dial," he said.

"Who am I supposed to call?"

"Call Nigel."

"Miles, I don't know . . . after what happened . . ."

"Listen to me. You're going to call him."

He told me what to say.

I steadied myself and dialed. The phone rang, but no one answered. I hung up and shook my head.

"Okay," he said to me. "Try again."

"Call Nigel again?"

"No, I want you to call Daphne."

I nearly choked when he said her name. I felt a burning shame that I tried to press down. My last conversation with Daphne involved stealing her purse and some borderline stalking. Not a part of my life I was eager to revisit. Then again, it occurred to me that Daphne—*that* Daphne—didn't even exist anymore. Miles pushed the receiver into my hand.

I still knew her number from the long weeks of trial prep. I pressed the digits in, lingered over the last one, then felt it depress. I closed my eyes.

"Hello," came the milky voice. It set off a firestorm inside me. I tried and failed to ignore the image of her coming out of the shadows outside my room, grabbing me and brushing her lips across mine. I looked at Sarah and encouraged myself to focus.

"Hello," I managed.

A pause.

"Jeremy . . . is that you?"

It was disturbing how much power she still had over me. Deep breaths . . .

"Yeah. It's me."

Another pause.

"I was just thinking about you," she purred into the phone. I could picture her, curled up by the window, legs tucked under, her long hair in a ponytail slung over her shoulder; those fire-blue eyes. "I want to see you."

I bet you do.

"Daphne, I need you to listen to me."

"Come on, why talk on the phone? I *miss* you." Her voice was melodic. "I want to *see* you."

"Listen to me. The situation has changed."

I repeated Miles's words exactly. We'd protected ourselves. We wanted to meet. No details. No fear. My voice was confident, firm.

This time there was a longer pause on the line. I heard voices in the background. Then Daphne spoke to me. All the purring and silkiness was gone. Her voice was all business now. I listened to what she said and nodded. Miles and Sarah looked on, eyes wide. Apparently, Miles was just as surprised as I was that his words hadn't led to hysterical giggles on Daphne's end. Glad I didn't know that *before* I'd spoken them. "I understand," I said, and hung up the phone.

I realized I hadn't breathed in a while. I exhaled and rubbed my eyes.

"Well?" Miles said.

"They want to meet us tonight."

"Really? Where?"

I smiled wearily and made a face that said, *Where else?*

"In my room."

I've never been on the victim's end of a burglary, but I was pretty sure this was how it felt. I hadn't been back to my dorm since coming out the hatch under my bed. Everything was in the exact same place, but it all felt different, foreign and contaminated. My Albert Einstein poster—the one that says "Do not worry about your troubles in mathematics, I assure you mine are still greater"—used to be cute (a little juvenile for law school, maybe, but a concession to the fact that I never had a college dorm room to decorate with clichéd posters). Now Mr. Einstein's face, larger than life on my wall, looked sinister, as if the benign genius in his eyes had slipped into lunacy while I was out. The troll dolls in a line along my desk used to guard my computer; now they struck me more like a druid assembly, here to hack at our shins with tiny adorable axes.

When we arrived, the door was still locked, but of course I expected to see Daphne waiting for us on my bed anyway. Locked doors had never been a problem before. But the room was empty and eerily silent. The only relief from the darkness was the moon shining through the blinds, splashing old Albert in silver light.

I flipped on the fluorescents, and the shadows vanished and the room became much, much closer to normal. I forced myself to sit in my old chair, a nice leather one that rotated and complemented the Stickley furniture. It felt the same, creaked in all the same places.

Sarah sat on my bed. There was one other chair in the room, wooden, yellow, and surprisingly uncomfortable. I bought it at a thrift store for seven dollars, the last chair from a long-gone kitchen table. Miles tried it, said *oomph,* and joined Sarah on the bed.

We left that chair open and waited.

No one spoke.

My mind started messing with me again. Were they standing us up? Did they think we were bluffing? Was this a trap? Why the hell did we come?

How many times was I going to lower my fists and show my neck?

How many more times would I get away with it?

I was about to curse Miles for . . . for *something* . . . (not fixing the mess I'd created?) . . .

And then I heard it:

Three knocks—slow, soft, and polite.

30

Two questions: first, who opens the door in a situation like this? And second, is there a cannon with a lit fuse on the other side? As any good lawyer would tell you, the answer to one question might affect your answer to the other.

I gave a last hopeful glance at Miles and Sarah, then stood up and went to the door.

Through the peephole, the man didn't look like a murderer. He was neatly dressed, in a plain and somewhat worn gray suit. In his left hand was a battered briefcase. His hair was a little ruffled, but he had a tidy mustache, thinner than a drug lord's and thicker than a magician's.

When I opened the door, he held out his hand.

"You must be Jeremy," he said in a tired voice.

I sat in my leather chair and left the wooden one open for him.

He sat hard and cringed, popped off the chair, and sort of half-stood and put a hand on his flank. He let out a little groan.

"Bad back," he said apologetically. "Just give me a second."

The man seemed like he was in real pain. He sort of hovered, half-standing, half-sitting, with his eyes closed. He kept one hand on his lower back; his lips moved like he was counting slowly to

234

wait out the spasm. I shot Miles and Sarah a look. Miles shrugged. Sarah cocked her head. The doctor in her couldn't resist.

"Have you tried a lumbar pillow?" she asked him.

He turned his head to her, still crouching, and half-opened his eyes.

"I heard they don't work."

"Actually, they're great," she told him. "Takes the pressure off your lower back."

"Well, you are the neurosurgeon in the room," he said, trying to smile but still wincing.

"Listen, just take this one," I said and stood away from my chair.

"Thank you, much obliged," he said and walked, still bent, to my chair, grimacing with each step. He settled down slowly into the chair, then let out a big sigh. "Very kind of you," he said.

I went to the wood chair and sat. The angle of the back against the seat was preposterous—an angle unknown to human spines in the history of sitting—and the wood planks jabbed into me. I accidentally let out an *oh*.

The man in the suit smiled sheepishly.

He was sitting in my chair!

The negotiation was off to a great start.

He looked around the room, soaking it in. He smiled at my Einstein poster. He shook his head at the stack of books on my desk. "I don't miss school," he chuckled, in a way that suggested he did miss it, a little.

"We don't want to play games," I said to him.

"Good, good."

He smiled pleasantly.

The man picked up one of the troll dolls from my desk and turned it over in his hands. "My sister used to collect these. She had ones for different countries. I remember, she had a whole cabinet full of them." He smiled at the memory. "Shall we get started?"

This guy was messing with me!

"Yeah, let's get started."

I handed him one of our packages.

The man took it. He pulled out the paper and read it slowly, taking his time. It contained every single thing we knew about the V&D: facts and rumors, puzzles and solutions, maps of tunnels, the location of their temple, lists of names. His face was passive, perfectly unreadable. Not blank—just mild. He might've been flipping through *Reader's Digest,* waiting for a haircut. When he was done, he handed it back to me.

"Okay," he said.

"Okay *what?*"

He didn't reply. He just sat there patiently with a polite smile, hands folded in his lap.

He sat there until I couldn't stand it.

"We want protection. We want you to promise you'll leave us alone. Me, Sarah, Miles, Chance. That's it. We have copies of this all over the place. If anything happens to us, they go out— newspapers, internet, you name it. If we're okay, they never see the light of day. We don't care about the V&D. All we want to do is live our lives. That's it. That's all we want."

I tried to think if there was anything else to say. But there wasn't.

"Well?" I prodded him.

"Well what?"

I wanted to jump the space between us and throttle him.

"Do we have a deal?"

"Okay," he said.

I almost didn't catch it. He said it quietly. No haggling, no comebacks. Just "okay." It seemed too easy. But then again, it wasn't a very complex situation. I didn't buy his Willy Loman act—behind those placid eyes I saw a snake-brain coiling. It seemed like the smarter someone was, the less there was to say.

"That's it?" I asked.

"Is there something else?"

"No."

"Okay then." He used his thumb and forefinger to smooth the two halves of his mustache. "I better get going. Seems like I'm always running behind. You know how it is." He chuckled. "Say, I hate to ask, but can I have this?" He picked up one of my troll dolls, one with wild pink hair. "Haven't seen this one before. I bet my sister would like it." He gave an apologetic smile.

I think my eyebrows were knitting tighter than if he'd asked me a math question.

"Sure. Fine."

"Thanks. Really kind of you."

He did a couple of mini-bows to me and shook Miles's and Sarah's hands.

He was at the door with his hand on the knob when he turned around.

"Oh, sorry, one other thing. Your friend Chance."

Suddenly, the entire room froze.

"What about Chance?"

The man in the suit shook his head. "Sad news. He was killed in an accident. Drunk driving, I'm sorry to say."

I looked at Miles and Sarah. Sarah's eyes were wide. Miles's were burning.

"It'll be in the paper tomorrow," the man said. "We were waiting to put the rest of you in the car, but I guess there's just one victim in this accident, after all." He scratched his head. "Well, good night."

31

For a moment, I thought Miles would jump across the room and tear the little man limb from limb. The look in his eyes scared the hell out of me.

But he didn't move. He just sat there, his eyes burning like coals. I heard the door close. The man with the mustache was gone, and he took all the air in the room with him. Miles just kept staring at the spot where he'd been.

Chance is dead. That's what kept running in my mind, over and over. *Chance is dead. Chance is dead.*

Miles shivered. I thought he was cold, but then I saw his eyes. They'd dimmed from burning to a low simmer. His shiver was like a lion's shaking off a hunt. He walked to the window and threw it open. Cold air rushed into the room. It stung. It felt like an exorcism, cleansing the room of that man's affable malice.

Miles turned to us and opened his hands.

"We're free," he said.

"What?"

"We're free. We did it. We have our lives back."

"But *Chance*."

Miles shook his head.

"Chance was an adult. He knew what he was doing."

"They *killed* him."

"They did. And if it hadn't been them, it would've been the Sandinistas. Or the Taliban. Chance was only happy in the middle of a war zone. I'm surprised he made it this long. You know what would've been a tragedy? Chance dying in a Boca Raton retirement home with pea soup on his chin. His only crime was getting Jeremy involved in all this." Miles rubbed his hands briskly. "Listen to me. We're moving on with our lives. This is a gift. This is as good as it gets."

I started to protest, but Miles raised his giant hand with such force that I took a step back.

"How can you be so cold?" Sarah snapped.

"Cold?" He stared at her. He almost roared. "You think I'm cold? I knew Chance better than either of you. I'll be mourning him long after he's just a footnote in your memory."

His eyes actually started watering.

"Miles . . ." Sarah said gently.

"I don't want to hear it. Chance is gone."

"This isn't about Chance," she said. "Miles, they're killing kids. Twenty-two-year-olds, right at the start of their lives."

"You can't beat these people!" he barked. "Say we tell people what we know. So what? We're only alive because it's easier for them than cleaning up the mess we'd make. But they *could* clean it up. We're alive at their *convenience.* That's it."

"You're right," I said.

Miles did a double take. Sarah looked at me like I'd betrayed her.

"What?"

"You're right."

"I don't think you've ever said that before," Miles mumbled.

"Exposing what we know won't help us."

"Thank God. At least someone's been paying attention."

"We have to beat them another way."

His smile dropped; he let out a low growl.

It was time to tell them what I'd been thinking about, ever since my trip back from New York. The final piece of the puzzle. Their Achilles' heel. The piece that had been right in our faces the whole time. We just hadn't seen it.

"Something's been bothering me," I said. "Remember what Isabella told us? Possession is a *temporary* state, right? You do the ritual, magic happens, and then bam, it's over. Right?"

Miles closed his eyes. He didn't say anything.

Sarah nodded. "Right."

"So how are they maintaining this for the entire life of the victim's body—until they're ready to skip to their next generation of hosts? We're talking sixty years . . . How do they do it?"

"I don't know," Miles snapped. "What am I, Grand Poohbah?"

"Miles, listen. What did I see, when I was in the tunnel over the ceremony? Remember? There were dancers, right? And drummers? And the priest with the crazy eyes? And behind them, what did I see?"

He tried to remember, then shook his head.

It had been there, right in front of us, all along. Sarah's eyes lit up.

"Behind the dancers?" she asked.

I nodded.

"And behind the priest, on the altar?"

"Right . . ."

"A machine. You said you saw a machine."

"That's right—"

"A machine, or something like that, in the dark, twisting and moving like the dancers were. That's what you said."

I nodded. Her eyes were bright, alive.

Miles didn't say anything. He just nodded slightly.

"Isabella didn't say anything about a machine, did she?"

He shook his head no.

"Of course she wouldn't," I continued. "It's totally out of character with the ritual . . ."

Sarah smiled, remembering my exchange with Isabella.

" 'What if someone were *using* voodoo . . .' " she recited.

" '. . . someone from *outside the culture* . . .

" 'In a way it was never intended,' " Miles finished.

I nodded.

"What if the machine . . ."

". . . was some kind of *extension* of the ritual . . ."

"Prolonging it . . ."

"*Sustaining* it . . ."

Miles shook his head as the idea unfolded.

"It's an addition."

"A mechanization."

"Assembly-line voodoo," I said, smiling.

"Then it stands to reason," Miles continued, "that if the machine is prolonging a temporary state—possession—indefinitely, then if we . . ."

". . . destroyed the machine . . ."

". . . we'd end the possession . . ."

". . . and then . . ."

". . . what then?" Miles asked. "Are the victims—what did Izzy call them?—the *horses* . . . are they still in there, somewhere?"

"Would they come back?"

242

"'When the god dismounts, the priest is himself again, *weary* maybe, dazed,' but . . ."

". . . but this is so much *longer* . . . not minutes but *decades* . . ."

"If you cut them off too long, do they die?" Miles asked.

"Don't we owe it to them to find out?" Sarah replied.

Miles laughed harshly.

"*Owe* them? What do we owe Nigel . . . Daphne . . . *John*? Those people *used* Jeremy. And when he had nothing left to offer them, they dropped him without a second thought."

"So what?" I said. "So they deserve to die?"

"No. And they don't deserve you risking your life to save them, either. Or me." He laughed. "Would they do it for us?"

"No," I said softly.

"It's not just Nigel, Daphne, and John," Sarah said. "It's everyone who came before or after. A new group of students every year."

"People we don't know," Miles said. "People who would slit each others' throats for an A."

Sarah leaned toward us.

"It doesn't matter if they'd do it for you. It doesn't matter why us. *Us* is all there is." She looked at Miles and me matter-of-factly. "I'm going. Whether you two do or not."

I met her stare and nodded.

"I'm in," I said.

We looked at Miles.

"Even if your theory is correct," he said, "you're talking about walking right into the sanctum sanctorum."

"That's right."

"You could be walking to your death."

"Maybe not," I said. "Think about it. They only need to do

the ceremony once per initiate, right? The machine does the rest. They already did Nigel. Maybe the others too. So there's a good chance no one's even down there now."

He didn't argue.

"Miles, you *know* about this stuff. *You* were the one who cracked the voodoo puzzle. I don't think we can do this without you."

He scratched his beard. He mumbled something that sounded like *what a clusterfuck.*

"Get in, smash the machine, get out?" he asked.

I nodded.

He closed his eyes.

"Can we set the place on fire, for fun?"

"Sure we can."

At long last, he sighed.

"Why not?"

Sarah let out a cry and hugged the big man.

32

I found the lever, more like a clutch, somewhere in the upper bowels of the fireplace. The room was perfectly silent in the middle of the night. My cheek was pressed against the marble, while my hand groped around inside the mantel. I heard it before I saw it—releasing the clutch led to the popping open of a tall panel by the desk. Sarah clapped her hands. "Perfecto," I heard Miles say, his voice echoing into a larger place.

Just this morning, we were sitting in Sal's, trying to think of a door they wouldn't be watching. We had a map—the one Chance and I had concocted with the help of the late Frank Shepard. We knew where we had to go and what we had to do, which was why Miles's leather satchel now contained a crowbar instead of postmodern gibberish. We just needed a starting point, a way down into the tunnels. Preferably one they wouldn't be guarding with a team of assassins. Which meant, strangely enough, that the best door for us would be one we didn't know existed.

Where to start? There was the hatch under my bed, extra handy if you were inclined to murder me in my sleep. Not to mention it was the first place I'd think of, if I were dumb enough to go after them (which apparently I was). No thanks. There was the elevator in the old house on Morland Street, but I'd been blindfolded, and anyway it was a natural second choice. There was Humpty Dumpty's library passage—but we didn't have his keys. There was the plant manager's office—wired with a burglar alarm. There was the sewer by Nigel's house. They sure as hell were aware I knew about *that*. I thought of the Puppet Man, coming toward me on his gangly spider legs, that long silver fang in hand.

There had to be a better way.

I've said it before—the brain is an amazing thing. Sometimes it tries to help you, even if you're too stupid to notice. I found myself struggling to ignore a sudden, pointless memory: leaving Bernini's office for the first time, walking away down that old hallway.

Stop it, I told myself: *focus on the problem.*

What did Bernini say, seemingly to himself, as I'd walked away?

V&D perhaps?

And what next . . .

That other voice, unexpected, much, much colder—a voice I now assigned to the priest with the twisted, yellow-eyed stare.

We'll see, he'd said.

Where had he come from? No one else had been in Bernini's office with us. No one had passed me in the hall.

It was suddenly clear.

There was another door in Bernini's room. Well hidden and, as far as they knew, totally unknown to us.

I had a less pleasant memory: my last visit to Bernini's office. His cool termination of my services. The way he let me get all the way to his door before he called my name and asked for his key back.

But that was perfect, wasn't it?

He had his key back.

A door I didn't know about, in a room without a key.

I thanked God for the anal-retentive, type-A, worst-case-scenario worldview of young lawyers, as I pulled my copy of *Crime and Punishment* off my bookshelf, opened it to the middle, and let the spare key to Bernini's office fall into my hand.

Perfecto.

Beyond the hidden door was a staircase that spiraled within a tall shaft. We took it down: Miles, then Sarah, then me, the air cooling as we wound downward. At one point, there was an indentation in the wall, the size of a stone. I peeked in and saw a tiny view of the city, through two small holes at the far end of the nook. I realized that we were inside the turret of the law school's west corner; I was looking out through the eyes of a gargoyle. The staircase continued down below ground level and eventually let us out into a cellar, which threaded us into the tunnels.

We followed the map, using a small compass of Sarah's from her father. He was a tycoon of some kind at a Boston investment bank that had started three hundred years ago as a maritime trading company. In a nod to the past, they gave nautical compasses to their new executives, and he had given his to Sarah when she graduated from medical school. This was the first time she'd taken it out of its leather pouch, which gave her a perverse satisfaction, under the circumstances.

The steam tunnels seemed darker now. Somewhere outside, a cold front was pulling the temperature down to minus four—a cold so extreme that all life seemed to pause—and the maintenance lights, usually so bright, were pulsing dimly as the campus struggled to heat itself. The only sound was the occasional hiss or drip far down the tunnel, and of course the slap of our feet, which we tried to keep to a minimum. I thought of the Puppet Man. Sarah was next to me. Miles lagged behind, his leather satchel over his shoulder. He was the only one who seemed totally at ease. He might as well have been strolling to a Phish concert.

I looked at the map in my hands and thought with a shiver: *two of the three people who contributed to this are dead*—Frank Shepard for about two hundred years, Chance Worthington for about two days. I was the only one whose name was still ticked in the Alive column.

We passed under Creighton and Worley. We knew we were under the Michaelson Chemistry Labs when the vapors hit us through the air vents overhead, and we passed a trash heap of old beakers and Erlenmeyer flasks, all shattered and discarded—a tribute to two centuries of clumsy students. We arrived below Embry House and took fork after fork to place ourselves directly below the Steel Man. I tried to hear the thumping of music as we passed beneath that famed party room—I imagined the beautiful people dancing in the style of my generation, rugby players and sorority sisters grinding against each other five floors above us.

And then, at the end of our map, we saw a door. It was one of many in a small deserted hallway. We were in a branch of a branch of a branch of the tunnels. No one would ever come this way unless they knew exactly what they were looking for.

We almost passed it.

It would've been an ordinary door, identical to dozens of utility closets and electrical rooms we'd already passed, except for the subtle glyph above the door frame:

Two small eyes—orange pupils and black irises—staring down at us.

I gave the knob a turn, and the door opened.

33

"Where are we?" Sarah whispered.

"I don't know."

"*This* is where you saw the ceremony?"

"No. This is nothing like that. Too small. Too . . . homey. The place I saw was like a cathedral."

"Well, where is *that*?"

"I have no idea."

The place we were in looked like a junior common room in one of the dorms, in a state of bad neglect. There were several couches with cracked and worn leather. There was a rug in the center of the room that had never been fancy, but now it was threadbare. The air was stale. I shut the door behind us and switched on a dim lamp. Old photos covered the walls, hard to make out through thick layers of dust.

On the wall opposite us were two doors.

"I guess we try those," I said.

"I wouldn't do that," Sarah whispered.

"Why not?"

"No lock on the door, out there in the hall. Don't you think that's weird? Why wouldn't they lock their door?"

"I don't know. Maybe we just got lucky for once."

"I doubt it. The only way you'd come through that door is if you were looking for it. I think this room *is* the lock."

"What does that mean?"

"I'm not sure," Sarah said. "I just wouldn't go touching everything."

"Look at this," Miles said.

We turned around.

On a small end table, he'd found two statues; miniature kings standing side by side, carved out of limestone. The pedestals put them at eye level with us.

They were intricately detailed, with lined robes and faces. You got the feeling they were meant to be brothers. One looked kindly, the other cold.

"Look," Sarah said. She was next to me, pointing at a plaque on one of the pedestals. It had an inscription in foreign letters. It looked like Greek.

"Miles, do they take your Classics degree back if you actually use it for something?"

"You mock," Miles said, "but what would you do without me?"

He leaned over the plaque and ran his finger across the raised letters.

"It's a parable," he said. He laughed. "About two brothers, sworn to guard a crossroads. Not just any crossroads. One path leads to glory beyond your wildest dreams. The other leads to . . . oh."

"What—death?"

"I wish. It's from *Paradise Lost*. 'To bottomless perdition, there to dwell, in adamantine chains and penal fire, who durst defy th' Omnipotent to arms.'"

"Penal fire?"

"Yeah."

"It's the crossroads between heaven and hell?"

Miles nodded.

I looked at the far wall.

"Two doors. Two paths. How do we choose?"

Miles put his finger back on the words. "According to the parable, you can ask each brother which way to go. But there's a hitch. By law, one of the brothers must always lie. The other must always tell the truth."

"No hint on which one's which?"

Miles read the rest.

He shook his head.

"That's all it says."

"What does it matter?" Sarah whispered. "They're statues. How are we supposed to ask them anything?"

I looked at the two men. Each had one arm raised over his heart, the other down by his side. At the base of each statue was a small rectangular stone that rose slightly above the stones around it.

"Okay," I said. "We push that stone. That's how we ask. Does it say anything about chances? How many chances do we get?"

"It doesn't say."

"We should be careful."

"You're right," Miles said. He reached out and pressed the stone in front of one statue.

"Miles!" Sarah cried.

The stone sank down under his finger. We heard the clicking of chains, and then, suddenly, the statue's arm began to move. Where the forearm met the elbow, there was a joint, disguised by the grooved folds of his robes. His arm actually rotated, like the hand of a clock, toward the statue's right. He came to rest pointing toward the right-hand door across the room.

"Well, it works."

"That was *stupid,*" Sarah snapped. "This isn't a game. Stop acting like it is. Someone could get hurt."

"We had to try. What'd you want to do, talk about it until we lost our nerve?"

"Don't be stupid," she said again, poking him in the chest with her finger.

"Okay, sorry." He rubbed his chest, then nodded at the statue. "Now we know. He wants us to go that way."

"We don't know anything," Sarah said. "Is he the brother who lies or the brother who tells the truth? Maybe he's pointing us to our death."

"Fine," Miles said. He pushed the other stone.

"Crap!" Sarah shouted.

This time, the brother statue rolled his arm in the opposite direction, toward the door on the left.

"Great! Which way do we go now, genius?"

"Miles," I said, "stop touching and start thinking. Of course they were going to point in opposite directions. One's lying, one's not."

"I knew that," he said, sounding hurt. "I don't hear you offering any brilliant ideas."

"Just give me a minute to think."

"Take your time," Miles said. "I feel really comfortable here."

I closed my eyes. This was just logic. And logic was just math. I was *good* at this.

Say that Truth equals $+1$. And a Lie is -1. Ask the lying brother, get a *negative* answer. Ask the truthful brother, get a *positive* answer.

But we don't know which one's which . . .

Come on . . . *think*.

It was a magic trick: we had to turn a lie into truth. In other words: how does a negative number become a positive number? . . .

Multiply it by another negative! Two negatives equal a positive!

So if you ask the liar, you have −1. How do you throw in another negative? Do the opposite of what he says! If he says go left, you go right! −1 times −1 equals +1.

But how do you know you're talking to the liar??

I mean, if you ask the truthful brother, then you're multiplying −1 times +1. You're back to the wrong answer.

Shit!

So the question is: How do you make sure that second negative is in the equation?

Come on . . .

I felt my brain stretching, groaning . . .

Almost there . . .

"I got it," I said.

Miles and Sarah stared at me.

"We ask either statue what his brother would say, and then we do the opposite."

"What?"

"Huh?"

"Think it through. We don't know who is who. So if you ask the liar what his brother would say, his brother would tell us the truth, but the liar would lie about his brother's answer. So we do the opposite!"

$$+1 \times -1 \times -1 = +1!$$

"Or, say we ask the truth-teller. His brother would lie, and he'd truthfully tell us which way his brother recommended. So again, we do the opposite."

$$-1 \times +1 \times -1 = +1!$$

It was kind of like a cartoon. Both their eyes drifted upward as they each worked it through. It clicked for Sarah first.

"Yes!" she said. She smiled. "How did you think of that so fast?"

"It's just logic," I said.

"Impressive," she replied. I felt all warm and goose-bumpy.

"Yeah, it's great," Miles said. "Except for one thing. THEY'RE FUCKING STATUES! You can't ask them anything. You just push a button and they move. Jesus Christ, and *I'm* the professional academic?"

Shit.

I felt the air go out of my balloon. He was right, of course. I'd been so excited about the logic that I'd forgotten the reality of the situation. Still, the answer was so clever, so pure, so . . . *V&D*. It had to be right. I couldn't see any other way.

The button. The gears and chains inside. That was the statue's guts—gears and chains, not blood and viscera. The joint at the elbow, hidden in the seams of his robe . . .

I walked over to the statue on the left and grabbed his head. I traced my finger over the line between his neck and his robes . . . could it be?

We hadn't come this far to give up or turn around.

I closed my eyes and twisted. Nothing, at first, and then I felt a gritty giving-way, as if the twisting was pulverizing the bits of dust filling the groove, and then the king's head turned. It rotated to my right under my hands, the sound of a mechanism clacking and trucking inside the statue, until his head wouldn't turn anymore. I opened my eyes and looked. The statue's head was now rotated to the right, and his lips fit perfectly against the opening of his brother's ear.

I looked at Miles and Sarah and gave them a wide smile.

"You see?" I sounded like a giddy idiot. But it was awesome!

I stepped in front of the second brother, the one who was now receiving instructions, metaphorically speaking, from the lips of his brother nestled in his right ear.

"Ask one statue what his brother would say," Sarah whispered.

She came over and put her hand on top of mine, and together we pressed down on the button in front of the second statue. His hand was already pointing to his right, from our previous attempt. There was a clicking—higher-pitched this time—and the arm ticked all the way to his left.

"YES!!" Miles shouted. He pumped his arms in victory. "You did it, by God, Jeremy, you really did it!" He ran and jumped toward the left-hand door and put his hand on the knob.

"MILES!" we both screamed at once. "MILES, *NO!!*" Were we seconds from death? By what means? Would the room start hissing with gas? Or maybe the opposite: the air would suck out until we were gasping on the floor, a couple of heartbeats away from the penal fire . . .

Would it be quick? Would it hurt?

Miles turned around, grinning.

"Just kidding," he said. "Ask one statue what his brother would say"—here he winked—"*and do the opposite.*"

Miles walked to the right-hand door and, without looking back at us, turned the knob.

There was a release of air, a quiet hissing, and then the door opened inward.

34

We passed into a small room, a library with a nautical theme. There were paintings of lighthouses and schooners on the walls. A globe in one corner, an astrolabe in another. The ceiling was painted with a nighttime mural: stars and a moon.

But what was truly notable about the room was the split that ran across it lengthwise, cutting everything in half: the far wall, a painting, the green carpet, even a chair in its path. The chair was silk: green, gold, and blue; its two halves sat on either side of the rift. You could see the yellow stuffing, but the split was perfect; the stuffing didn't bulge or spill out from the halves.

There was an archway on the far wall, with a bar across the door. Miles walked over and gave it a good shove.

"Locked."

I knelt down and looked at the split in the floor. The edges were sharp. I tried to see into it. It seemed like the bottom, far below, was moving.

Sarah held out a coin and let go.

A few seconds later, we heard a faint splash.

"It's water," she said.

She put a hand on both sides and leaned in. Her head disappeared.

"Be careful."

She ignored me.

"I think there's a current."

She was right: when I looked closely, the water was moving toward the far wall.

To my right was a giant mirror in a gold frame. Below it, a glass bowl sat on a table, filled with small planks of wood.

"Very *cute*," Miles said.

He was suddenly next to me, with that self-satisfied look on his face. He leaned forward, resting his hands on a wooden chair.

"What?"

"The moon above. The water below. It's the classic triad. They're practically shouting it at us."

"Huh?"

Miles shook his head patiently.

"The moon. Water. What is the one thing that symbolizes *both* in nearly every culture?"

Suddenly, Miles grabbed the chair and shouted with glee: "*MIRRORS!*"

He swung the chair with all his force into the colossal mirror on the wall.

There was a tremendous explosion. Glass flew everywhere.

"A-HA!" Miles shouted victoriously.

He was holding the remains of the chair in midair.

Behind the mirror, there was a plain wall.

The last pieces fell with a jangle.

"Oh," Miles said. He looked at us. "Oops."

Sarah and I exchanged glances.

"Oops?"

"Oops."

"You just killed the mirror."

"I said oops."

Sarah scrunched her face into a perfect Miles impression. *"It's the classic triad,"* she lectured, pretending to push a pair of glasses up the bridge of her nose.

"Piss off," Miles said.

Sarah and I looked at each other and burst out laughing.

"It *would've* been cool," Miles mumbled. His face was turning bright red. "Come on—if there was a tunnel or something behind the mirror? That would have been awesome. What the hell do you know anyway . . . think you're some kind of genius, just 'cause you played with dolls in the other room . . ."

He stomped off to the far corner of the room and plopped in a chair, sulking.

We nearly doubled over, laughing.

Finally, I wiped my eyes and walked the room.

On the bookshelf, I found a model ship, the kind you'd see inside a glass bottle, but larger.

"Hey Miles," I said. "Mind if I look at this, or did you want to smash it first?"

"Screw you."

I took the ship off its base and turned it over.

"Weird."

On both sides, several planks were missing, like the smile of a very bad boxer.

I grinned.

I took the boat to the table under the broken mirror. I grabbed a plank of wood from the glass bowl and held it up to the boat. It was a perfect fit.

Sarah clapped.

Every plank snapped into place, not one to spare. The boat looked whole again, except that the old ship was made of pale balsa wood; the new pieces were cherry brown. But the problem was cosmetic—the boat felt perfect, balanced and new.

"Cool."

"I want to put it in the water," Sarah said.

"Well *obviously*," Miles mumbled from his corner. He still wasn't making eye contact.

"Let's do it," I said.

"You would," Miles muttered.

"Could you grow up, please?" Sarah said. "If you know something, say it."

"It's the Ship of Theseus, clearly," Miles said.

"The ship of what?"

"Theseus. It's a paradox. An ancient puzzle."

"Oh for God's sake. Enlighten us."

"The Ship of Theseus was getting worn out, right? But they kept it going by replacing planks. Take an old plank out, put a new one in. So the question is, when does it stop being the Ship of Theseus?"

"I don't get it."

"If you replace one plank, is it still the Ship of Theseus?"

"Of course."

"What if you replace half the planks? Is it still the Ship of Theseus?"

"Yes."

"What if you replace all the planks?"

"Sure."

"Okay, now say someone picks up all the discarded planks and builds a second boat. Which one is the Ship of Theseus?"

Sarah and I answered at the same time.

"The old one," I said.

"The new one," she said.

"Exactly." Miles rubbed his hands together. "It's not just about some boat. It's about what it means to *be* something." He pointed at the smashed wood on the floor. "Is that still a chair? Is that still a mirror? Are you the same person you were a year ago? Is this boat the same one you found on that shelf?"

I threw my hands up.

"Great. Typical philosophy. We could debate all night, and we'd still have no idea what to do."

"I have an idea," Miles said. "Take those damn planks out and drop it in the water."

"Are you crazy?" Sarah snapped.

"It makes perfect sense," Miles answered. "Think about the V and D. What they're doing. They don't want the ship to change. They want the same old ship to keep sailing, forever and ever. They don't want to turn the voyage over to a new crew, a new ship, new planks. You put those pieces in, the philosophy's all wrong."

"But the *physics* is right. My boat won't sink. Yours will."

"Trust me."

"This from the guy who smashed the mirror."

"I'm telling you."

"We get one chance," I said. "It's twenty feet down."

"You're right," Miles said. He sighed. "Let me just see one thing."

He took the boat from my hands. He pulled out the brown slats of wood.

"Hmm . . ." he said, thinking hard, or rather pretending to.

Before I could say anything, he took a massive step and dropped the boat right into the split.

"YOU BASTARD!"

We ran to the edge. The boat went down with a splash then sank underwater.

"You fucking arrogant prick," Sarah shouted. "How dare you? People's lives are at stake. Maybe you don't care about them, but don't you care about yourself?"

"I have self-esteem issues," Miles said.

"Shut up and look!" I shouted.

The boat had hit the water and submerged from the force, but now it popped back up and rocked its way in the slow current toward the far end.

"I'll be damned," Miles said.

I started to get excited, but then I saw the bubbles escaping the boat. I could imagine the water flooding into the hull.

"Oh shit."

The boat started to sink.

"NO."

It was still moving, slower than we needed. Halfway down the stream, it was halfway submerged.

"Shit," I said. "Shit, shit, shit. Come *on.*"

"Go . . . go . . . go . . ." Sarah called.

"Oh no," Miles said.

He was looking at the far end of the stream.

"What?" I slid toward the end with him. "What *is* that?"

There was a tunnel at the end of the stream, tall enough for the boat to pass through, sails and all. But what Miles saw was spanning the length of that entrance: a wire, pulled tight across the passage, near the top of the opening.

A wonderful phrase from my childhood adventure books suddenly came to mind:

Booby trap.

"Miles," I said, "what do you think happens if our sail hits that string?"

He shrugged. All the smugness was gone. He met my eyes and made a motion with his hands that said: *ka-boom.*

Sarah was a couple of feet away, her eyes locked on the boat, chanting: "Float . . . float . . . float . . ."

"Sarah."

I showed her the wire.

Her eyes went wide.

She looked back at our boat and chanted: "Sink . . . sink . . . sink . . ."

I joined her.

What else could we do—run out the way we came in?

Miles was already there. He tried the knob and cursed.

The boat was inches from the end. It was almost three-quarters underwater, still drifting in the current, the sails still high enough to hook the filament. The bubbles were pouring out the sides.

"Sink . . . sink . . . *sink* . . . SINK . . ."

The ship hit the end, sputtering air, drowning, and by a fraction of an inch the sail cleared the wire.

The boat disappeared into the shadows of the passage.

This triggered a rumbling that began far below and worked its way up to us. It seemed to be inside the wall. There was a clicking sound, and the bar slid across the massive door, back into its socket. Moments later, a panel clicked open in the bookshelf, and the boat was deposited back in its spot.

Miles marched to the door and gave it a heavy push. It swung open.

He shot us a victory smirk and strode through.

I looked at Sarah and shook my head.

"You know, he's right half the time. The problem is, we don't know which half."

She took my hand and smiled wearily.

"Let's just get through this, okay? Then we can go somewhere, get a nice little house, have kids, grow old. What do you say?"

"Where would we go?"

"I don't know. How about Jamaica?"

"What do you think of Texas?"

"Texas?" She gave a *why not?* shrug. "I've never been to Texas."

She kept holding my hand, and we walked under the arch.

35

We found ourselves in a room that was somehow vast *and* claustrophobic.

Vast, because the far wall—and the only other door—stretched away from us like a hallway in a bad dream. The kind that keeps extending the more you run.

Claustrophobic, because the side walls and low ceiling loomed in on us. Every few feet I saw narrow slots that ran from the floor up the side walls and across the ceiling. There were elegant sconces with candles on the walls. Miles pulled out his Zippo and lit a few.

To my left, I noticed a bizarre mosaic on the wall, made out of tiny slick tiles. It traced the form of a demon, a grotesque creature with massive lips and hands, and an odd phallus that hung limp.

Miles walked up next to me.

"Ugly little fucker," he said.

Sarah was across from us, examining a mural on the opposite wall. This one resembled a subway map but with no stops labeled. She studied the branching paths.

I put my hand on the demon and let my fingers trace over the tiles.

"What is it?" I asked him.

"It's a totem of some kind. A god from some ancient religion."

"Which one? What does it mean?"

Miles squinted his eyes.

"South American, maybe. Or Pacific Islander . . one of those Easter Island heads."

"You guys have no idea what you're talking about," a voice said from behind us. It was Sarah. She was laughing.

She started walking toward us, and her foot came down on a floorboard that sank inward with a series of sickening clicks, like an old man cracking his knuckles. Sarah's head jerked up at us. Her eyes were wide.

"What did I just do?" she asked.

Before we could guess, there was a grinding noise from within the walls. My fingers were still on the tiles. I felt a vibration pass in a wave under my hand. There was a tremendous noise, like a machine rumbling to life, and then there was a *release*—the noise a carnival ride makes after it's raised you up ten stories and the claws suddenly spring open.

We heard a screaming metallic cry. It started slow and then accelerated, rising in pitch. Then there was a flash of mirror and the blade—as tall and wide as a man—came tearing out of the slot with blinding speed. It arced down, sliced a hair above the floor in the center of the room, then disappeared into the slot on the far wall. The screaming slowed, then stopped.

Then it built up again, and a moment later the blade tore back across the room, straining its cable like the pendulum of an asylum clock.

"Oh, shit," Sarah said.

The blade swung back and forth at the far end of the room, in front of the lone door.

"It's okay," I said. "It's okay. It's not that fast. We can time it."

"Time it wrong, and you're salami," Miles offered.

Every pass of the blade made a palpable *whomp,* a pulse of wind that reached us. I counted from the time it disappeared into the

266

slot until it reappeared and ripped across our path. At least three seconds. No problem.

"We can make it."

No sooner had I spoken, than the noise roared louder and a second flash of silver released from another slot in the wall—this one about a foot closer to us. Now two pendulums were slicing past each other, out of phase.

"*Shit.*"

I counted again. They were off, but the cycles were steady—I could hear the motors grinding above. The noise was terrible, and the smell of burnt oil was filling the room. But there was a moment of opportunity, once the blades crossed paths. One or two seconds, but long enough. If we took turns, we could make it, one by one. We just had to be patient.

I started to say so when the third blade fell, a foot in front of the second and closer to us. It came tearing out and cut a lunar path across the room.

Now three blades were crossing; it was getting harder to see the door behind them. The cables whined and the motors squealed like animals being branded.

"I no longer think we can make it," I announced.

"That," Miles said, staring at the walls, "really isn't the issue anymore."

I saw what he was looking at.

The blades came out of slots, all about a foot apart. I hadn't paid attention before, but the slots continued from the far end of the room, where the blades were swinging—all the way to us. In fact, there were only six inches between the door we came through and the first slot. Miles was more than six inches thick. So was I.

Maybe Sarah could suck in, but then what? Spend infinity watching a giant pendulum slice past your nose? Plus or minus a few toenails?

"Maybe there's just three," I said hopefully.

I barely got the words out before *hiss, clank, release* and a fourth monstrosity *whomped* across the room.

That broke the spell.

Miles grabbed the doorknob behind us and twisted it frantically. Locked. He put all his weight into it. Nothing. He rammed his massive form into the door. It didn't even buckle.

"This," he shouted, poking a thick finger into my chest, "is the last time I listen to you!"

Miles kept slamming his shoulder into the door. I turned to Sarah. Her eyes were locked on the colossal blades, six of them now, mesmerizing. She was paralyzed. This wasn't a room designed to kill. This was a room designed to make you lose your mind. The killing was an afterthought. Another blade dropped, and this time I really felt it—my hair blasted in the breeze.

I grabbed her shoulders and shook her. I shouted her name, but it was hard to hear over the roar. It sounded like a trash compactor closing in on thousands of glass bottles. I pulled her back. Her feet dragged like she was unconscious. She looked at me blankly. She looked at the blades and started screaming.

I had lost count of them. I yelled at Miles—he was getting nowhere with the door but probably breaking his shoulder.

I saw the image of the demon, grinning at me with those big lips.

Sarah knew something about the demon. She said so.

"Sarah!" I yelled, trying to get her to hear me over the machines. "Sarah, you said it *wasn't* a totem . . ."

She blinked at me. She shook her head like she couldn't hear me.

"You said we didn't know what we were talking about . . . *What is it?*"

I turned her toward the mosaic.

"Please, we need to *do* something."

"I don't know . . ."

"You *do*. I need you to *focus. Come on.*"

The sound roared and a blade fell so close to us that Miles had to jerk us backward with his massive arms.

"We are going to *die,*" I yelled at her.

That did it. Sarah nodded. Her eyes seemed to clear.

"It's not a demon," she said. "It's a homunculus."

Miles roared. "Demon, homunculus, it's the same thing!" He looked at me. "The alchemists made life from scratch. They called them homunculi."

"No," Sarah said, shaking her head vigorously. She had to shout over the machines. "*Listen to me.* Not alchemy. *Biology.*"

"There's no *time,*" I said. "Can you stop this or not?"

"I don't know," Sarah said. "But I know what *he* is."

She pointed at the demon.

"Talk fast," I pleaded.

"He . . . it . . . is a map. Of the nervous system. It shows where our nerves are. The more nerves, the bigger you draw the body part."

"What?"

"From neurology . . . the hands, the lips, the genitals . . . that's where we have the most nerves. That's why they look big in the picture. It's a symbol."

"That ugly little shit is *us*?" Miles shouted.

"So what's that?" I asked, pointing to the subway map.

"I knew I'd seen it before," Sarah said. "It's the brachial plexus."

"The *what*?"

"A map of the nerves in our shoulders and arms. Look. The median nerve. The radial nerve. The ulnar nerve."

We were running out of space. The door was impossible to see across the room. We had feet left to go.

"Sarah, honey, this has got to get practical really fast."

"It *is* practical," she said. "Doctors use these maps to figure out where an injury is . . ."

"Like . . ."

And then she saw it. Her eyes literally welled with joy.

"That's it!" she cried.

She pointed.

"Here. See this?"

She jabbed her finger at a missing tile in the subway map, a small hole in the mural.

"So what? It's old."

"No. This isn't an accident. This is what doctors *do*. This *means* something."

We heard a hiss and Miles pulled us back. His shoulder slammed against the back wall, just as another blade swung past.

"What, Sarah?"

"If someone got hurt, *here*—" She pointed to the gap in the mural. "If this nerve got severed . . . you'd have a *specific* injury . . . I need to *think* . . ."

"NO TIME!"

". . . C5, C6, C7 . . ."

"Come on, Sarah . . ."

". . . roots . . . then trunks . . . then divisions . . ."

"Come *on*."

"... splits to the median nerve and crosses ..."

"COME ON"

"... you'd lose sensation in ... in ..."

She was squeezing her eyes shut and shaking her head.

Miles pressed himself flat against the back wall and yelled, *"Why do I have to be so fucking fat?"*

The next blade would pin us all.

She cried: *"He'd go numb in the lateral three-and-one-half fingers of his right hand!"*

She bolted across the room toward the homunculus.

I heard the rumbling of the next machine. There was a flash of silver. Behind me the blade came free, split the subway or the brachial plexus or whatever the fuck it was and tore at me. I jumped. The blade flew toward Sarah. It would split her in half.

"SARAH!"

She dove to the floor and slammed her fingers toward the demon. The noise was unbearable. I hit the wall, saw flashes of light, and moaned and rolled over onto my side to see her reach the demon and press the shiny tiles of his outer four fingers. They sank inward with a click and she screamed or laughed and rolled to her side as the blade ripped past.

It disappeared into the wall and a tremendous clamping sound rang out. It didn't come back out. All down the room the blades swung on their paths into the walls and didn't come out again. The noise decreased with each return, until one or two last blades disappeared and it was totally, unnaturally silent. There was only the smell of rank gasoline and the total absence of thought in my head—perfect stillness.

At the far end of the room, the door had slid open.

I felt a joy surging inside me.

Sarah was on her feet. She was okay. She was smiling at me and tears were streaming down her face. She put her hand on my cheeks and I realized I was crying too. I grabbed her and hugged her tighter than I've ever hugged anyone, and I just kept saying *Oh my God, Oh my God* in her ear, over and over. Then I felt the crushing hug of Miles around us.

"You did it!" he cried to Sarah. "My God you fucking *did it*! What did you *do*?"

Sarah beamed. "It's just science." She pointed at the brachial plexus. "It's a map of the nerves in someone's arm. This missing tile, here, it's *intentional,* like someone severed the nerve. I just had to figure out where a person would go numb if you cut that specific nerve."

"Oh," Miles said. "I knew that."

Sarah was smiling and we ran toward the door. "Let's get out of this room," she said, laughing. She took off, Miles behind her, me last.

And that's when the bad thought came into my head, so quickly that I didn't even see it at first. It was just a sensation. We ran toward the door.

I felt the thought unpacking itself. I became aware of it, of what it was trying to tell me. I couldn't verbalize fast enough. Sarah was at the door, running through it. Miles was on her heels, his momentum vast. I couldn't get the words out fast enough, but my arm just shot forward and grabbed at them.

Why hadn't I seen it sooner? It was so obvious. Three rooms. Three puzzles. The first one logic: the two kings. A lawyer's puzzle. The second: the Ship of Theseus. A philosopher's riddle. The third, the homunculus—only for a neurologist could that puzzle exist. Three of *us*—a lawyer, a philosopher, a neurosurgeon.

272

Oh God, they were just waiting for us.

My hand closed over a shirt, and with the strength that only terror can give you, I pulled back and Miles came with me as Sarah disappeared through the door.

I fell backward and Miles came down, half on top of me, crushing the wind out of me.

A second later, I heard Sarah scream.

36

I pushed Miles off me and ran to the edge of the door. I expected to see Sarah, to figure out some way to help her. But what I saw instead was a hole in the floor, and a giant trapdoor hanging down. And below that, emptiness. Just a vast hole that sloped down at a steep angle into nothing. The false floor was long. She would have made it several feet into the room before it collapsed below her and sent her spiraling down.

I tried to see down into the hole. I got on my hands and knees and let myself hang over it. Cool, earthy air hit my face. But I couldn't see more than a few feet. The chute just disappeared into blackness.

I felt my world start to unravel. There was a gnawing sensation in my brain that made me want to start shaking my head like a wandering lunatic. I shouted *Sarah* into the hole. My voice echoed down and back again and mocked me. But nothing real came back. No call for help. Not her soft voice, calling my name. I yelled again. Nothing.

That's when I felt Miles's hand on my shoulder.

"Jeremy."

I was hanging too deep into the hole, holding on with my hands and trying to see something, anything. Miles pulled me back.

"You're gonna fall," he said.

The room was tiny. Just big enough to get the three of us to the middle, on our way to a door at the far end, before the trap sprung. There were candles burning in holders on the walls, the room flickering between shadows and light.

Miles asked how I realized it was a trap. I told him about the puzzles, the way each one was designed for one of us. Like they wanted us to solve them.

Miles shook his head. It was a gesture I'd seen before: a mix of surprise and admiration for the V&D and their tricks—except that this time, there was less surprise, less admiration, crowded out by something I'd never seen in Miles's face before: defeat. He looked defeated.

"It was a test," he said. His eyes were sad. "A final warning. If we were smart enough to get it, we were smart enough to turn around and honor our deal. And if not . . ." He looked at the trapdoor. "Then they'd have to handle us another way."

I stepped toward Miles.

"What are you saying?"

"Jeremy . . ."

"What are you *saying*?"

"You know what I mean."

He said this surprisingly gently.

"You don't *know* that," I told him.

"Think about it."

"You can't be sure."

"Remember Chance? Remember Sammy Klein?"

"Shut up."

"We didn't listen. We went back on our deal."

"Shut up."

"They even gave us a last chance. She didn't—"

"Shut the fuck up."

"She didn't *see* it."

I went for him. All I felt was rage. I wanted to tear him to pieces—*stupid fucking know-it-all*. He grabbed my arms and twisted me around. He overpowered me and forced me down.

"Jeremy, stop. *Stop.* This isn't going to help anything."

"We have to go get her."

"We can't."

"We have to. We have to save her."

"How? How, Jeremy? How could we save her?"

"We go after her."

We both looked at the hole in the middle of that flickering room. The hole was impossibly dark. Inestimably deep. I tried to imagine what was at the bottom. Given the deviousness, the ghoulishness of what we'd seen so far, the possibilities seemed limitless. Would we fall at breakneck speed into a pit of random spikes, where a dozen skeletons were already impaled? Or maybe we'd land in a pit of half-starved dogs, creeping toward us, snarling, mangy fur glowing faintly with moonlight. Would they throw in a sword and shield to reflect the stars and add some excitement?

We looked at that hole for a long time. It occurred to me that if we wanted to save Sarah's life—if we wanted to even have a *chance*—we had to go now.

Miles spoke softly behind me.

"Jeremy, if you were going to jump, you would've done it already."

He walked back across the blade room to the door we'd entered a hundred years ago. He tried the knob, and it opened. He waited for me at the door.

I turned back to the hole.

If this were a movie, I would've jumped. I would've said something heroic, or at least clever: *I'll be back! Hasta la vista, baby! All in a day's work!*

But it wasn't a movie.

And I didn't jump.

God help us, we left her there.

I felt a strange buzzing in my head. It was a giddy feeling. My body was pumping me full of joy, excuses, illusions, distractions. We sat in Miles's apartment on the red futon, flipping channels and trying not to look at each other. We ordered Chinese food and waited for it to come. There was nothing on TV. We passed *Hogan's Heroes,* an infomercial for a gym machine, a Steven Seagal movie dubbed in Spanish, reruns of classic game shows. The badness made it almost impossible to pretend we were actually watching. Miles lit a joint and took a long drag. He offered it to me. I'd never smoked pot before. Never even wanted to. But right now, all I wanted was to stop the feeling of pointlessness that was creeping around the edges of my awareness, looking for a way in. I took the joint. It was wet on the tip. I sucked in and let the raw smoke go into my mouth. I held it there for a second. I knew what to do next. I'd tried cigarettes once in high school and mastered the art of letting the smoke go down my trachea and bloom into my lungs. I wanted that peaceful look I'd seen on potheads' faces. I wanted to find truth in Pink Floyd. I wanted to find my own hand hilarious. But I didn't inhale. I just held the smoke long enough to fake it and let it out a moment later. I passed the joint back to Miles.

I couldn't stand the silence. I asked Miles a question I'd been saving for a late-night chat. I asked it now, just to break the tension.

"Hey Miles."

"Yeah?"

He didn't look at me.

"Why'd you quit law?"

He took another hit. He didn't say anything.

"You had an offer from the best firm in the country," I said. "People would kill for that. And you turned it down. Why?"

Miles closed his eyes.

"I don't know," he said. "Maybe it was a mistake, in retrospect."

"You must've had a reason. Do you remember?"

Finally he sighed.

"It's gonna sound stupid now." He shook his head. "Something I heard on the first day of class, in Torts. It always bothered me. A man sees a baby on some train tracks. He's just walking by. No one else is around. There's a train coming. It's way off in the distance. All he has to do is move the baby, right? Just pick it up and move it off the tracks. But he doesn't. For whatever reason, he keeps walking. And Professor Long told us: the law has nothing to say about that. Remember? Because there's no duty between him and the baby. Not in the legal sense."

"That's it? *That's* why you quit?"

"No. I started thinking. Say we all get mad. We pass a law that says you have to move the baby or you go to jail. Next time, the guy moves the baby."

"That's good. The law worked."

"Sure it worked. But the guy hasn't changed. See? He didn't *want* to move the baby. He just didn't want to go to jail."

"So?"

"*So?* So it's not free will. He's just a slave. The law didn't make him good."

"The law's not *supposed* to make him good. It's supposed to stop him from being evil."

"So where does morality come from, then?"

"I don't know. Religion."

"Fine. He moves the baby because God wants him to. Isn't that just a different kind of law? Maybe he's scared of going to hell. Isn't that just another kind of prison?"

"Parents, then. Culture."

"More rules. More law. When does it come from *inside*, Jeremy, absent anything else . . ." Miles shook his head. "I turned to philosophy. I studied Aristotle and virtue ethics. I studied Kant and Mill and Rawls and Nozick. I mastered communitarianism, egalitarianism, utilitarianism, structuralism, deontology, Straussianism, postmodernism, objectivism, contractarianism . . ."

I started laughing. I didn't mean to. I couldn't control myself. It was an unhappy sound—the worst laughter I'd ever heard. I felt like the last hinges in my brain had sprung open. I just laughed. At first Miles thought I was laughing with him, and he smiled uncertainly, but then he heard the edge in it and stopped. He looked at me, his mouth half-open. I just laughed until I thought I'd go insane.

"You're talking about *goodness*," I said. "You're talking about goodness, *and she's down there*."

Miles looked startled.

"You asked about my career."

"*We left her down there.*" I was shouting. I couldn't stop. "Miles, you're talking about *goodness* and WE LEFT HER DOWN THERE."

279

"It's just *philosophy*."

"It's *nothing*—if you *don't get off this couch*. I want you to shut your big fucking mouth because it's all *bullshit*." My head was going to explode, the blood was rushing so hard. "Get up. Get off your fat ass and get off this couch because we are going to save her. We are going to get her out of that dark place and make her okay. Do you hear me, Miles? Do you?"

He didn't say anything. He blinked a couple of times. His eyes were red from the pot. He scratched at his beard.

"I'm going to take a shower," he said.

He left the room. I wanted to move. I wanted to go after her. But my legs wouldn't budge. And suddenly I realized what my legs already seemed to know: if I went down there after her, I might die. If I went alone, without Miles, it was virtually guaranteed. Let him take his shower. Ten minutes under the hot water and he'd come around.

This was *Miles,* I kept thinking over and over. My mentor. My protector in high school. I remembered the time we walked down the hall together, and this guy who used to pick on me passed us and said something ugly. In one motion, Miles had him up in the air, and he held him there with one arm for a long time. No words, no threats, no violence even—just the gentle lifting, like a father lifting a child. Miles was valedictorian of his class, and he could lift a bully with one arm. For me. Miles was my hero.

When the water stopped, he stepped out of the bathroom. He was wrapped in a towel. His massive frame, somewhere between fat and muscle, was pink from the hot water. But the thing that shocked me had nothing to do with his colossal size or his bareness. He'd shaved off his beard. His face looked naked, almost babylike. I barely recognized him at first, and then suddenly he looked just like the Miles from high school, like he'd traveled back in time seven years. As if you could reach inside yourself and produce the person you used to be, just like that.

But when I saw his face, I knew.

"I understand what you're saying," Miles said. "But I can't help you."

He walked into his bedroom and shut the door.

I heard it in his voice. There wouldn't be any discussion. Not this time.

I walked to the entryway and picked up his satchel. I strung it over my shoulder.

As I left his apartment, for some reason I thought of Miles proposing to Isabella—one giant kneeling before another.

I walked the campus one last time. I passed the music school with the statue of Beethoven outside—larger than life and cast in black metal, his eyes and hair blazing. I passed the bridges over the river and saw the line of bell towers, one red, one blue, one green. The campus was quiet. The crew teams still had an hour before first light, when they'd practice on the river, rowing as a unit like an eagle pumping its wings. I passed the library with its massive columns and the statue of our founder with his three lies, and there I flashed back to that first day, passing the tourists on my way to Bernini's class. I wondered what had gone through Sarah's mind, down in that hole, if she wondered why I hadn't tumbled down after her. Then I found myself past the yard, facing Centennial Church.

The bell tower was shingled with chalky shades of blue, red, and brown, striped like snakeskin. Spotlights went up the sides of the tower and ended in the clouds. I felt an unbearable sense of need rattle me, and I fell to my knees and looked up. When I saw the cross, for the first time in my life it meant something new—no longer did I see a symbol of membership, of fraternity or conversion. Now it was something internal: the intersection of my spine and shoulders. It was a cross inside me, a steel frame, holding me up against the unstoppable urge to crumble. I wanted a religious experience. I wanted a voice and I was instead consumed by an almost infinite silence. The harder I begged that building to speak, the more quiet, the more alone I felt, kneeling in an empty lawn and looking up at a silent building. And yet, in that moment, I had the truest religious experience I believe there is: for I was suddenly filled with the desire to be good, even if no one was watching.

I did one last thing. I wrote a letter to my dad and put it in the mail. It's hard to even call it a letter—it was just one line. It said:

You are not small to me.

I retraced my steps from Bernini's office to the steam tunnel door with eyes above it. I passed through the three rooms. The doors were all open now. The mechanisms were silent. It felt like an abandoned movie set. Or, even better, it felt like something I remembered from my childhood, an amazing, unexplainable feeling that was new to my generation, since we were the first generation to grow up with computers. It felt like a computer game, after you'd solved all the puzzles and done everything you were supposed to do for that level. All that was left was to move on. But if you postponed that—if you walked around that world just a little bit longer—it took on an uncanny feeling. The characters were still there, little animated men running through their programmed routines, tending bar, sweeping porches, working the docks of the pirate shipyard. But it no longer felt like a real world, because your tasks were done and the characters had nothing left to say to you, and you saw through the illusion of their activity.

I found myself past the last room and standing above the hole where the trapdoor still hung open. I let my feet stick out over the edge.

I took a deep breath, and I jumped.

37

I fell, and the walls of the hole arced and I went into a slide that sent me hurtling. Miles's satchel was across my waist; I had one hand over it and one protecting my head. I was rolling over myself now, smacking different parts on the packed dirt of the walls. And yet there was something thrilling about it. I felt free. I felt hope. I was going to rescue Sarah. This was an adventure, and nothing was going to stop me!

The walls leveled out as I fell until they became ground below me and a ceiling above, depositing me in a wild roll until I skidded in a mounting pile of dirt. I plowed to a stop. My eyes were closed. I froze for a moment and listened. Nothing. No explosions, no snarls, no voices, not even crickets chirping. Just the light sound of air moving through cracks.

Did my fingers and toes still move? Check. Vision intact? Check. Wooden spikes through my torso? Negative.

Things were looking up.

It smelled pungent down here, thick and muddy. The rocky walls were covered with writing, more mathematical than pictorial. They still looked primitive. Maybe this was once the home of the Einstein of cavemen.

My body was sore, but I was okay.

I saw a hallway chiseled through the rock. I moved too quickly and was almost seen by three people at the end of the hall, but they were absorbed in conversation and I pressed myself against the wall faster than I realized I could move.

At the distant end of the hall were three women. Their lips were moving, but I couldn't hear them speak. They were young. They reminded me of pretty mothers at a playground. Their skin was almost luminous, lit by a shaft of pale light from slats above them. They seemed lighthearted. One of them laughed. The women moved away together, so gracefully that it wasn't at all clear they were walking. They disappeared around a corner.

I went down the hall after them. I stepped slowly and hoped no one would come around the bend ahead and see me. But it was completely silent. Every step I took, gravel crackled under my shoes. I clutched Miles's bag and felt the metal inside. It was comforting.

I got to the spot where the women had turned and was hit with a blast of cool, fresh air. The dirt path I'd followed forked and continued also in the other direction, around another turn. For a moment, I started to follow the women, but something told me not to. I turned and went left instead of right. I can't tell you why. But I was glad I did. Because the path brought me to a stone stairway within a tight, ascending passage lined with columns on either side. The steps were wide but the stairway was steep, the end high above me. As I neared the top, I saw I was heading toward a slanted opening, like the entrances of Assyrian temples I'd seen in history books. No sound, no movement from that opening as I climbed. But when I reached the top, I looked through the door and saw a room I'd seen before. An altar in the center. A pole that loomed from the floor to the high stone ceiling. And beyond all that, a machine, quietly thrumming and moving in the shadows.

38

The machine reminded me of a spider, the way its long spindles bent in unnatural places, producing movements that were alive but definitely not human. Not even mammalian, for that matter. It creeped me out. It was machinelike in an ancient way, like the Gutenberg press. It could have been hundreds of years old. How long had these people been replicating themselves? How many centuries had they lived?

The machine was also larger than I ever imagined, seeing it through the slots of that vent, looking down. The thin spindle arms spread out from the central mechanism; they filled the room and towered over me. The arms bent and gyrated at joints, like bones. They traced out the points in space of the ritual dance without really capturing what was alive about the dancers—the way stars could be connected into bears and scorpions without blood or brains.

I wanted to get out of here as quickly as possible. I wanted to rescue Sarah (*if she's still alive,* the wicked voice in my head whispered) and leave this place. But I knew what I had to do first. If my theory was right, this machine was the artificial heart that kept the possessed imprisoned. Smashing it to pieces, prying it apart—that would make noise. That would give me away. But if I could do it fast enough, I could free Nigel, Daphne, John, and everyone else.

And the people coming to capture me would no longer have bodies to grab me with. That was the theory, anyway.

You know the old joke about the economist stranded on an island. He decides to build a shelter and says: *First, assume a hammer.*

If I was wrong, I wouldn't have a chance to find Sarah.

But if I went looking for Sarah, somewhere in this huge place, I might never get back here and have this chance again.

The tie-breaker was simple: I knew what Sarah would want me to do.

I reached into Miles's satchel and pulled out the crowbar. I moved into the room and walked the steps up to the altar and the machine behind it.

And that's when I saw something that made my heart stop and took the air out of my lungs.

There was a person chained to the slab on the altar. His voice was muffled with a gag. His wrists were raw and purple from the shackles. When he saw me, he started struggling violently against the chains and looked at me with wide, pleading eyes.

It was John Anderson.

I ran to the altar. What did I feel? Horror, for sure. John was stripped naked. His arms and legs were bound at four points. He was pinned to the sloped rock. When he saw me, he started fighting. The chains were loose enough that he could swing his arms up until the give ran out. They snapped tight and the muscles in his arms and chest flexed. All of this made a terrible noise. I looked over my shoulder to the door. We were still alone, for now. I motioned for him to be quiet. He had a wild, terrified look in his eyes, but I think he understood. He fell still.

What else did I feel? He certainly looked like the football star I knew he'd been in college. He actually looked like an ancient Greek statue come to life, except for the fact that he had arms. I felt that familiar sting of jealousy at the blond hair, the handsome face, the perfect six-six body. And should I be totally honest? Should I admit that I felt, deep down in a place I usually ignored, a brief flash of glee? Did I remember him gloating at the Idle Rich, leering at me and kissing Daphne on the top of the head? Am I a monster if I admit that some part of me looked at John and said: *Who's on the slab now, asshole?*

I stuffed that down. I worked the crowbar into the loop of the bolt securing one of his chains. I came down on it with all my weight. It didn't even budge a hair. I tried again. All I did was send a frightening vibration through the bones in my arms. They would snap before the chains did.

John locked eyes with me. He was terrified. Where was all the cockiness? What had he seen down here that made him look so scared?

"Listen," I whispered. "You need to stay quiet. I know what to do. I'll be right back."

At that, he started jerking again wildly, rattling the chains. *Jeez, buddy,* I thought—*a little help, here.*

I studied the machine. The weak points were obvious. The arms that dipped low as they traced out the enchantments; the joints and gears that wheeled those precise orbits in the middle of the apparatus. I could do this.

I was twenty feet from the machine when I heard the scream. I pressed myself against a column and looked toward the sound. It came from a doorway at the distant end of the cathedral. The room was shadowed, but I saw movement, and suddenly Sarah emerged from a dim shaft of light. She was held on either side by medieval men, large executioners in leather and metal. Men with hungry eyes that cherished, above all else, having orders to follow. One of the executioners had a long, baroque knife, and he held it against her neck.

They were followed by dozens of figures who slowly filled in the room below me, pressing up to the altar. They carried candles and wore masks: an eggshell face with antlers; a patchwork harlequin; a Casanova; a Scaramouch. I saw a shimmering elephant, made from jewels, carried on ivory poles. Its tusks were burning candles.

A familiar face arrived on the altar. It was the priest with the gnarled beard and the cruel voice. No unnatural phosphorescence now—his eyes were just black dots surrounded by unnatural white. They were coldly hypnotic. His nose was flat and broad, and his cheeks were coarse, like the surface of the moon. His mouth and eyes were bone dry—when he spoke, the fissures in his lips accordioned.

He placed his hand on Sarah's forehead and whispered to himself, eyes closed.

Then he looked over at another figure, in golden robes. It was Bernini.

He whispered into Bernini's ear. Bernini nodded, then cupped Sarah's face in his hand.

"Why did you come?" he asked her, shaking his head. "We would have let you live. You realize that, don't you? Now we have to harm you." Bernini frowned, disgusted. "We are not barbarians."

I raised the crowbar in my hands like a baseball bat. *One good swing,* I thought. But I'd have to cross the length of the altar first,

289

in plain view. Even if I made it, what then? I was outnumbered. Helpless.

Sarah moved so quickly she caught the henchmen off guard. She broke free with her right arm and landed a punch across Bernini's face.

"I know *exactly* what you are," she spat.

He nearly collapsed. The man was eighty years old, for God's sake.

With everyone watching Bernini, I took a careful step, crowbar in hand, toward the machine.

Bernini brought a finger to his lip and inspected the blood.

He sighed.

"It's okay," he said to her gently. "I understand."

The priest lit the silver box. There was a cascade of red sparks, and then a plume of smoke and salmon light burst through carved inscriptions. It was on a chain, being swept back and forth by the cruel-voiced priest. The light reflected on his cold eyes. The smell hit me—acrid smoke with strange spices. The priest was chanting to himself and swinging the box.

The light grew, and the half-dressed men surrounding us began pounding their drums. The women dancers advanced from the shadows and began their wild movements. I saw whipping hair and spinning bodies.

"Is he ready?" Bernini asked, looking at John on the slab, naked and bound.

John went crazy, thrashing against the chains on his arms and legs. One of the thugs put his weight on a lever, pulling the chains tight and pinning John to the stone.

A loose rock cracked under my foot.

Shit.

I jumped off-course into a shadow.

The priest dipped two fingers into the box and painted a bright stripe of ash across John's forehead. He did the same to Bernini. Smoke was filling the room. The ash reflected the light. I could barely see through the haze. I moved behind a column and came face to face with a masked figure with no eyes. I swung the crowbar toward his skull.

Just before contact, I saw it was a statue. *One inch from breaking my wrists and bringing the entire V&D down on me.* The drumming grew louder. Gears were turning inside the machine. Leather belts threaded the wheels and pulleys, pulling the jointed arms in competing directions, making them twist and bend in a skeletal dance.

The men pushed Sarah toward a wooden pole. The *sun pole,* Isabella had called it, linking the sky to the underworld. They tied Sarah's arms behind her, binding her to the pole. She was in *the center of hell.* Bernini spoke to her soothingly. "An animal is sufficient . . . *truly* . . . a lamb . . . or a goat . . . *But* . . ." A cold chill ran down my spine. "Only because you're here . . ." He shook his head. "Only because you've left us no choice . . ."

Oh, God, no.

He smiled sadly. "I would not have you die for nothing."

"You son of a bitch," Sarah yelled.

The medieval executioner turned his knife to her.

I broke into a run.

The executioner lifted the blade over his head.

Point-down toward Sarah's heart.

One push . . . I thought, *running . . .*

The priest tossed his head back and howled.

. . . one push . . . crowbar through the gears . . .

He raised his arms and a stream of light shot above him.

291

. . . shove it right through the spokes . . .

The priest nodded and the executioner brought down the knife.

It cut through the air.

I screamed—louder than I imagined possible, from some- place deep inside—a guttural *NO* that cut through the room and echoed back from every stone. The executioner froze, his knife just above her neck, my crowbar less than a hair from the central spinning gear. My voice shook with fury. *"Let her go,"* I shouted, *"or so help me God I will kill you all."* Our eyes were locked. Nobody dared move.

There was silence in the room now.

The dancers crouched on the ground, feral, their long wet hair stuck to their faces. The drummers were still.

I saw the stare of masks from all sides.

A hundred lifeless faces accusing me.

"If you hurt her," I said, *"you all die."*

My words echoed.

Bernini came at me, hand up, palm forward. *Caution!* it said. *You have no idea what you're doing . . .*

"Stay back," I yelled.

The medieval men were inching closer from all sides.

"STAY BACK. ALL OF YOU."

I pressed the crowbar against the spinning metal, just slightly— a stream of sparks shot out. The gear slowed almost imperceptibly, but the second it did, the room filled with unbearable screaming from the masked figures below me. Bernini's face rippled with pain. He let out a terrible squealing noise as if I were twisting a knife between his ribs. The screams came from all around me, hundreds of voices. *Stop,* Bernini cried.

I pulled the crowbar back, horrified.

For a moment he just stood there, catching his breath. He coughed a few times, a wounded, rattling cough. Then he looked at me with those penetrating eyes. I thought of the first day of school. He looked fragile, and above all else, tired.

"Let her go," I said to him.

"If I do," Bernini said quietly, "you will hurt the machine."

"If you don't, I'll destroy it."

"No," he said, "you won't. You'd have nothing left to bargain with."

"So what? You'll all be dead."

He shook his head. "Not fast enough to save her."

The executioner leaned into Sarah and pulled up slightly against her neck with the knife.

"So you see," Bernini said. "We have a stalemate."

For once, I was a step ahead of him.

"Not exactly," I said.

I raised the crowbar, ready to press it forward and slow the gears again.

Bernini raised his eyebrows, unsurprised.

So calm. Like he knew what I was thinking before I did.

"You'll torture us, then?" he asked mildly.

I nodded. "If you make me."

"We won't let her go, Jeremy. You know we can't. You'd only be torturing us for sport."

I hated this man! How could he be so sure I was bluffing?

"We'll see about that," I heard myself say.

To my own shock, I shoved the crowbar forward and slowed the wheel.

Bernini's head jerked back and his eyes rolled up. He cried

out. His torso twisted and he fell forward on his knees. His arms locked in rotation, one inward, one outward. Veins popped up along his skin.

Shrieks, from around the room—hundreds of terrible cries.

I felt a wave of horror. And at the same time, I felt powerful. I *loved* her. They wanted to *murder* her. Was I wrong to do this? Was I wrong to stop?

I pulled the crowbar off the wheel and the screams stopped instantly. The pain was unnatural, and it vanished with unnatural speed.

"Let her go," I cried, my voice breaking.

Bernini stared at me, half-collapsed, on his elbows.

For the first time ever, I saw him look surprised.

"I didn't . . . think . . ." he gasped, wiping a sleeve across his mouth, " . . . you . . . had it . . . in . . . you . . ."

I was going to shatter. There was nothing left.

I was an empty vessel.

I looked at Sarah, and she mouthed, "I love you."

Bernini sighed.

"I think, Jeremy," he said, "that you deserve to know the truth."

39

"It must have hurt," Bernini said, "when you didn't make the cut. I'm sorry about that. Your friends had the physical presence of presidents. Prime ministers. Very valuable. You . . . You do not. Not *quite*."

I thought of the mirrored ballroom. How they watched us.

"And their minds, Jeremy. *Supple*. Capable of abstraction. John less than the others, but that was mostly laziness. Riding on his looks. He had the *capacity* to hold one of us. He would have survived the transfer." Bernini shook a finger at me. "You would have gone insane."

I felt a mix of rage and shame.

"But we're past that, now," Bernini said. "There *is* a way out of this, for both of us. But you must open your mind. Can you do that? Can you indulge your old law professor one last hypothetical? I mean to say, before you put that crowbar through my heart?"

There was a flash of the old Bernini—the hint of a smile.

"I'm done with your games."

Bernini shook his head.

"This time, I promise you, it's no game."

He rose slowly. His eyes twinkled. Suddenly, he was the professor again.

"Suppose, Jeremy, that we weren't down here in this unfortunate place." His eyes danced around the cathedral. "Suppose instead you are the night watchman about a thousand yards that way, in the largest library in the world." He gave that wry grin. "*Imagine* it. Four thousand years of knowledge. Original Shakespeare folios. Handwritten notes on nuclear theory by Rittenberg and Kingsley. Priceless. Just last year, Professor D'Martino found a lost book on rainforest herbs and deduced a new treatment for Parkinson's. Somewhere in there is a cure for cancer. A framework for peace.

"You might guess security is tight for such a building. There's a fire system, of course, but who would spray water on a priceless collection? So, instead, they spray a chemical that will douse flames without harming paper. Ingenious, really."

He raised a long finger.

"You might also know that there is a noble tradition in the College of completing four tasks before graduation. Forgive me here, I'm only the messenger. First, of course, is affixing a pat of butter to the ceiling of the freshman dining hall. It's said that a young Richard Lymann constructed a catapult for the task. Second is running nude through the freshman yard. Third, regrettably, is urinating on the statue of our beloved founder. And fourth, of course, is to have . . ." (here he blushed a little, although he never lost the glimmer in his eyes) "er . . . *relations* . . . in the stacks of the library.

"Now, say that one evening, a couple has slipped past you and remained in the stacks after closing, determined to cross number four off their list. Yet a fire has broken out and is spreading quickly through the building. You have only to push a button to release the chemical spray and end the destruction. The problem, however, is that the chemicals are quite toxic and will surely kill the amorous couple."

He cleared his throat and folded his hands over his knee.

"What do you do, Jeremy? And this time, I'm afraid, *none of the above* is not an option."

He thought I couldn't commit? He was wrong.

"I would not push the button," I said.

Bernini raised his eyebrows, as if to say: *What did I expect?* He looked at me and shook his head.

"You already pushed the button, Jeremy."

"What are you talking about?"

But I knew. In my mind, I couldn't block the image of the crowbar sending out sparks. The screams from the crowd.

"I would *not* push the button," I repeated. "They're just books."

"I see. And what if they weren't . . . just books? Tell me, Jeremy, how long would it take you to read all those books? One lifetime? Two? Ten?" His voice grew louder. "And not just to read them, but to *understand* them? To *practice* what you've learned? To test your cures? To perfect your peace talks?"

Suddenly, he was filled with an anger I didn't know he was capable of.

"You have *no idea* what's at stake," he snapped at me. "You think this is about cheating death? I *long* for death. I wish I had the luxury. I've seen every manner of human cruelty. Witch burnings. Lynchings. Pogroms. Gulags. Child armies. Genocides. My eyes are *tired*."

Bernini spat on the ground.

"The universe is biased toward *evil*. Simple thermodynamics. It is always easier to destroy than to build. The Romans built a republic. How fragile! They slipped, and the world plunged into one thousand years of darkness. *One thousand years!* Can you *imagine* that? A thousand years of oppression—kings and religious tyrants and castes and slavery. One thousand years of pestilence, poverty, superstition . . .

"Ah! But then came the Renaissance. Enlightenment! Freedom and equality escaped from the shadows and swept the world. But some of us didn't forget . . . We didn't forget how *fragile* it all is . . .

"You think good can survive without cost? The people who ended slavery are in this room. The people who defeated Nazism and Communism. *In this room.* Drawing on our wisdom. Our fortune. Our carefully cultivated power. Imagine *this* mind in *that* body." He pointed at John. "We have spent *centuries* perfecting the means to fight evil. For the first time in history, good has an advantage."

Bernini let his magnetic eyes travel around the room, then they came to rest on me.

"But it's happening again, Jeremy, isn't it? You *can* feel it, can't you? The armies of cruelty are massing. Reason is giving way to superstition, thoughtfulness to ideology, humanism to tribalism, honor to greed. Citizens become fools and savages. Crowds become mobs. Ripe for the Leviathan! Read your Hobbes! Read your Aristotle!

"No, our work is more important now than ever. Appearance is the new god. Could Lincoln become president today with his strange face? Could Roosevelt in his wheelchair? Today, the perfect mind needs the perfect body. That doesn't occur by chance."

"But we're getting *better*," I shouted at him. "*Every* generation, there's less hate, less prejudice. More democracy, more freedom. Look at the *world*!—we have *more* law, *more* constitutions."

Bernini's eyes suddenly narrowed.

His voice turned cold.

"You dare lecture *me* on law? I've dedicated my *life* to law. What can the law do against barbarians? Against suicide bombers and nuclear terrorists? Can you reason with madness? A constitution is not a suicide pact. We must *fight evil.*"

"How? By killing people, taking their bodies? By putting yourself above the law? You're fighting slavery with slavery. Murder with murder."

"Don't we send armies to fight the enemies of humanity? How many die then? Thousands? Millions? *We* only take three a year. That's our oath. Three a year to stop the wars before they start.

"I am offering you the chance to join us. You and Sarah both. You can have *everything*. A perfect body. Infinite time. You can build on what you have and over time you will know what we know. You will be one of us. You will save millions of lives with what you'll learn to do."

"Look at her," I said, my eyes on Sarah. "*Look at her.* You were ready to kill her. Is that what you are now?"

He waved me away.

"That was *necessary.*"

I thought of the books I used to read. The ideas I used to believe in.

" '*Necessity is the plea for every infringement of human freedom,*' " I recited. " '*It is the argument of tyrants. It is the creed of slaves.*' " I begged Bernini with my eyes. "There is always another way."

"See what I have seen," Bernini growled, "and then tell me there's another way."

"You were supposed to *teach* us. Help *us* fight. We're ready."

A wave of laughter passed through the faceless crowd below me.

But Bernini didn't laugh. His voice splintered.

"Teach *you*? I have seen the *soul* of your generation. Your television. Your video games. You are frivolous, violent, undisciplined. There is no inner life. Only selfishness, greed, amusement. No sacrifice. No duty. No honor. No virtue."

"Then *show* us." I thought of Jefferson. "*'Enlighten the people generally, and tyranny and oppressions of body and mind will vanish like evil spirits at the dawn of day.'*"

Bernini let out something like a small cry.

His face began to tremble.

"You will not lecture me on enlightenment." His hands were shaking. He pointed a finger at me. "My father believed in enlightenment. My true father, the father of my born body. He used to speak to me of enlightenment, read me philosophy at night. He was a gentle man. Pious. All these centuries later, I remember." His eyes welled with tears. They spilled over and streamed down his face. "Then came the Grand Inquisition of the Church. They had to make sure his faith was real. So they burned him to death. In front of my mother and me. *They burned him to death.*"

He was shaking.

"Professor," I said.

"*Enough.*"

"Professor," I said softly. "What if you become the thing you're fighting?"

"*ENOUGH!*" he cried.

He put his hands over his face.

"*Enough.*"

He stayed like that for a moment, bent over, racked.

I waited until he raised his head and faced me with clear eyes.

As always, he knew it before I even said it.

I could see my grandfather in him then. The dignity. The kindness. The two men weren't so different.

"It's over," I said gently. "Whatever you choose, I'm going to destroy the machine now. Let your last act be good. *Let her go.*"

Bernini stared at me. I watched his face.

He was reading me.

Measuring me.

Then he turned to the executioner and nodded.

"Release her."

The room broke into a roar of protest, fury.

"No," the priest said.

The executioner looked from Bernini to the priest with his dull eyes, trying to find a clear order to follow.

Bernini stepped forward and grabbed at the executioner's arm. The priest came forward too and the three of them wrestled for the knife until Bernini was forced onto his back and the priest guided it into Bernini's chest. He gasped.

I pushed the crowbar into the largest gear of the machine and held it there with all my might as the wheel bucked and ground against the metal. Screams erupted all around me as the machine rattled and the people convulsed. The executioner tried to pull the knife out from Bernini, but he held it there with his last strength just as I held the crowbar firm against the tremendous force of the locking gears. Tormented bodies lurched toward me, crippled but clawing at me, trying to pull me off the machine, trying to tear the crowbar out of my hands. My eyes swept over the room and I saw Bernini fading, still clutching the knife into himself and away from Sarah, the crowd twisting and screaming from behind that infinite sea of masks. The leather belts of the machine strained inward, pulling the arms toward the center like a spider recoil-

301

ing in on itself in fear or pain. The wires that wrapped the arms like nerves ripped apart, sending sparks through the air and lighting the whole machine in a white glow. With all my strength I twisted the crowbar in and out of the gears until the whole thing was coming down, fire running up and out toward the farthest arms. All around us, bodies began to collapse—the youngest first, the ones who had been possessed for the shortest length of time. The older ones held on, screaming in unfathomable pain. I dropped the crowbar and tried to cover my ears. Then I gave up trying to block it out and ran to Sarah, who had slid down the pole to the ground, still bound, squeezing her eyes closed. I untied her and she wrapped her arms around me. I saw a brown hand reaching out from one of the many robes on the ground. I pulled the mask off and it was Nigel, perfectly still. Sarah felt the artery in his neck. "He's still alive," she said. He stirred. The youngest ones were waking up. They were dazed, unaware of their surroundings. I wondered, what would they remember? How would the university cover this one up? Gas leak? Small explosion in a rich person's secret club? Strip them down and concoct a story of sex and bad drugs and amnesia and best not to discuss these things and embarrass one's self and one's alma mater? And of course we hope this won't affect your giving relationship with the university. I thought of the wall of unbroken portraits. The school had an endowment larger than the wealth of most nations. The past could always be fixed.

I told Sarah I didn't want to be anywhere near here when they woke up.

She agreed.

We moved toward the door, trying not to trample the people under us.

The Faculty Club

Suddenly, someone grabbed my ankle.

It was Bernini. His face was pale. He looked at me desperately.

I had to lean in to hear him.

He said, "What have I done?"

Did he mean taking all those lives?

Or setting them free?

Before I could ask, his eyes went blank.

40

"Let's go over the plan one more time."

Sarah smiled at me. It was a bright day. We walked through the park, hand in hand. It was cold out, but the sky was blue and the sun reflected off the snow. Couples and families were strolling around us.

I tried to brush a piece of hair from her face, but my hand was shaking. I was still trying to recover from the shock of it all, even though now, two weeks later, it felt about as real as someone else's dream. Somehow the final surprise had been the worst of all: when we got home from that underground cathedral, Miles was gone. Vanished. No note. No clues. We didn't know if he'd run away in shame or if *they'd* taken him.

He was my oldest friend, and I had no idea if he was alive or dead.

Sarah took my hand and kissed it.

"The plan," she said again.

I nodded, steeling myself.

For me, the plan was to finish law school. I would take the Incompletes on my transcript, if the school would let me, and start over in the fall. It was something I could never recover from, not totally. There would be no law firm job. No big salary. No guarantees. For Sarah, the plan was to search for a program that would take her based on her real transcript, F's and all. She wanted to try family medicine. Something about learning to care for people from the day they were born until the day they died called to her now. I guess it was the circle *and* the line, just like Isabella said. We were searching for balance. When our training was done, Sarah and I would go back to Lamar, together. I'd open a small practice, just like my grandfather had done sixty years ago.

It was a good plan, but it was filled with question marks. Our résumés weren't what they used to be. *We* weren't what we used to be. For the first time in our lives, nothing was sure anymore. I felt terrified.

I also felt happy.

"I got you something," Sarah said.

She handed me the package she'd been carrying. It was wide and flat, cloaked in a black velvet wrapping. I set it down on a ledge and tried to untie the strings, but my hands were still too shaky. Sarah leaned in and used her surgeon's fingers. She undid the knot and folded the velvet flaps open, revealing a flat, polished piece of wood, with ornate engraving.

It was an old-fashioned shingle that read:

JEREMY DAVIS, ATTORNEY AT LAW

Acknowledgments

I would like to thank Jodi Reamer and Emily Bestler for their unparalleled wisdom, insight, guidance, belief, and kindness. I couldn't have dreamed up a better agent or editor. And thanks to Amanda Burnham for gracing the book with her amazing illustrations. For research on certain topics, I turned to Milo Rigaud's 1969 work, which I won't name here to preserve the surprises in this book. Professor Bernini's mine car hypothetical is based on the famous trolley dilemma, which, according to the *Oxford Handbook of Contemporary Philosophy*, was conjured up by Philippa Foot and developed by Judith Jarvis Thomson. The library hypothetical was a favorite practice case of the Harvard Speech and Parliamentary Debate Society. Bernini's course is an homage to two wonderful classes named Justice, Professor Michael Sandel's at Harvard and Professor Bruce Ackerman's at Yale Law (though any errors are my own). Thanks to Noam Weinstein, Anne Dodge, and Nicholas Stoller for reading the book and providing excellent comments. Laura Stern, Alec Shane, and many others contributed invaluably to the production of this book. Most of all, I would like to thank my parents, sister, and Jude, for everything.